Georg[i]e

Marion Grace Woolley

GreenSunsetBooks

www.greensunsetbooks.co.uk

First published in 2012 by
GreenSunsetBooks
92 Mosse Gardens
Fishbourne
PO19 3PQ
www.greensunsetbooks.co.uk

Copyright © 2012 Marion Grace Woolley

Marion Grace Woolley has asserted her right to be identified as the author of this work.

All characters in this book are fictitious and any resemblance to actual persons, living or dead, is purely coincidental.
Reference to existing organisations is on a fictional basis and not intended as a true representation of such organisations.

All rights reserved.
No part of this publication may be reproduced or utilised in any form or by any means electronic or mechanical, including photocopying, recording or any information, storage and retrieval system now known or hereafter invented without the prior permission of the publisher.

Cover Art Dan Ben Matthews © 2012
Cover Design Adrian Floyde @ www.prepared-4.uk © 2012

A catalogue record for this book is available from the British Library.

For Harri

A story about women

Also by Marion Grace Woolley:

Angorichina ISBN 978-0-9562766

Acknowledgements

As always, I would like to thank my dad, for nights spent with *Puddle Lane*, *Johnny Morris* and the handmade phonetics wheel.

Also, my mother, whose imagination in the realms of bedtime storytelling is second to none. Literacy is one of the greatest gifts that I possess, and undoubtedly the one that I would miss the most. Thank you for that gift and thank you to the public libraries that supplied the means to cultivate it.

To my family: Marilyn, Merrick, my brother William and nephew Damian.

In the writing of this book, I wish to extend my gratitude to:

Martine, my continual taskmistress, for demanding the next chapter. Without you, there may never have been one.

Sophie Haesen and family, for the use of their house near Görlitz, Germany. Also, Lisa Steinert and family, for making my stay such a pleasant one. The peace and introspection found there allowed me to complete two novels, of which this is the first. For that, and for teaching me to paint eggs, I am greatly indebted.

:JR: 'Heartface' for watching the sun come up over Charles Street and explaining to the bouncer that 'yes, we have been here before.' With much love and affection, always.

Daniel Matthews, Pollie & Paul Rafferty for their artistic support.

As always, thanks to my promotional team, Andy Heer and Fred Cairns, for their time and input.

Georg[i]e is a story inspired by the courage of others. People who have fought against convention in pursuit of self-acceptance. During the research of this book, I was constantly astounded by the bravery, humour and depth of those who had come forward to discuss very personal aspects of their identities in public. One of the first video blogs that I discovered in my research belonged to LaMuerta27. Thank you to him and to all of those documenting their transitions.

Finally, to Tina Smart at GreenSunsetBooks. Thank you for your ongoing support, and for recognising the strength in an unconventional story.

CHAPTER ONE

It stung like a bitch. I could feel the lumps of moussaka forcing their way up the back of my throat as the rancid smell of sour vomit rose like an acid cloud.

I thought I was going to die.

Before I had a chance to start praying, another wave of nausea hit, and orange liquid spewed forth onto the pavement. I tried to reach up and hold my hair back, but the moment my hand left the pavement, my body lurched to one side like the Titanic. I was blasted. I had no idea my body could hold so much fluid, or lose it.

Oh, shit. I rested my forehead against the wall. It was rough and dug into my skin. I didn't care. I had to rest. The moment I closed my eyes the world started spinning with gripping G-force. My eyelids fluttered, and I heaved once again into the growing puddle that was fast encircling my hands and knees. Christ, I hadn't been this drunk in as long as I could remember – which at that moment wasn't very far back.

I tried to reach out again and managed to press one of my palms against the wall, but any attempt to push myself to my feet was futile; I seemed to slide sideways instead. It was about then that the tears started. It slowly began to sink in to my booze addled brain that I was in trouble. What if I couldn't get up at all? What if I fell asleep here in the alley and choked on my own puke? It happened, didn't it – people really did die this way?

Oh, Christ. I hiccupped and my cheeks filled with awful, burning mush. I opened my mouth and let it slosh to the pavement, closely followed by a second spasm. Tears were streaming down my cheeks, and my bottom lip began to tremble like a school girl – a wrecked school girl.

I suddenly felt very cold.

"Oh, my God. Look at this!" I heard a man's voice shout from somewhere behind me. I was completely torn between relief that I might finally be rescued, and mortal dread at the state they would find me in. My flashy silver halter-neck mini was drenched at the skirt, and my indiscretion was so bright orange and smelled so terrible, that there wasn't the slightest hope of disguising it. I knew within seconds that any concern would turn to laughter, but there was nothing I could do about it.

"ehp," I managed to mumble, saliva dripping from my lower lip. "Ih 'ehp."

"Hey, are you alright?" I felt the guy squat down next to me and put his hand on my exposed back. "Had a few too many?"

I nodded and then wretched. He stumbled back to avoid getting his shoes coated and almost lost his balance, which would have landed him sitting in it.

"Ooookay. What's your name?"

I took a deep breath. I wanted to tell him, really I did, but instead I just burst into fresh tears. I felt so miserable. Blub, blub, blub – that was my name.

"Hey, is she okay?" somebody else asked behind me.

"I don't know." He tried again, leaning closer and speaking louder. "What is your name?"

"Hobey...ph..." I took a deep breath. I was *so* tired. I just needed to close my eyes for a moment...my forehead rested back against the bricks.

"Hey, you okay there?" the other guy asked, approaching us.

"Hmmm," I nodded, grazing my skin.

"I think we'd better get someone."

"No," I managed. "Uh-uh."

"You look like you need help."

"No." Really, I didn't want to go to the hospital. It's every weekender's worst nightmare. I'd accompanied friends before. The lights were blindingly bright. Nurses prodded and poked you and asked you questions that you had to answer – just the thought of it made me sick. Literally.

"Oh, God!" The guy next to me said, taking his hand off my back and standing up. "My shoe!"

"-horry."

"Where do you live?" the second guy asked.

"South heet."

"By the park?"

"Hmm." I nodded again.

"She needs medical attention," the first guy said, sounding a little annoyed.

"No! No hoptal...home." I tried to wave a hand to emphasize how much I didn't want to go to the hospital, but lost my balance and was saved from falling in my own mess by the second guy holding out his arm.

"Ew, you're going to get cooties on you."

"Shut up, Seb. She needs help." He sounded very young. Was he laughing at me?

"Isn't that suit dry clean only?"

Yes, he definitely laughed at that. "Come on, help me get her to her feet."

They each took an arm. I didn't have time to argue. I found myself standing. The first guy let go of me and the second held my arm loosely as I leaned forward against the wall again. I took several deep breaths. Droplets were dripping from my skirt onto my feet, which weren't in the least protected by my Jeffrey Campbell sandals. My cousin had brought them back from New York with him. The addition of day-glow orange did nothing to improve their style, and I couldn't look down without feeling as though I would fall over.

"George, what are we going to do? I have *got* to be there by sun-up or he's going to kill me."

"It's two AM. You're hardly late."

There was silence for a moment as the second guy rubbed my back and the first one gave a drawn-out sigh.

"She doesn't want to go to the hospital. There's not much we can do."

"Home!" I squeaked pathetically in a last ditch attempt to stop them from walking off and leaving me. I had no idea who they were, but I felt infinitely better than I had on the floor, and that was thanks to them.

"See," the second guy said, "she wants to go home."

The first guy gave another audible humph. "George, don't do this to me. I've been looking forward to it all week."

"Well then, go."

"Without you?" There was something whiney about his voice.

"Look, what if she's been drugged?"

"Then I shouldn't leave her with you." He laughed, but for the first time I suddenly felt a chill run down my spine. Who were these people? I couldn't even lift my head to look.

"Uh..." I panted, trying to roll my face to one side to look at the first guy standing at the end of the alley. He was lit from behind by a large yellow street lamp that hurt my eyes.

"It's okay," the second guy said, stroking my back. "He's joking. I promise."

The realisation that I could potentially be in mortal danger had been a sobering one. I almost started to drift back to myself. As my brain struggled to regain control of my body, it decided to take another attempt at clearing out the trash. I grunted and rested my head against my arm to vomit.

"This is going to take forever," the first man groaned. "I can't do it. I haven't got time to go home and change – this is Cavalli, you know."

"So's this, and I wear it better."

"Honestly! I'm not joking."

"Then go!"

"You're really taking her home?" There was another pause in which I guess the second guy nodded. "Fine," he said, letting out a third sigh.

"Look, I'll drop her off, then come over."

"Do what you like. Call me if she tries to attack you or anything."

"Uhm…" I tried to protest, but the wall started spinning again. I heard the sound of his shoes tap off down the street, leaving me alone with the person he wouldn't leave me alone with if I were drugged. I wasn't drugged, I knew that much. I was just utterly smashed.

"Hey, you alright?" he asked, brushing my hair over one shoulder. It was a little late for that, but I appreciated the gesture and nodded against the wall. "Think you can walk?" I shook my head. "Can we try?"

I started to cry again. The thought of walking was just too much to bear.

"Hey, okay, it's alright…" He rubbed my back some more. I stopped blubbing and started just to feel stupid instead. What a state I must look. I gave up praying to be sober and settled for praying not to remember any of this in the morning.

Quite a bit of time went past. He kept rubbing my back, it was kind of soothing. He didn't say much, just occasionally "there, there" and "it's okay". I started to get colder and colder, and as I got colder I also started to feel a little more aware.

"I'm going to call a cab," he said eventually, and I just nodded. My forehead was actually stinging now; the bricks were like sandpaper. I hoped I had enough concealer at home to cover it.

A moment later he returned. "Okay, take hold of my arm."

I did as I was told and allowed him to lead me very slowly back out onto the street. The lamps above were horrific, and I started to get a throbbing headache.

"Won't take me like this," I said, surprised that I was able to string a sentence together. I pulled at my skirt to illustrate the point.

"It's alright, it's a Hackney. Just get in, act natural, and rest your head against my shoulder if you need to, okay?"

"Okay."

He walked up the street a little, and I staggered along on his arm. He was about my height, maybe an inch taller. He was wearing a black suit which, even in my drunken state, I could tell was good quality. It had silky pinstripes through it, and he wore a crisp white shirt beneath. I burned with embarrassment as I realised his cuff was slightly orange. I hoped I would never see him again. Ever.

His face was hidden by a black trilby, and I didn't have the willpower to focus. I simply let myself get dragged along to the waiting car and slid gratefully onto the smooth leather seat, thankful for the protective glass between us and the driver – the one that protected him from the smell.

"South Street," my gallant rescuer announced as we sat back in the dark. I did indeed rest my head against his shoulder and instantly started to drift into oblivion. But just on the very edge of oblivion, the spinny monster lurked, and I sat up suddenly, cold sweat prickling my brow.

"Hey, you alright in the back? If you're sick it's fifty pounds."

"We're fine," he said. "Can I open the window?"

"Sure, but it's twenty if you throw up on the outside. Someone has to clean it, you know."

"She won't be sick. We just need some air." With that, he leant over me and wound down the window. It was a blessed reprieve. I gulped in the crisp night like a goldfish. It helped to ward off the worst.

I managed to hold it together until we got to my street and even managed to point out my house. Very inelegantly, I misjudged the curb and found myself staring once again at the pavement, saved by my outstretched arm.

As I struggled to right myself, I heard the taxi door slam behind me, along with some mumbled words from the driver which sounded like "…if that were my daughter…"

As the cab drove off, the guy appeared by my side again. "Come on, let's get you inside."

I thought about telling him that I was fine, that I'd make it from here, but I honestly wasn't sure that I could. I started walking to my door. The stench of gut lining was suddenly overpowering and, halfway up my path, I leaned into the hedge to retch again.

He came and held my hair back whilst I vomited. When I was finally ready, we completed the marathon to my door. He helped me to locate the spare key under the mat, then guided my hand unsteadily to the lock. Once the door was open, I reached in and flicked the hall light, squinting against the onslaught of reality.

It didn't cross my mind to stop him; I just allowed him to support me in by my elbow. If he hadn't, I would probably have lain face-down on the stairs and slipped into a coma. Instead, he directed me into the kitchen and sat me down on a stool at the breakfast table. I crossed my arms in front of me and rested my head as he went about running the taps and opening draws.

I had no idea what he was looking for. Just as I started to drift off, I felt a cool, damp cloth against the back of my neck. He helped me lift my head, and wiped around my mouth and fringe.

"We need to get you to bed."

"Hmmm." I was so, so tired. I wanted him to go away now. Thanks very much for getting me home safe, really appreciated, but leave me alone.

To be honest, I don't remember much more about it. I remember being forced to drink water from a pint glass. Something about "rehydration". Then I remember leaning over the toilet with him holding my hair again whilst all that water came back up. Somehow I got to my room. I remember taking my dress off, so I must have been alone. Then I was in my grey T-shirt, the one I sleep in. I think he wiped my face again. I was sitting on the edge of the bed or something…

I woke up.

Every part of me ached like hell. My hair was matted together with crusted sick, my mouth was like sand and my arm felt like I couldn't move it. When I pulled back the cover it was swollen. It took me about ten minutes to remember falling out of the taxi. I wiggled my fingers to make sure that it wasn't broken, then pulled the covers back up over my face.

I would have stayed like that for the rest of the week, only I needed to pee. It was a monumental effort, but I dragged myself to my *en suite* and rested my head in my hands as I sat on the loo. My stained, silver mini was soaking in the sink and the whole cubical smelled of yuck.

Oh so very slowly, images of my homeward journey began to surface. I wiped, dipped my hands in the cold water, then rushed downstairs to see if the telly was still there.

CHAPTER TWO

Everything was still there. Nothing was broken or missing as far as I could tell, and the front door was locked, its Yale bolt clicking into place as he closed it on his way out. Or at least, I hoped it had. A deep rumble from upstairs raised the awful thought that perhaps my dad had found it open when he came home.

Dad worked nights; he was a porter at the hospital. He usually left around ten and got back in the early hours, five or sometimes six. We often passed on the landing, me blow-drying my hair for a night out whilst he was getting his first cup of coffee.

I listened to him snore for a moment, building up the courage to face my own reflection. A large oval mirror hung in the hallway like a picture frame, but I was no Mona Lisa. Thick black circles sagged beneath my eyes, accentuated by blurred mascara. My forehead was red, the rest of me was pale as milk, and my hair looked like an electrocuted scarecrow. I turned away in disgust.

By the time I dragged myself through the shower, a second awful thought had seeded itself in the otherwise barren wastelands of my brain.

That man knew where I lived. He had been in my house, knew the street and the number, and I didn't even know what he looked like. I hoped to God that he wouldn't think to check up on me. Last night had been one of those occasions in life that had happened. Undeniably. But maybe, just maybe, if I tried hard enough to forget, it never did.

There was a knock at the door.

Oh boy. This was going to be it, wasn't it? Some spotty teenager. Or, maybe, if I was lucky, a suave young professional - perhaps with flowers - here to make sure that I hadn't died in the night.

I thought about pretending to be out.

The knock came again and, with a heavy heart, I went and opened the door.

"Forget something?" It was Orla, my best mate. She stood in the doorway holding my little silver clutch bag in one hand, her curly red hair making her look almost devilish in her delivery.

I stepped back to let her in, and we convened around the breakfast table in the kitchen. She looked deceptively like she'd been in bed by nine: her makeup was immaculate, her hair lacquered and defused. She wore cute red kitten heels, a matching knee-length skirt, a black vest top and denim jacket. Nothing ever looked bad on her.

In contrast, I sported this season's pink and white striped bath robe and a head towel.

"Two questions," she said as she perched on a stool. "Where on earth did you get to last night, and what happened to your face?" She drew a finger around her forehead in case I hadn't realised which part of my face she was referring to.

I waved a hand and went to make coffee. "Nowhere, and it's need to know only."

"Well, I need to know. You just walked off and left your bag. I thought you were coming back. You know your money and your phone and everything is in here?"

"Yeah, thanks for bringing it back."

"That's it?"

I shrugged.

"Uh-huh. So, what did he do this time?"

The kettle clicked, and I started spooning instant granules into a cup. Before I knew it, she was standing next to me, rubbing my back just like that guy had done last night. "Sweetie, you know whatever it is you can tell me, right?"

"It's not that. I just really don't want to think about it right now."

"Hangover?"

"Yes."

"Look, go upstairs. Get some clothes on. I'll make coffee and then we can go for ice-cream at the Centre, okay? Best cure for a hangover there is."

Reluctantly, I trudged up the stairs and started going through my wardrobe. I could feel a serious bout of the glums coming on. Everything just seemed to suck. I would be twenty-six next month, and I was still living at home. My job was crap, I had no money, I'd almost drowned in my own vomit, and my boyfriend was cheating on me. As far as prospects go, they weren't sparkling.

I pulled on jeans and a faded Button Moon T-shirt. My bottle blonde hair was starting to show at the roots, and it took five whole minutes of intense, eye-aching concentration to plaster over the abrasions above my brow. The last thing in the world that I felt like doing was going for ice-cream at the local shopping centre, but I'd learned a long time ago with Orla that the best way to get rid of her was to humour her until she got bored.

When I finally re-emerged in the kitchen, my coffee was getting cold. I left it, and we headed out.

There was something to it: ice-cream is good for the soul. That and the two Panadol I'd taken.

"Did you try to kiss a lamp?" she tried again, once we'd exhausted comments on the size 22 woman window shopping at Zara, and the unruly kids who almost upended a bargain jewellery stall.

"Something like that."

"Quit being mysterious. What happened?"

"You want to know the truth?"

"Well, duh."

"I had a little more than I thought."

"That's it? You got tipsy and decided to go home?"

"Sort of. I got tipsy, and I went to the toilet to pee. Whilst I was there, I heard a voice in the cubical next to me."

"What sort of voice?"

"A male voice. A woman and a man, to be precise. Getting it on."

Orla frowned. "I'm not going to like where this is going, am I?"

"Well, I certainly didn't."

"It wasn't Mark?"

I looked down at my empty ice-cream saucer. I just couldn't bring myself to admit it, not out loud.

"Oh, God. Phoebe, I'm so sorry! Are you *sure*?"

"Yes, I'm very sure. I peeked under the wall. He was wearing his red trainers that night, the ones with the white line around them. They were definitely his feet."

Orla glanced down at the table. I sensed her drawing her own feet under her chair, as if feeling guilty for also wearing red shoes. "That's just awful. But where did you go?"

"To the bar. I ordered three of their biggest cocktails and downed each one of them."

"Ouch."

"Like I say, I was already a bit tipsy."

"Hence the quick exit?"

I nodded. "Yeah, I was so ill. I got about as far as the end of the high street, then I was sick in an alley."

"How did you get home?"

"Some guys stopped. One of them helped me."

"Fee! Do you have any idea how dangerous that was? You should have called me."

"You had my phone."

She paused for a moment, then reached forward for my bag and pulled out my mobile. I'd transferred it from the clutch bag before we left.

"What are you doing?"

"Let's see if Mark called."

"What? Why?"

"He came looking for you about half an hour after you disappeared. I had no idea where you'd gone. You could have been with a dishy fella for all I knew, so I just said that I hadn't seen you – which I hadn't."

Only Orla could try and make up an alibi for the innocent truth. Two seconds after she turned my phone on, it beeped with a message. "You have voice mail," she said, pressing a couple of buttons and passing it to me.

"Hey, babes." It was Mark. "Where are you? Look, I'm kinda tired. I think I'm going to call it a night. Give me a call when you get this, beautiful."

I passed it back so that she could listen to it. She made a face like she'd just been sucking lemons, then put it down again. "He is such a piece of work. I don't know what you ever saw in him in the first place."

"Me neither." I tried to smile, but deep down I knew exactly what it had been. I honestly thought that I had seen a future there. We'd been dating for almost three years. He made me laugh. He was educated; he had his own place, his own car, a good job. I thought we were set.

"Oh, Fee." She reached out her hand and placed it over mine. "It's not the end of the world. Who knows, perhaps they weren't even his shoes – they're in fashion now. Plenty of guys are wearing them."

I felt a flash of annoyance. Orla was my best friend. She was only trying to cheer me up, but to suggest that I didn't know the sound of my own boyfriend's voice, or what he was wearing, was a little insulting. I just wanted to be on my own.

"Look, if you don't mind, I'm going to head home, okay?"

"No problem. Do you want me to come with you? We could watch old movies. I know where there's a tub of cookie dough ice-cream with your name on it."

"No, if it's all the same, I'll pass. I'm actually kind of tired. I need to sleep."

I picked up my bag, gave her a hug, and headed for home.

As it was, I did end up on the sofa with my duvet and a bag of toffee popcorn, watching an old Audrey Hepburn movie. I didn't feel much like eating, but I didn't feel like thinking either and it helped stop me from doing that.

Around half-eight I heard my dad get up. The shower ran for a while, and then he came downstairs, towel wrapped around his pudgy middle-age spread. He made a beeline for the kettle.

"Morning, love."

"Morning, Dad."

"Did you have a good night last night?"

"Yeah, it was great."

"Where'd you go?"

"Just Kabana, nowhere fancy."

"With Orla and Mark?"

"Yeah, and a couple of girls from work."

He went through the fridge and pulled out bacon, eggs, and a Tupperware container of beans.

"Going to make a fry-up, do you want some?"

I shook my head. Even though Dad had always worked nights as long as I could remember, it still didn't seem right to me to start the night off with a full English breakfast. I continued to watch TV with the subtitles on whilst the bacon sizzled and snapped in the pan. Eventually he scraped it onto a plate, poured himself a coffee and went back upstairs to get dressed.

About five minutes later my phone went. It was Mark, and I hit the 'reject' button. He left a message, much like the last one. I fixed my attention back on the telly with double intensity.

Around quarter to ten, Dad left for work. Suddenly the house seemed very quiet. I kept turning the telly up to try and fill the void, but somehow I couldn't concentrate as well as I had before.

I found myself reaching for my phone.

I listened to the message again.

"Hey, babes, have you dropped off the face of the planet or something? Give me a call when you get this."

I held it in my hand for a while longer. Then, just as I was about to call him, he called me. This time I answered.

"At last, I thought you'd been abducted by aliens or something."

"We need to talk."

There was a pause.
"Yeah. Yeah, we do. Come over to mine."
"Now?"
"Yeah."
I hung up.

CHAPTER THREE

I pressed the intercom, and he buzzed me in. Mark lived in a posh modern apartment about twenty minutes away. The stairwell was all plate glass and stainless steel railings. He was standing in the doorway by the time I got up there. It dawned on me that perhaps, after three years, a girl might reasonably be allowed to expect a spare key.

"Hey, you made it."

Did that really deserve congratulating? Sure, the city can be a big bad place, but getting on a bicycle and peddling five miles hardly seemed a game of chance. Though I supposed, with the attitude of most night-time drivers, it was more of a chance than I generally gave myself credit for.

"Come in," he said, standing back and allowing me to pass. He went to the kitchen area and poured me a glass of red wine. He already had one himself.

"Thanks," I said, taking it and putting it on the counter.

He frowned. "Aren't you going to sit down?"

I shook my head. No. I wasn't even going to take off my coat.

"Should I be worried?" he asked.

"I don't know, should you?"

His frown deepened, and he put his own glass of wine down next to mine, leaning back against the counter with his arms folded. "Okay, so what do we need to talk about?"

I suddenly felt like I'd lost my nerve. I'd built myself up so much that I'd practically cycled here under steam power. But now that the shit was about to hit the fan, I wasn't sure that I wanted to do it. Sounds ridiculous, doesn't it? I wouldn't say that I'm someone who avoids confrontation. I don't like it, but then nobody likes it. Well, except maybe a few dramatic types who thrive off it, but generally it's not the norm.

I was upset. Of course I was upset. It really, really hurt to think that my boyfriend - this man standing here in front of me now, whose face and body and smell were all so familiar to me - could be sticking his dick into another woman. It made me feel dizzy.

But what if Orla was right? What if I was wrong? I mean, I'd only seen his shoes; I hadn't seen his face. I'd heard his voice, but then I'd already admitted to being a little tipsy.

If I was wrong, he might never forgive me.

And if I was right...

I glanced over to the door where a few pairs of shoes were lined up. One pair were the red trainers he'd been wearing last night. I bit my lip and gazed at them.

I was sure.

"Did you have sex with another woman last night?" I asked abruptly, turning to him.

He didn't move, and I didn't breathe.

Then suddenly he leaned forward, almost double, and gave a hoot as he clasped his hands behind his head.

"Thank fuck for that," he said, straightening up. "I thought you were about to tell me you were pregnant!"

I didn't know what to say. I think my mouth opened and closed a few times like a fish. I was completely stunned.

"I -" I tried, but nothing came.

"Seriously, babes, you had me going for a minute there. You sounded so peeved on the phone earlier; I thought it had to be bad."

"But -"

"Honestly though, I'm glad you brought it up. We really do need to talk."

It's not me, is it? Men don't generally reply to the question 'Did you sleep with someone else?' with 'Thank fuck, I thought you were pregnant.' That really wasn't a normal reaction, was it?

It's that feeling, like your whole body isn't there anymore and you're just a pair of eyes hovering in mid-air. I looked at him and waited. I didn't have to wait very long.

"Oh, Phoebe, baby, I'm so sorry. I really didn't want to do this to you. But when you said that we needed to talk, I just knew you were right. I can't lie to you, babes. There's someone else."

The back of my throat felt like glue. It was hard to swallow. "I know," I whispered.

He seemed to calm down a little, and folded his arms again. "Oh," he said.

"I was in the cubical next to you."

He seemed to take this in for a moment, then nodded. "What did you see?"

"What kind of a question is that?"

"Just a question, how much do you know?"

I felt like one of those code crackers during the war, only I'd got the code mixed up and somehow my message read: 'pink rabbit in underpants drinks lemonade in Peru.' None of it really made a lot of sense.

I took a deep breath and tried again.

"I heard you, with a woman, in the women's lavs last night. You were screwing her."

"Yeah. I was."

"That's it, 'yeah I was' – that's all you're going to say?"

"Well, what else is there to say?"

In the ensuing silence I realised he had a point. What more was there to say? Did I want him back? No. Did he want me? No.

I turned slowly and let myself out.

"Ah, Phoebs," I heard him call, without any real conviction.

I made it to the bottom stairwell before it hit me. My astonishment melted away like the ice age, replaced by granite hard hatred.

What the fuck kind of man did that to somebody? What kind of shit-for-brains could brush off three years of my life like it were a minor inconvenience? *Three years*. Three years in which I could have been doing something, and someone, else. Sure, booze made me sick, it made me throw up in the street. But this was a whole other kind of sickness. I was sick with anger. Hell yes, I was angry with myself for settling for mediocre. I knew our love affair was no Casablanca, but I'd stuck with it anyway. I'd rather assume this was 'normal' and that everybody lived half fulfilled hopes, than accept that maybe he just wasn't that crazy about me.

But there would be plenty of time to kick myself later. I was not about to step meekly into the night and close the door behind me. Storming back up the stairs, I began hammering on his door. He opened it with a look of mild surprise.

"You bastard!" I exploded. Until then, I hadn't realised that I held such venom inside me, or that I was capable of such all-consuming fury. "You fucking bastard," I slapped him hard across the face and pushed him backwards into the room. I went to hit him again, but this time he caught my hand. When I tried to kick at him, he pushed me away, and I almost tripped over the couch.

"I'm sorry, alright?" His voice was thick.

"No! No, it's *not* alright! It's not alright!" I couldn't see for tears. "Are you leaving me for her?"

"Yes. Really, I'm sorry."

I'd known the answer, but still felt compelled to ask. "Well, who the fuck is she?" I screamed.

He didn't look at me, but after a moment he moved towards the door. "I think you'd better go."

"No, I won't go! Who is she?"

"You're hysterical."

"I'm *allowed* to be, you shit fuck son of a bitch."

He looked almost as impressed by my creative use of language as I was. But, all the same, he didn't invite me to stay. Instead, he came over and took me by the wrist, dragging me towards the door.

I flailed out for anything I could grab hold of and managed to find a white enamel vase with a single red rose in it. Without pausing to admire the romantic imagery, I brought it down across the side of his head. He ducked just in time, and I caught the side of his neck, which was lucky in a way otherwise I might be facing a murder charge. Almost as quickly, he swiped it to the floor and retaliated with a savage left hook to the jaw.

I went down like a sack of potatoes. It was shock more than anything. I couldn't believe that he'd hit me. So, okay, I was about to bludgeon him with a decorative ornament, but I hadn't meant it. Not like this. I'd been in a frenzy. I had no idea what I was doing. He had very deliberately smacked me in the face.

I slouched there on my knees for a while. He loomed above me, pinching the bridge of his nose. I was too shocked even to cry. How had it come to this? All I had to do was keep walking and get on my bike; it would have been such a dignified exit. But instead, here I was, bloody lip and battered ego.

Slowly, he lowered his fingers from his eyes and reached down to me. I took his hand, and he pulled me up.

"I'm sorry," he said again.

"You arsehole."

"Yeah. I know."

At least he wasn't his usual cocky-mouthed cuntish self. He finally had the decency to look ashamed.

I walked to the door and opened it.

"I never meant for it to end this way," he said.

I slammed it shut.

CHAPTER FOUR

Orla had been amazing after that. I'd called her when I got in. It was at times like this that I appreciated Dad working nights. I don't know what I would have said if he'd seen the state of me. 'I walked into a door' would have been a clear lie. It was obvious someone had smacked me one. He would have guessed that it was a bloke, and no doubt made the short hop of logic to Mark. I would probably have had to hold him down, or chain him to something, to stop him from going over there.

But Orla was coolly philosophical about it all.

"You have no idea who she is?"

I shook my head. I guessed, in some circumstances, things like this would lead a woman to suspect even her closest friend. But I was spared that because, when I came out of the toilets, Orla had still been sitting at our table, sucking the face off some guy.

"So, what are you going to do about it? Do you want him back?"

I shook my head and sipped from my glass of Black Bush, which we'd opened in commiseration. "No, I don't want him back."

"You want to forget about him?"

I nodded. Yes. I'd like to forget all about him.

She didn't push me, and we sat watching various types of free-to-view trash until the early hours. I offered her the sofa, but she eventually opted for home. I crawled up to bed myself, feeling a smidge better for Orla's suggestion that my over reaction might have been in part due to a come-down from the horrific hangover I'd suffered. We all act irrationally when our bodies are out of sync.

The next three weeks passed in a blur of office, filing, phone calls, e-mails and purchase order forms. I worked for a local disability charity as an assistant administrator. It was only part-time. Enough hours not to qualify for the dole, but not enough to earn any money to move out, afford a car, or have a life. There was nothing I could do about it though. Between rising unemployment and plummeting financial stability, I was just damn grateful to have a job. If I hadn't been laid-off by the time the market picked up again, then at least my CV would be current and I'd stand a better chance of getting out.

Working for charities is fine, but the problem with the Voluntary Sector is that everyone is so very passionate. If you want to make big money, you join the Private Sector and go into business. People work for charities because they are committed to a cause, be that autism, cancer research or the elderly. Passion is what it's all about. But passionate people are often strong personalities, and when you put all of those strong personalities in a room together...

Add to that "founder's syndrome," of which we had a classic case. Our organisation worked only in the local community, and had originally been founded by the church. When it split, they appointed a fairly formidable lady to take over management decisions and shepherd the trustees. Nobody was left in any doubt that it was Sheila's organisation.

Doubly depressing when you knew you couldn't stage a walk-out because there was nowhere else to go. Every other day was a 'yes, ma'm, no, ma'm' day. But at least it kept me busy. Whilst I was at work, I wasn't thinking about he who shall not be named. During the other half of the week, when I wasn't working, I went jogging in the park, cooked large quantities of food for freezing – possibly enough to survive a nuclear fallout – and read a lot of books.

Mark didn't call or try to make contact in any way, and I didn't ask about him. It was as if three years had never happened, and the more I looked back over those three years, the more memories only seemed to feature myself. For such a solid relationship it was remarkable how much time we spent apart. I always thought it was a classy, grown-up, no-pressures relationship. The type you're supposed to have once teenage hormones wear off and allow you to let go of his leg and wipe his lipstick emblazoned name off your mirror. Preparation for marriage.

I didn't like to think about it. If I thought about it, I would start to wonder how many other women he'd slept with. Had she been the first? For all I knew there could have been a string of them queuing up outside the door each night, maybe even prostitutes.

Several occasions arose where I found myself turning the pages of my book automatically, without actually having read a single word. After I'd scanned the same paragraph four times, I called Orla, and she agreed to come with me to the family planning clinic.

The tests were fairly undignified. Anything involving the removal of your underwear whilst lying on your back with your legs wide open generally is, when not preceded by a romantic meal and a little slow dancing. But the results came back quickly, and thankfully Mark hadn't given me anything except crippled self-esteem.

I was holding up like a trooper. There was only one really bleak moment. My period was due; I felt bloated and unattractive. I'd managed to cultivate a pubescent-sized spot on my chin, and I'd made the fatal mistake of tuning into a soppy love song slot on local radio.

In times of extreme stress I take out the shoebox in my wardrobe. It happens maybe two or three times a year; the rest of the time it's buried under my casually discarded clothes and lost socks.

Inside the shoebox are all my baby trinkets and a picture of my mother. It's not the best picture in the world. It was taken in the mid-nineties, but she's smiling with such genuine happiness, and I'm there, wrapped up in her arms. I must have been about twelve, and Dad says it was her forty-fifth birthday.

She died a year and a half later, of a stroke. We were shopping at Waitrose. We had just stopped in on the way home from school. I went to the pasta section to get Bolognese sauce and shells.

As I came back down the aisle, I could see a group of people had gathered. I wasn't sure what they were looking at so I went up and tried to peer through. One of the men glanced down. He physically turned me away and pushed me on the back. "You don't want to see this," he said.

But it was too late. I'd already caught sight of her. She was lying on the floor, propped up by an older woman who looked like my head teacher. Mum's face was all drooped down on one side and her eye was looking right up; there was hardly any pupil there, just white.

I remembered screaming and shouldering my way back past the man, shouting: "That's my Mummy!"

She was dead before the ambulance arrived, but I stayed with her all the way to the hospital. There wasn't anybody else there that I knew. I think the paramedics tried to make it look like they were helping her so that I didn't panic, even though they knew she had gone. It worked because I remembered thinking that it would all be alright if we could just get to the hospital. Dad would come, and we'd all be alright.

That was almost thirteen years ago.

I loved that picture of my mum, and I'd hold my baby tag from the hospital, the one they put around your wrist the day you're born so you don't get mixed up and sent home with the wrong family. There's a rattle, a teething ring, and my christening gown - which looks like a doll's nightie.

I cried really hard then. Mark was the sort of problem that only a mother could fix. You need your mum to tell you about all of the heartaches she went through before she met your dad. To tell you it's all just part of life, and remind you that there's still plenty of hope. Dads are great too, but they just can't have those conversations in the same way.

It all came pouring out, and I felt much better afterwards. I found a secret stash of chocolate in a cupboard that I'd forgotten about and ate it whilst watching the comedy channel.

So, Mark wasn't the one for me. Big deal. Life moves on, the earth doesn't spin off its axis, and watching people cycle into lampposts doesn't become any less funny.

At the end of those three weeks, Orla finally imploded. "This is silly, lady. You're living in some kind of bubble! All you do is work and bake cakes that you never eat. Not that I'm complaining, they're yummy, but you need to get out of the house."

I could feel it coming. Another Orla directive that you had to follow in order to put it in the 'done' pile and move on to the next issue.

"I don't feel like going out," I said, in a half-hearted attempt to squirm out of it.

"But you never will if you stay cooped up in here. Come on, just a little outing."

"I haven't got anything to wear," I lied.

"Rubbish! Your wardrobe is vast. Anyway, nowhere fancy, casual is fine. I'm not suggesting we go on the pull."

"Good!"

"I'm just suggesting drinks. Somewhere nice, like Henry's."

"Well..." It had been a long time since Orla and I had been out for 'just drinks' together. I was always with Mark, and she was usually trailing some bloke along. We would bump into colleagues and friends, which always resulted in a nightclub after several bars ranging from ear-bleedingly loud to slightly seedy.

Henry's, on the other hand, was nice. It was a suave, almost sophisticated cocktail bar with light wooden flooring, dark upholstery, and majestic iron chandeliers.

"Okay," I relented.

I managed to dig out a sleeveless black cowl-neck sweater and a pair of three-quarter length jeans with Chinese dragons embroidered up one side. Understated and under the radar. I was hoping not to attract any unwanted attention.

We took the bus into town and ordered Charlie Chaplins, made with apricot brandy and sloe gin. It felt kind of strange just the two of us being out. I couldn't remember the last time. We'd been friends since school and had learned to drink at a tender age in the park with the same group of lads we occasionally still drank with in the pub. Orla worked as a receptionist at a local solicitors' firm. She thought about training once, but then decided academia wasn't really for her. Not that she isn't smart – she's razor sharp – just that it's a lot of money, and you have to be really sure that's what you want before you go spending it. I can understand that. I'm an assistant administrator for the exact same reason. One day, when I figure out what I want to be, I'll go for it. But right now I'm just getting by.

We were sitting on bar stools along the shiny, varnished counter. We'd just drained our second glass when she excused herself and went to find the loo. I was feeling really relaxed. It had been a great idea to come out for the evening, and maybe this was exactly what I needed. I had been holed away for so long.

I was fiddling with a beer mat when I happened to look up and notice someone watching me from the other end of the bar. He was quite far away, but I was fairly sure that he was staring at me. I looked away, then looked back. I did it again and, just as I was about to hold his gaze, the corner of his lip twitched in a smile. Orla sat down next to me.

"You okay, trouble?"

I tried to ignore him. He'd probably been looking past me at the window, which looked out onto the street. It was dark now. A few people were walking past with their shopping, trying to pick out a suitable restaurant.

We ordered another drink and talked about her latest love affair. Orla fell in love like lemmings fall off cliffs. The guy she'd been snogging in the club the night Mark unceremoniously dumped me, had been her sports instructor. She trained at the pool twice a week. She'd always been a water baby and sometimes swam in local trials. Apparently this new guy had made quite a splash. They'd been out for dinner twice in the past week.

"I haven't bedded him yet," she explained. "It could get awkward in the water if I did that. I need to be sure that he's either happy to have a bit of fun, or maybe that he really means it. I don't want any of this complicated in-between stuff."

"Wow, you almost sound serious about the guy."

"Well, maybe. He's very hot."

I laughed. Orla never uses the word 'serious' about any relationship, so who knew, this could really be something.

We stayed at the bar until quarter to eleven, interspersing cocktails with soda and lime. I was surprised when I asked whether we were going on anywhere and she didn't pull out an itinerary.

"I don't want to wear you out on your first night, honey. We need to build you up slowly, get you in training."

"I'm grateful, really, I am."

She gave me a reassuring pinch on the shoulder and headed to the loo for a final call before we started for home. As I waited, I noticed the guy at the end of the bar again. He was definitely still there, and definitely looking in my direction.

I stared down at my beer mat and tried to ignore him. We'd be gone in a couple of minutes. Then, out of the corner of my eye, I saw him get up and start walking towards me.

The person who arrived by my side oddly bore little resemblance to the person I thought I had seen. I believed that I had been looking at a young man with cropped black hair and pale skin, dressed in black.

The person who stood next to me still looked young-ish, and had short-ish black hair, pale skin and a long black overcoat. But all of a sudden I found myself a little uncertain.

"You're looking better."

I gaped for a moment. The voice sounded familiar.

"I'm sorry…," I eventually managed, holding out my hand.

"George," he said with a smile.

I racked my brain, then settled for nodding effusively and shaking on it.

"You don't remember me, do you?" He leaned on the bar and looked down with a self-deprecating twitch of his lip.

"I'm so sorry. Where did we meet again?"

"You sure you want me to remind you?"

I stared at him for a moment before a sudden, cold realisation hit me.

"Oh, God," I whispered.

"Hey, don't sweat it. Really. It's forgotten."

"If you'd forgotten, you wouldn't be here talking to me."

He shrugged. "Look, I'm sorry. I didn't come to make you feel bad. I just recognised you from the end of the bar."

"Yeah, sure, recognised me in a bar, drinking – what a surprise, huh?" I wanted the seat to disappear me.

"Well, you know, you shouldn't let your body win. Beat it into submission."

I grinned and tried to think of something to say.

"Look, I'm just glad you're feeling better. You have a nice evening." He smiled again, gave me a little wave of his fingers, and left.

I was still staring after him when Orla came back.

"What's up? You look kind of spaced. Too much brandy?"

"No. I just bumped into someone."

"Someone from work?"

"No, just someone who helped me out once - that night when I got home really drunk."

"What, the man who helped you in the street?"

"Yes, only…"

"Only what? You're scaring me."

"Well, only, I don't know. Must just be me."

"Just you?"

"Yeah, just me. Let's go."

I grabbed my coat and we left.

CHAPTER FIVE

That night I couldn't sleep. I tossed and turned for over an hour before trying to lie as still as possible on my back, arm resting across my forehead. I gazed into the darkness, daring sleep to attack.

I tried to think about work. There was a ton of filing I needed to do the next day and several e-mails I had to reply to in order to arrange dates for meetings between various staff members. I also tried to imagine Orla with her new bloke – could this actually be the one? I only remembered him very briefly from the bar. I think he was handsome, but the only thing that mattered was that Orla thought so. I even fleetingly thought about Mark, who was probably tucked up in bed with that floozy with the green wedge heels.

But none of these thoughts lasted terribly long. Eventually they all melted away to the man at the bar. Granted, I had been a little tipsy again. Nowhere near as blasted as I had been the first time around, but it was still truthful to say that I'd never seen him through sober eyes.

What I did see more clearly this time, was that he had several attractive features. Firstly, he had magnificent bone structure. High cheekbones and an angular jaw. He had short, cropped black hair and a swept fringe, shiny with gel. His eyes were oval and, I think, green, with thick lashes and an arched brow.

He was extremely good looking in an almost feminine way. Androgynous.

But his clothes were definitely those of a man, and his scent was familiar. *Declaration*, perhaps.

I felt that thick scent enwrap me as I closed my eyes and drifted off into long awaited dreams.

The next day at work was a surprise. I walked in to find my colleague Miriam's desk covered in flowers. There was a bouquet the length of a palm tree lying across her fax machine, and the whole room smelled of oriental lilies. There was also a helium balloon tied to her chair, with a big red heart on it.

"Is it your birthday?" I asked, trying to make sense of the situation.

"Duh, what planet are you living on? It's Valentine's Day."

I frowned. She was right. It was 14th February, and I hadn't even noticed.

"Planet Singledom," I replied, and she suddenly looked apologetic.

"Oh, crikey. Sorry, Fee, I forgot."

"Yeah well, no big loss."

"His big loss," she said, in a belated attempt to back Team Phoebe.

Lunchtime came and went. I bought a potato with chicken curry from the café opposite and sat at my desk writing an update for the website. Thankfully, Madam was out of the office, so there was nobody breathing down my neck, and Miriam took the opportunity for an extended lunch break.

She was just sauntering in when I noticed that she'd brought someone with her. It was a delivery woman in a blue jacket with *Floral Tributes* emblazoned on the breast.

"Phoebe Gelber?" she asked, looking around expectantly.

I raised my hand, and she deposited a narrow white box in front of me.

"Happy Valentine's Day, Ms. Gelber," she said and brusquely walked out.

I assumed I'd got the late shift. After about one o'clock the muscles in her face probably stopped working, and you had to pay extra for a smile. Still, I was more than surprised by the gift and tentatively lifted the lid.

"Wow," Miriam said, peering over my shoulder, "he must be really sorry."

It was a single stem rose with a gift card. I opened it. Maddeningly, it simply said: **?**

Our Advocacy Officer, Eddie, walked in and, seeing us gazing at the table, also came to have a look.

"Well," he said, breaking our reverie, "you must have impressed."

"What do you mean?"

"It's her ex," Miriam blurted out. "He's been a bad boy."

"Are you quite sure about that?"

We both looked at him. "What?" I eventually asked, exasperated by his smug expression.

"Goodness, sweetie, it's all about the colour. That's an orange rose."

"*And*?"

"Alright, keep your knickers on. Only, if I were going to send my boyfriend a sorry note for playing away from home, I'd send him a red rose, to affirm our love. Or maybe a white one, as a sign of surrender," he chuckled.

"But this one's orange," Miriam repeated, a puzzled frown crossing her face.

"What does that mean?" I asked.

"It's desire, sweetheart. Fascination."

Now it was my turn to frown.

"If it were red-tipped at the end, it would mean that they were falling in love with you. But perhaps it hasn't gone that far yet. Whoever sent it knows their roses though."

"And you know this because-?"

"I'm green fingered, can't you tell? It's something all gay men know. We brush up on these things – flower arranging, choosing the right colour scheme for our boudoir, red or white wine with a meal."

"You're kidding?"

"Yes," he said, deadpan. "Look it up on the internet. Right, anyone for coffee?"

I waited until he left the room before calling up the search engine.

"He's right, you know," I called to Miriam, who'd returned to her own desk. "Fascination, desire and passion."

"Does that sound like Mark?"

"Not unless he underwent a frontal lobotomy and got a gay best friend."

That evening I went home via the bakery and treated myself to a cream-filled chocolate éclair. Dad came down for coffee around nine o'clock and stopped to admire the rose, which I had placed in a glass flute by the television.

"From Mark?" he asked, scratching his head and blinking in the harsh living room light.

"Who knows," I shrugged.

Then, at around ten-thirty, the strangest thing happened.

Mark called.

I stared at the screen of my mobile for several rings, stunned into inaction. Finally, I answered it.

"Hey, Phoebs?"

"Hey, Mark."

There was a very long pause.

"Can I help you?" I prompted, sounding like someone in a call centre for the terminally brain dead. Maybe I was a call forwarding centre; perhaps he meant to call Prostitute, but I was just above that in the alphabet. Or perhaps I could offer him electro shock therapy, to his balls.

"I, uh, I just wanted to call. See how you're doing."

"Why?"

There was another long pause. I thought it was a reasonable question though. Why, after almost a month without even a text, did he feel the need to call me up and talk?

"Has she dumped you?"

"Oh, don't be ridiculous, Phoebe." Ah, that sounded more like the normal Mark. Arrogant cock. "It's just - it's Valentine's Day, and I thought you might be, well, you know…"

"No, what?"

"Lonely."

"Is that why you sent me the flowers?" A slight exaggeration. It was only one flower, but that didn't really roll off the tongue.

Yet. Another. Paaaaaauuuuussse.

I glanced at the clock.

"What flowers?"

Aha! Sounded like the truth. He would have said 'what flower?' if he knew there was only one.

"The rose."

"Someone sent you roses?" Again, plural. So it wasn't him! I felt rather smug at my own cunning.

"Oh, nothing," I breezed. "Anyway, Mark, I'd better get going now. There's something on telly I want to watch."

"Oh, okay. If you're sure you're alright?"

"Absolutely. My world didn't revolve around you, you know. I actually do have a life."

And with that, I hung up before the silence sent me to sleep. What had I ever seen in that boy? When you really stopped to listen, he had the personality of a brick. And, like bricks, it was all architectural with him – the suit, the tie, the swagger.

My eyes slowly drifted to the rose.

Big speech that, Phoebe love, but I bet you wouldn't have been half as brave if you really were sitting here alone on Valentine's Day. I had a sudden image of the room with no Dad, nothing worth watching on TV, and no rose, surprised at how depressed I suddenly felt. But the rose was there, and everything was good again. How on earth could that one thing have such an effect?

I wasn't alone. I just didn't know who else was in the room with me. *Fascination, desire and passion.*

I turned the TV off and, despite how late it was, I decided to run myself a long, hot bath. I burned a cinnamon candle, poured a glass of *vin rouge* and allowed myself to sink into steamy reflections.

CHAPTER SIX

I didn't hear anything more from Mark. I assumed my caustic words had left him licking his wounds. I was fairly sure that he'd only called because his own date had fallen flat and he wanted to reassure himself that my life was just as miserable.

By the time Friday rolled around, my rose was starting to wilt, and there was a note on my desk from my boss – Her Almighty. Apparently the Administrator, to whom I was assistant, was still on sick leave. No surprise, she'd only been in two weeks out of the last twenty. Some mysterious illness, the main symptom of which seemed to be a pronounced phobia of work. I was inclined to give her the benefit of the doubt – that it was actually stress-related – which was fully understandable, given that we worked for Madam Mao. But at the same time it meant that we were down a key member of staff, which was more stress for everyone remaining.

The note simply said that there would be a Funding Conference on Monday, could I please attend in her place and pay particular attention to payroll giving. Deep joy. Something to look forward to. Yawn.

"Aw, lucky you," Miriam said. "I wish I got a day off next Monday to sit and network. They always have good lunches at those things."

"Yeah, but you know it comes at a price. One day slacking means all my weekends for the next month. She's trying to prime me to become a fundraiser."

"Ouch," she grimaced. "You think?"

"I know." Part-time hours, full-time work; half the staff, double the effort – all carried over on the sheer good will of Voluntary Sector workers. Still, another string to my bow. At least when the market picks up again I'll have funding experience behind me and a shot at a better paid job. Maybe even a place of my own.

I folded the note into my pocket and stared at the thirty-seven new e-mails awaiting my attention. Everything from requests for disability statistics to enquiries as to whether I would like a stiffer cock. It was always so difficult to know where to start.

Orla blew me off at the weekend to spend time with her handsome merman. I didn't really mind; Dad had Sunday off, and we went to the cinema and bought take-out. He usually wore shades on his days off, unaccustomed to even clouded-over sunshine. Occasionally people would think he was blind, you could see them giving him a wide birth as we walked along. That or they thought he was a member of the mafia, packing a tommy gun beneath his raincoat.

Monday came. I opted for flowy grey trousers, a white blouse with matching grey neckerchief, and black kitten heels. Young professional chic. I even scraped my hair up into something resembling a *chignon*. There would be tea, coffee, biscuits and a buffet. No e-mails, filing, or chance of running into my boss.

The venue was impressive. A spacious hotel just out of town. Dad let me borrow the car, for which I was extremely grateful.

After signing in and pinning my name badge to my breast, I topped up my coffee and sat towards the middle-back of the room. It was a big event. Two hundred organisations had sent representatives to listen to the doom and gloom forecast of forthcoming closures, mergers and downsizing. Most organisations were kept afloat by local authority service tenders, providing things like care homes and day centres that the council outsourced because they didn't have the capacity to run them internally. Now nobody had any money, so there was no money for service provision or day centres. Those that couldn't make themselves pay like a business were more than likely going to fold.

Our organisation was certainly one of those in danger, which is why I was sitting there trying to pick up tips on applying for funding. Every organisation was trying to train up staff. Most organisations had no money to employ a fundraiser, and there was no money for them to apply for if they did employ one. The wonder of the capitalist system hitting home for the most needy. I'd never done a degree in it, but no one who worked in the Voluntary Sector for any length of time could remain oblivious to the downturn.

Eventually everyone settled into their seats, and the introductory speeches began. Someone from the National Council for Voluntary Action opened by reaffirming that we were living in difficult times, but optimistically predicted that the sun would shine through once again. She was a little less specific about when, exactly, that would be. But assured us that it would happen.

I was reading the list of attendees included in the welcome pack. There were several other disability organisations we worked closely with, and a few names that I recognised.

"Ah, here we are, ladies and gentleman," the orator announced. "Squeezing us in between busy schedules. I'd like you to welcome your local Voluntary Action Council Manager, George McCally."

I glanced up at that moment and almost fell off my chair. It was George, George. George from the alley the night I was sick, George. George who recognised me in the pub. I sank down slowly in my seat and raised the attendee list a little higher to cover my face. *Shit*.

I was fairly sure there was no possible way he could see me sitting back here, and if he did he'd wonder why I was trying to hide behind a sheet of paper. I slowly lowered it and tried to assume a casual, yet professional, poise. I managed to force myself to look ahead so that I didn't seem bored, whilst trying to mould an expression of concerned interest.

"Sorry I'm late. Most of you probably know that the National Lottery are launching their new Communities Scheme today over at Bryerbank, so I'm hopping between the two." He gave that same self-deprecating smile he'd given at Henry's, though his presence was anything but low on confidence. He wore a loose-fitting black suit with a green, open-collar shirt. I wondered whether it was designer again, like the one I'd thrown up over.

I flushed hot with embarrassment at the memory of that night and crossed my fingers that he wouldn't look in my direction.

He spoke for a further ten minutes about changes to local authority spending and what that meant for grass-roots organisations. But there was something about him, about the way he moved, playing to all sides of the room and allowing his voice to rise and fall, emphasizing each new point. Everybody was listening.

Well, everybody except me. I was just watching and wondering. Somewhere at the back of my mind I remembered an e-mail conversation with George McCally. I couldn't entirely recall what it had been about, but I think he was trying to arrange a meeting with the Dominatrix and, as usual, she was near impossible to pin down. She had the infuriating habit of agreeing dates with important people and then pulling out with less than a day's notice. Of course, she never had to deal with the carnage herself because she had her Administrative Assistant to do that for her. It was so bad that sometimes important people would start to play the same game back, and she would walk around in a huff, unable to understand why she couldn't get a meeting with so-and-so or whatchamacallit.

So this was George McCally, manager of the local Voluntary Action Council. I was absolutely stunned. I guess I'd just assumed that George was a balding fifty-something, brushing crumbs from his pot-bellied pinstripes and counting down to retirement. Yet here he was, sleek, self-assured, and just the right side of arrogant.

He made several quips during his speech and roused a laugh or two from the audience. I honestly couldn't tell you anything he said, but I was captivated. The dull world of paper and pen pushing suddenly seemed a little more glamorous.

"Thank you, George, a pleasure as always to have you here," the grey, anaemic orator said, shaking George's hand with a thin smile. "We'd better let you get back to Bryerbank."

My heart sank. *No!* I heard an inner squeal. *Don't go!* But off he went, with a final wave at the audience.

The rest of the day dragged like a snail on Valium. It was all I could do to keep my eyes open. Lunch was the same: everybody wanting to tell you about the work of their organisation, expecting you to be just as passionate and interested as they were.

Perhaps, if the day hadn't opened with George, I would have been. Maybe I would have thrown myself into every conversation and networking opportunity. But it had started with George, so I wasn't listening.

I stopped myself. What the hell was wrong with me? Was I developing a crush on a guy I'd thrown up over? Someone who had wiped sick from my mouth and held my hair back whilst I worshiped the porcelain god? I scrunched my eyes shut and groaned under my breath.

"Are you alright, dear?" a kindly woman from Help the Aged leaned over and asked.

I snapped my eyes open and sat up straight. "Oh, fine. Just remembered I'd forgotten to buy something this morning."

"Oh, for a moment I thought you were ill." She looked concerned.

I spent the next five minutes reassuring her and listening to the effect government shortfalls were having on meals-on-wheels in the region. I managed to escape by offering to fetch her a second helping of lemon cheesecake, then went in search of a newsagent.

I bought a small pack of cigarettes. I hardly ever smoke, only one or two at parties. I never buy them for myself. But all of a sudden I felt like doing it. There's something about smoking and thinking. I lit up and sat on the low wall by the shop. I maybe had two puffs of the entire thing, but whilst I sat there with it in my hand, I felt as though I could focus.

I knew what it was all about. It was about Mark. This was backlash rejection. I was fixating on anything that looked good. Sex with Mark had been slowly waning in the last months of our relationship. At least now I knew why. But at the time I hadn't even noticed. That's how mundane we'd grown. We'd fall into bed after a night out, a few drunken romps and morning cuddles. But nothing mind blowing. Not for a long time.

It completely beats me where these things go wrong. The passionate fire that brings you together, burning like a delicious flame. Then it slowly fizzles down to embers and goes out altogether. And you don't even notice. The most important thing between two people gradually goes limp, and neither of you give it the world-shattering recognition it deserves. Nobody reaches for the life vests, calls 999 or screams for the defibrillator. You just potter along quietly and assume everything is as it should be.

What I was experiencing was eighteen months of repressed sexuality screaming to go wild. It'd simply latched onto the closest, and, in predictable style, the least appropriate candidate. It's like the way babies look at the first thing after being born and call it 'Mama'. I saw the first thing after being dumped and went, 'you'll do'.

CHAPTER SEVEN

I sat in the boutique staring at Orla. "That's stunning," I said and meant it.

She was wearing a figure-hugging red velvet dress with black lace trim that stopped mid-thigh. She squeaked at my compliment and clapped her hands together.

"Really? You really mean it?"

"Totally." The fabric looked like it had been wound around her. It was a truly eye-catching dress.

"God, he's going to bust something when he sees this."

Orla and Andrew, the merman, were off to his graduation ball. Apparently he was only temping as a swimming coach whilst he finished his Master's in Physiotherapy. I was impressed. I had him down as a jock; instead he was an edumercated jock. Nice going, Orla. Perhaps this really was one to watch.

"Sold!" she shouted at the shop assistant, who was busy straightening dresses on the sales rack by the window. "Now, what are you going to get?"

"Hah, with whose millions?" I asked.

"Come on, you have to treat yourself now and then. Let me help."

"Really, I don't want anything."

"You have to. It was pay day last week, and I'm feeling flush."

I'd been Orla-ed again. She wouldn't let it drop until I picked something. I went over to the discount rail whilst the assistant helped her to undo the zip on her frock. I fingered through, looking for the cheapest thing I could possibly tone down into daywear.

To my surprise, I found a pretty blue beaded dress that looked slightly vintage. I was doubly surprised to see that it was in my size, so I took it to the dressing room. It fitted perfectly, and I had a pair of heels at home which would match.

Reluctant to admit that Orla was right to push me into shopping, I folded it and took it discretely to the counter.

"So, let's have a look," she grinned, reaching under my hand and holding the dress up in front of her. "Oh, Fee, that's beautiful! Really it is."

"Now all I need is an occasion to wear it."

"Mark would have a cardiac if he saw you in this!" She paused and peered over the top of the dress. "Oh, shit, shouldn't have said that, should I?"

I shrugged. "I'm over it. Though I can't deny the thought of him having a cardiac is kind of appealing."

She laughed. We paid and headed for ice-cream.

On Wednesday, Orla sent me an e-mail. It read:
Andrew's got a friend! He's single, muscle-bound and yum. Pleeeeez say yes!

No, was my brief reply.

Pleeeeeeeeeeeeeezzzzzzzzz. Pretty witty bitty? x x

No. Tough titty.

I logged out of my personal mail folder and started reaching for an envelope into which to put information brochures about our training courses.

The phone rang. I answered.

"Aw, come on, Fee. You'll love him. I *swear*. And even if you only have one date, at least you can take pictures of his abs to hang on your wall."

I rolled my eyes. Orla-ed again. "Is he solvent?"

"Completely in the black."

"Name?"

"Ferris."

"As in wheel?"

"No, he's part Canadian."

"Like that explains anything."

"Seriously, Fee, he's witty, charming, funny. And the body – oh, my god, the body!"

I could hear drips of saliva hitting the desk. "If he's so cute, why don't you go out with him?"

"I've got Andrew," she whined.

"So, you've had more than one on the go before." I heard myself say it before I could stop the flashback of Mark in the toilets. How many had he had on the go?

"No, this one's different."

I was still surprised to hear her say it. "Day?"

"Friday."

"Time?"

"Eight o'clock."

"Place?"

"Dexars."

"Certainly not. I hate that place. It's a dive."

"Well, then you name the place."

I thought for a moment. "Henry's."

"Classy. Okay, I'll inform him of the change of venue." With that, she hung up.

I shifted my hours around and went home early on Friday. I wanted a jog and a long, hot soak before getting ready. Most of my brain was saying 'chill out, relax!' After all, it really didn't mean anything. It was just a date. I didn't even know the guy. There was absolutely no obligation to ever see him again. After all, I was just doing this to shut Orla up.

But another corner of my brain was screaming: *It's a HUGE deal. You don't even know the guy. You're doing this for Orla – are you even ready?*

So the entire time I was 'relaxing' in the bath, my stomach was churning like the back end of a cruise liner. I towelled myself down and tried to decide what to wear. I briefly considered my black cowl-neck and jeans ensemble. That would certainly give the right message: back off. Then I considered a dress and jeans combo, casual but fun. But no.

I tried on several outfits. Nothing seemed right. I had no idea what he would look like. Maybe another jock in jeans and T-shirt. Or maybe a tuxedo! Who the hell knew?

Well, fuck it, I thought. The first, and probably last, time I get to go out for cocktails in a while. I reached for the blue beaded dress.

I opted for low kitten heels instead of the killer blue ones. I sprayed a little perfume, applied a little powder, and admired myself in the mirror. Even if I was completely overdressed, I still looked fabulous. My treat to myself.

Dad wasn't up yet, but I put the coffee maker on for him so that it would be fresh when he eventually surfaced. I grabbed my clutch bag and stepped out into the night. Despite myself, I felt a flutter of excitement. Breathing in the cool air, it felt as though the darkness held promise.

Anything could happen.

CHAPTER EIGHT

When I arrived, Ferris was already sitting on a bar stool. I knew it was him because he rose when he saw me, the only single woman in a fairly deserted establishment. It was still a bit early for the Friday nighters. Henry's was a mid-point between pub and club.

"Phoebe?" he asked, raising an enquiring eyebrow.

He certainly was all that. Almost army-short brown hair, crystal-cut blue eyes, an extremely handsome jaw line, and the hint of substantial muscle mass beneath his tight shirt sleeves. But I was just glad to see that he'd come in trousers rather than jeans. Beyond that, I could have overlooked most things. He was a good couple of feet taller than me, and gently removed my coat before I'd even realised what was happening.

"Hi," I smiled. I couldn't remember Mark ever taking my coat for me, even on our first date.

"What would you like to drink?"

"White please, just house."

He nodded to the bartender and placed an order for two glasses of house white, then we adjourned to a small table in the corner, away from the speaker and the bright lights. Soft, 1930s piano music filtered around us, and a waiter brought our drinks over.

"So," he said, fixing me with his summer-sky eyes.

"So." We both laughed nervously.

"Did Andrew tell you anything about me?"

"Only that you did three years for GBH and now front a money laundering outfit." I was good at making extremely straight-faced comments like that. It was the only reason they worked. He genuinely laughed. "No, actually, I hardly know Andy."

"Ah, right. You and Orla been friends a long time?"

I detected the slightest twang of an accent. "Yeah, a really long time. Since school. You're Canadian, right?"

"Heh, kind of. My dad is. I grew up there until we moved to England when I was nine. I studied there for my degree, too."

"Where abouts?"

"Ontario."

I smiled and tried to think of something else to say. Geography was always a dead-end subject with me. I had a rough idea where Canada was though.

"I'll bet Orla was trouble at school," he said, magically saving me from the embarrassment of complete silence.

"Oh, yes. She still is."

"Red heads, huh?"

I smiled.

"But blondes have more fun, right?"

I smiled again. His accent was getting more pronounced as he relaxed. He oozed clean, chiselled wholesomeness. It put me on edge. It was flattering to have his attention but, in having it, I felt that I had to live up to what he was hoping to see. And what was that exactly? Cool sophistication? That would match the dress. Girl-next-door, easy going? That was more my natural style. Maybe hard-to-get, flirtatious tease? Orla would know; she could suss any man's motives at fifty paces. But what were my motives? I drew a complete blank.

"Guess so," I said, and cringed at the false clink in my tone. Like someone playing a bum note on the tuba during a brass recital.

He actually seemed to register it, and sat up a little in his chair. "So, Phoebe. Tell me about yourself."

And I did. I told him where I worked, omitted the fact that I still lived with my father, tried to make out that my job was far more important and complicated than it actually was. I danced my coy mating rumba all over the table, tucking my hair behind my ear, smiling brightly whenever he made a comment, casually adjusting the strap on my dress when it slyly slipped over my shoulder. Half of it was second nature, the things all women do when caught in the lamplight of the perfect genetic specimen of the species.

Of course, I was careful not to bore him. I peppered my answers with questions about himself, which, infuriatingly, he always threw back at me after a measured moment of introspection.

And the night moved on. Eventually the bar started to fill with the slightly squiffy shouts of drunk twenty and thirty-somethings on a good night out. We left Henry's and found a small pizza restaurant around the corner. Again, it was almost empty as its previous occupants had traded places with us at the bar. We were experiencing social jetlag.

We decided on a bottle of South African white. He ordered lasagne, and I opted for tagliatelle. We shared chocolate mousse for dessert, and coffee to finish.

Time flew by. The alcohol loosened me up, turning me into my bubbly self. His accent was practically Inuit by that point, and his quick Atlantic wit made me laugh out loud. He was a fun guy to be around. He'd travelled quite a bit, he wasn't pushy, and he wasn't intrusive. He was attractive, well mannered... sort of perfect in his own little way.

He insisted on paying the bill. We got up to leave, and he helped me into my coat.

"Which way are you walking?" he asked.

"I'll get a taxi from the bus station."

"I'll come with you, make sure you get home safe."

"Really, it's fine. But thank you, I've really enjoyed tonight."

"I'm glad," he said. "Can we do it again?"

Thanks to the alcohol, I couldn't stop myself from smiling and nodding. "Sure."

"I'll call you then."

I turned and walked away down the street. I hate goodbyes, even on dates. It's so awkward standing around looking for a taxi. It breaks the magical spell of a wonderful night. Much better to just part on the spot, go your separate ways and wish you hadn't.

I didn't realise quite how far from the bus station I was. Thankfully the streets were well lit, but a sudden rumble from above made me stop to look up. The temperature dropped, and I felt a wet splash against my nose.

Before I knew what was happening, I found myself running along the road, coat held over my head. I lost my shoe and had to dash back for it.

I reached the high street, which was still a good few minutes walk from the bus station. Halfway along, a brightly lit department store glowed like a beacon, its wide overhang calling out 'shelter!'

Plunging beneath it, I slowly lowered my coat. Five or six other people were sheltering from the downpour, unlucky punters kept from their pints. I walked to the far end of the store front to peer out at the night's sky, trying to decipher whether it was likely to stop any time soon.

A man in a long black coat was standing there, smoking a cigarette. I stood next to him and frowned up at the rain.

"Following me?" he asked.

I looked round in surprise. "George!"

He took a drag on his cigarette. "Nice weather we're having."

"No kidding, my coat's soaking," I said, removing it and rolling it up in my hands like a muffler.

"Nice dress," he smiled, appreciatively.

I had completely forgotten what I was wearing, and felt myself blush. 1920s flapper meets modern-day main street. Now I really was overdressed.

"Thanks. I'll try not to throw up over this one."

He laughed at that. "On your way home?"

I nodded. "Yeah. Don't think I'm going anywhere for a while."

Our eyes slowly drifted to a gloomy pub across the street.

"No point freezing out here. Last orders?" he asked, taking a final drag on his cigarette and crushing it beneath his shiny leather shoe.

We slid into a wooden snug. It truly was an old man's pub, probably hadn't seen a lick of paint since the First World War. The ceiling was stained yellow from pipe smoke and cigars. The table was disturbingly sticky and, instead of optics, drinks were dispensed in miniature pewter barrels.

I asked for white wine again. George came back with my drink and a whisky chaser for himself.

"So," I started, in much the same vein as my first date of the night. "You're George McCally."

He paused, tumbler halfway to his lips. "I guess I am," he said slowly.

I let the suspense build for a moment before telling him. "We know each other, in passing. I work for a charity on Dorset Street."

He took a sip from his tumbler, then swirled the glass and watched the liquid spinning.

"You work for Sheila Hewing, don't you?"

"The one and only." I thought that I detected a hint of amusement as he switched glasses for the chaser. "I think we exchanged e-mails once when you were trying to set up a meeting. I'm her admin support." I was taking a risk revealing myself. It would be death for my career if he decided to phone her on Monday and tell her that her part-timer was a drunken wreck. But once again I was slightly polished, and somehow I didn't think he was about to bust me.

He simply nodded.

"I saw you at the conference the other day."

"Ah," he smiled, causing small dimples to appear on either cheek.

"Sounds like you have a busy job."

"It can be. Hard to stay sane sometimes. But then I don't have to work for Sheila Hewing." That sealed it. We were on the same side.

"She's certainly built a reputation for herself."

"So why do you stick it?"

The question threw me slightly. "Well, I haven't got anywhere else to go. It's not like people are throwing jobs at me."

"Times are tough." He took another sip of whisky. "But have you looked? There's always something out there."

The bell for last orders rang, but we didn't rush.

"Hey, cheer up," he said. "What's on your mind?"

I hadn't realised, but I was staring at the table. It was the stupid alcohol talking again, but I was angry. Why hadn't I ever asked myself that question? Why hadn't I left? Were there really no jobs out there, or was I just comfortable being uncomfortable? Did I actually enjoy the spiky atmosphere of my office? Was I so sad that I thrived off the drama it created?

"Oh, nothing," I sighed. "Just one of those months."

He placed his glass down and looked across the table at me, eyes narrowing.

"Give me your hands," he said.

"What?"

"Come on, give me your hands." He held his own hands out across the table, and I gingerly placed mine on top of them.

"What are you doing?"

"I read palms."

I laughed and waited whilst he examined the web of lines. As he ran his thumb across my left palm, a shiver shot up my spine. I found myself staring at him.

"What do you see?" I asked, trying to cover my own awkwardness.

"Well, the left one's what you're born with. The right one's what you make of it."

"So nothing's written in stone?"

He grinned and looked up at me. It was like electricity. My breath simply stopped. For a split second, magnetic energy passed between us, through our eyes and the warm, soft touch of his hands on mine. I watched the smile slowly drop from his face. He felt it too.

He cleared his throat and gently pressed my hands together between his, before removing them and reaching for his glass.

"So, what do they say?"

"They say that you'll receive an unmissable job offer in the very near future."

"You know, I've always fancied being a traffic warden."

"There you go. Don't need me. You can read your own future."

"It's the uniform," I grinned.

He swirled his glass and sucked down the last of the liquor. I felt like an idiot for being so obvious. Shit, Phoebe, when will you learn not to open your bloody mouth once you've been drinking? It always ends in disaster.

"Okay everyone, time to make a move," the landlord shouted from behind the bar. "Drink up now."

We drained our glasses and headed back out into the cold night air. The rain had stopped but it had left behind a strong chill. I eased back into my coat, which was now warm and damp as opposed to just damp.

We stood outside for a moment, waiting, whilst a handful of regulars filtered around us and disappeared into the shadows.

"Will you get home okay?" he asked, pulling a pack of cigarettes from his coat pocket.

"Yeah, I'll take a taxi." I allowed the sentence to hang for a moment until he looked up.

He smiled. "Would you like one?"

I nodded. They were extremely slim cigarettes. I hadn't seen that brand before. They seemed elegant, and matched his expensive looking outfit.

"Let's stand over there, in case it decides to rain again." We moved into a dark stone stairwell, part of an old office building. He drew out his silver Zippo.

"Indulge me," he said, exhaling a stream of smoke. "What's made it such a tough month?"

I shrugged and pulled my coat tighter around myself. "Just everything. You know how it can get sometimes."

He nodded.

"I caught my ex fucking around." I took a long drag and looked down at the pavement as I exhaled.

"Ah."

"It's okay. I'm over it. I think I was over it even before it happened. But it still takes you by surprise."

"You'd been together long?"

"Three years."

We stood in silence for a while.

"I'm sorry," I mumbled.

"What for?"

"For being such an arse. Every time we meet I'm either drunk or acting like an idiot."

He smiled, and I felt very aware of how close the confined stairwell was forcing us to stand.

"You know, you probably saved my life that night. I was so ill."

"That was the night you caught him at it?"

"Yup. In the girls' toilets. Classy, huh?"

"Ouch." He flicked his cigarette at the ground. "Well, that explains that."

"Yeah, I don't make a habit of it." I flicked my cigarette at the ground too, listening to it hiss out in a puddle.

I knew what I was doing. I'd been drinking, sure. But I still knew what I was doing. There was a hot pain deep between my legs, and I needed someone to fill it. I turned to him, pressed so close together in that shadowy space.

"I'm sorry," I said. Our faces were so near that I could feel his breath against my cheek. For a moment, we simply stood like that. Then slowly, very slowly, I moved my lips to within an inch of his, hoping that he would complete the move, sick with the sense that it was all in my head.

He didn't move, but I continued. Ever so gently, I brushed my lips against his. Then a second time, slightly longer, lingering, waiting for him to reciprocate.

He did. Pushing against me. Softly opening his mouth, he bit down teasingly on my bottom lip, our hot breath vivid in the cold, dank surroundings.

I reached my hands up to his face, pulling him more urgently towards me, and he followed, falling into a deep surrender. I held my head back as he kissed down my neck and then slowly ran his nose back up to my chin; our lips met again, enveloped in the scent of his aftershave.

"No," he said, suddenly pushing me back against the wall.

I tried to move back to him, to place my arm around his neck.

"No," he repeated, emphatically holding my hands down by my side.

"What's wrong?"

"This is. Not us. Not here. Not now."

He stepped out of the stairwell.

CHAPTER NINE

I watched his slim figure stride off out of sight along the high street.

I was in denial about what had just happened. Firstly, I was supposed to be on a date with a broad-shouldered Canadian. If I was kissing anybody, it was supposed to be him. Secondly, George McCally!? What was he doing sheltering from the same storm on the same high street on the same day and at the same hour as me? If fate had put him there for me to run into and go as far as having a drink with, then why had fate drawn the line at the rest of the night? And, finally, what on earth did this mean for my career? Maybe he would make that phone call on Monday after all.

Just seriously, what the fuck?

I stood there shivering for a moment, wondering whether I had completely misread the signals. Perhaps he was married. Maybe he even had kids, how would I know? Perhaps it was a pity kiss - he felt sorry for me after my desperate sob story.

Eventually I built up the courage to step out of the doorway and walk the final few yards to the taxi rank.

I hardly slept. Dad coming home at six woke me up. I had a headache from the alcohol wearing off, took some Panadol and tried to get back to sleep. It didn't work.

Instead, I slipped into the shower, then towelled myself down and threw on some clothes. I quietly walked out into the back garden and cut a handful of early delphiniums and forsythia. I tied them with string from the kitchen draw and walked down to the bus stop.

It took two changes to get to the cemetery. Mum was buried quite a long way from the gate, down a winding stone path between rhododendrons and a birdbath modelled in the form of The Three Graces.

Her headstone was carved from black marble with a gold etching of a dove in the top right. I cleared out the decayed remains of my last visit and replaced them with the fresh flowers.

"Hi, Mum," I said. I took a pair of nail scissors from my pocket and trimmed the grass around the sides, where the lawnmower couldn't reach.

Once I had finished cutting, I put the scissors back in my pocket and took out a tea light. I liked to light a candle. Somehow it made me feel closer to her.

The grass was still wet, so I took off my scarf and folded it on the ground before sitting down.

"It's been a weird couple of months, Mum. I told you last time, me and Mark are finished. He was cheating on me. Orla's been amazing though. I'm really lucky to have her. You'd laugh if you saw her now. I'll bring her some time, maybe for your birthday. She's all grown up, like me. Still causing trouble."

My words sounded stinted. I didn't always talk that much when I came to visit. Often we'd just sit here together, quietly, watching the world go by. But today I felt like talking. I felt that I needed to talk. I just couldn't work out what to say. Nothing seemed to get to the heart of the matter.

"Dad's good. Still working nights. We saw a movie the other day; you know how soppy he gets over rom coms." I smiled and felt tears. "I met someone, Mum. But I don't know what happened. I thought it was so right, but I think I made a total fool of myself."

I wiped my eyes on my sleeve. It had been a long time since I had cried there. This wasn't a sad place anymore. At least, it wasn't supposed to be. But suddenly everything was too much. A couple of months ago I thought that I knew where my life was headed. I had a man I'd been with for three years. He was probably going to propose at some point, then we'd move in together, maybe one day have kids. There was a lot that wasn't great about my job, but it was generally okay. Now, here I was, wondering why I couldn't leave it. Wondering if there was something else that I could have been.

Orla was wrapped up with her new guy, Dad was at work all the waking hours I needed him, and something had to be wrong with me because I honestly didn't fancy Ferris, the muscle-bound Canadian stud. What the hell was that about? Most women would fall over themselves for a date like that. Instead I was throwing myself at a Good Samaritan who clearly thought that I was insane. I wasn't far off agreeing with him.

Everything felt fairly fucking miserable.

"I miss you so much, Mum."

I was home again by half-nine. By the time I'd made myself a cup of coffee, Orla had sent me a text. I was surprised. Perhaps Andrew had woken her up early. It asked how the date went, and I texted back saying it had been 'really good' because just saying 'fine' would have raised too many questions.

I flicked on breakfast TV and fell asleep on the couch.

Sunday was gym day. I had a lot of unspent aggression to work out. I was starting to recognise my emotional biorhythm. My reaction to rejection was firstly one of mortification. What was wrong with me? What should I have done differently? Then, as with Mark, though perhaps not as explosively, it turned to sizzling indignation. What fucker had the right to make me feel so shitty about myself? Seriously, who has the god damn right to do that?

I ran several miles on the treadmill, pushed some light weights to tone my arms, then threw myself in the pool to recover.

As I was walking home, gym bag swung over one shoulder, my mobile rang.

"Hello?"

"Hey, Phoebe? It's me, Ferris."

"Hey!" I said, perhaps a little too enthusiastically. "How are you?"

"Good, thanks. I was wondering the same about you."

"Yeah, good too."

"Great."

There was a pause. "Um, I was wondering if you fancied going out tomorrow night. I know it's a Monday, but I've got meetings the rest of the week and I'd really like to hook up."

Hook up. Interesting turn of phrase. Like hooker. Or hook, line and sinker.

Where did that come from? I shook my head to clear it. "Tomorrow? That'd be fine. I have the day off actually. I'm part-time."

"Oh, that's great. I'm afraid I'm working until five, but shall we say seven? How about Henry's again?"

"Sure, can't wait."

There. A hundred miles from rejection. A second date with my very own Mountie. Perhaps I could find him a uniform, and we could ride off into the sunset.

At half-seven I got another call.

"Phoebe?"

"Yes?"

"It's Sheila. I have an emergency."

I felt my heart sink. This wasn't the first time she'd had one of those.

"I've got a meeting tomorrow afternoon, and Ann was supposed to type up the minutes, only she's still on sick leave and I forgot to ask Miriam to do it. Would you mind terribly shifting your Wednesday hours and coming in tomorrow? It'll only take an hour or so."

It was like being Orla-ed from a very great height. "Okay."

When morning came, I pressed the lift button like it were the button for my very own suicide bomber jacket. I'd had Monday all planned out. Sofa surfing, comedy channel, hot chocolate, possibly meet Orla for lunch and ice-cream; doze, laze, long hot bath, spend a couple of hours deliberating over outfits and eventually roll up at Henry's looking like a movie star on the red carpet to romance.

As the lift pinged open on the third floor, I stepped out, shuffled along the corridor and into my office.

"Oh," Eddie said, turning away in my chair.

"Christ, Eddie, it's my day off and you've already stolen my job." I went over to him, but he didn't turn back. "Eddie, are you alright?"

He nodded quickly but kept his hand to his face.

"Hey," I said softly, kneeling down beside him. "What's up?"

He let out a chocked sob, and I reached over to offer him a tissue.

"I'm so sorry, Phoebe. I didn't think you were in today."

Miriam also worked part-time, which meant that on Mondays our room was like a ghost town. "I wasn't supposed to be, but you can guess who called. Gave me the headless chicken spiel. I swear, she couldn't manage a smile on Prozac."

He almost laughed.

"I don't know about you, but I need a strong cup of coffee."

"That would be great."

I used this excuse to give him a few moments by himself. When I returned, handing him his cup, he looked a lot more composed.

"I'm sorry," he apologised again.

"Don't be. Being in work on a Monday, it should have been me crying."

"I appreciate it, lovely. I promise I haven't got snot on your desk."

I laughed. "Gives it a pretty shine."

We sipped for a moment in silence.

"It's Tim. He's leaving me."

I was shocked. Tim was Eddie's civil partner. They were only married a year ago. Everyone in the office had attended the ceremony.

"Oh, Eddie, I'm so sorry. What happened?"

"He met someone else. Through a chat room."

"Oh, Eddie."

"A woman!"

"Shit."

Eddie nodded and took another tissue. "I just feel so stupid. You know, I thought we were going to raise children, grow old together. I thought -" His voice broke.

I went over and wrapped him up in my arms. Poor Eddie. I knew exactly what he thought.

"You must think I'm so selfish carrying on like this when I hardly said a word about you and Mark."

I shrugged. "Our personal business isn't anybody else's business." He nodded against me. "I promise I won't tell anybody."

"It's not a state secret. It's got to come out some time."

"Only when you're ready."

"I knew he was bi when I met him. I just – I thought all of that was behind him."

"It scares me sometimes, how people can be anything other than what you think they are."

"Or how willing we are to ignore what they really are in order to invent what we'd like them to be."

I smiled. "Yeah, that too."

He pulled away from me, blew his nose on another tissue and let out a long sigh. "Anyway, I'd better get back to work. People to do, things to see, headless chicken shit to clean up."

He got to his feet, and I gave him a final hug.

"You, me, The Cambria. Tomorrow, after work."

"Okay."

I watched him leave. My heart went out to him. Me and Eddie had never been closer than office acquaintances. We'd shared a spliff outside the Christmas party, but never been for a drink as friends. Although it's sad that it took a personal tragedy to bring us together, I was sort of glad that he'd opened up to me. I wondered if he had many friends to see him through the rough times. At least I had Orla.

CHAPTER TEN

I booted up the computer and set to work typing out the handwritten minutes that Sheila had left in my in-tray. It took forty-five minutes, and despite promising myself that I wouldn't open my e-mail folder, I did. There's an irresistible pull towards electronic communications. You think you'll just pop in and check if you have any mail, and suddenly five hours of your life disappear. You know this before you even go to your mail box, yet still you do it to yourself. The allure is too great.

Glancing at the twenty-nine e-mails that had accrued over the weekend, I marvelled at who exactly sent them, considering that the concept of a weekend is fairly universal.

I decided to sort it all out during regular hours, and was just about to close the window when I noticed one towards the top of the list from George McCally, VAC Services.

It'd been sent about an hour ago. When I opened it, there was no personal message, just a forwarded job advertisement for an Executive Assistant to the Manager of the Voluntary Action Council. It was a full-time position but the pay was more than double my current salary. I stared at it open-mouthed for a moment before reality kicked in. The Manager of VAC was George. Considering how last night ended, I was at a loss to understand why he still decided to forward it to me.

At exactly the same moment that I was wondering this, a new e-mail landed in my in-box. Again, from George. This time it was a personal message. It read:

Dear Phoebe,

Please excuse my actions. I would very much like the chance to explain. Let me know if you are available to meet this evening.

He listed his personal number. I added it to my phone and closed the programme.

By the time I'd cycled home, I'd made up my mind. If I'm honest, I don't think there was ever any real doubt.

The Millers, 6:30, I texted.

I knew it was pushing it trying to get a conversation in with George before meeting Ferris across town, but I could blag running late. The Millers was a nice bistro overlooking the river. It had a heated outside seating area, and I felt like smoking. I was thinking about taking it up as a full-time hobby.

I took a shower and contemplated what to wear. Tough decision. I couldn't help looking at the blue dress with a mixture of emotions. It was stylish as all hell. It had led to a sexy embrace, and then a kick in the shins. I didn't want to dress up to meet George; he hadn't earned that privilege. But I couldn't meet Ferris dressed too far down otherwise he'd think that he'd done something wrong.

I decided on classic understated: a black wrap-round dress with seamed stockings and ankle boots. Not much of an outfit, but the slight heel on my boots made my legs look fantastic, and I went a little smoky with my eyeshadow. It was a work night, and Ferris would understand. As for George, I didn't really care what he thought.

I applied a little extra lippy on the way out.

The bus to The Millers seemed to take ages, winding through late afternoon traffic. As I walked through the door I saw George already at the bar. He had his back to me, his trademark smart jacket and loose trousers. He was also wearing a trilby, like the first night we met. I went up and stood next to him.

"Hey," he said, turning to me. "You came."

I shrugged, trying to play it cool. "Said I would."

"Do you mind if we go outside?"

We sat down on a wooden bench by the heaters, and he pulled out his long, slim cigarettes and offered me one. I took it and allowed him to light it.

My phone rang. He took a sip of his beer as I answered it.

"Yes?"

"Phoebe, it's me. I've been delayed at work, I'm so sorry. How does eight sound? I'll understand if it's too late."

"Eight? No, that sounds fine."

"Excellent, see you then."

I put the phone on the table.

"Going out tonight?" George asked.

"Yeah, I have a date."

I watched his expression carefully. The faintest flex in his jaw, a slight narrowing of the eyes as he glanced down at my phone, then smiled back at me. "Nice guy?"

"Yeah, he is, actually. Canadian. I was on my way home last night when I bumped into you."

Another subtle flex of the jaw, then a drag on his cigarette.

"About that…" he began, then trailed off.

"Yeah. About that." I nodded.

"Phoebe, it wouldn't have been fair."

I took a moment to absorb this. "You're married?"

His reaction wasn't what I'd expected. I guess I was going by Mark's example, waiting for the casual laugh and the change of subject. But instead, George looked pained, as if I'd said something I shouldn't have. Unhappily married, then.

"No, Phoebe. It's not that."

"Seeing someone?"

"No."

I was running out of suggestions. "So it wouldn't have been fair on who, exactly?"

"On you."

I frowned and took a drag on my cigarette, then a sip of wine.

"Look, Phoebe, you really don't know much about me."

"True. You know where I live, what colour pyjamas I wear, how pathetic I look when I'm drunk and where I keep the kitchen cloth. You've got a running start."

He gave a broad smile. Pinching the bridge of his nose with the hand that held his cigarette, he eventually looked back at me, smile gone.

"I like you a lot. You know that, don't you?"

What was this leading up to? I like you, but I'd rather be friends. I like you, but you're not the one for me. I like you, sort of like I like chocolate cake, but not as much as I like double fudge cake with cream…

I sighed. "So, what's the problem?"

He went quiet and looked down at the table whilst slowly exhaling smoke. For some reason he looked drained.

"George?"

He reached a hand up and slightly loosened his tie. "Phoebe," he said, slowly raising his dark green eyes to mine. "Do you know much about the work that I do?"

I shook my head. "You manage VAC."

"Yeah. But I've worked for a few different charities before I got there."

"RSPCA. You're a puppy smuggler," I joked, trying to lighten the mood.

His smile was fleeting. He put out his cigarette and immediately reached for another. His hand stopped on the packet, then withdrew.

"Look, I really have to go soon. You wanted to meet. I honestly don't mind about last night. It's okay. I understand. It's complicated." I slipped my phone back into my bag for effect. I knew that it would speed things up.

"Yeah. It's complicated. I really shouldn't have done what I did."

"Takes two."

He took a deep breath and looked up at the sky. "Phoebe, for six years I worked for Stonewall."

I ran the name through my grey database. It sounded familiar but I couldn't quite place it.

"It's a charity that fights for equality for gay people."

This time he did reach out and took another cigarette. I watched him light it. Something wasn't quite connecting in my brain. I knew what I was supposed to be thinking, but somehow that final wire just wouldn't quite spark. I just sat there, looking at him as he took a slow drag and ran the back of his hand across his chin.

"I really do need to go now," I said, quietly. "I really have to, umn. Ferris - he's…" I let the sentence trail off as I reached for my bag. I stood up and took a last sip from my glass. Imitating normal behaviour whilst waiting for the faint ringing in my ears to die out.

George cocked his head slightly as he blew out smoke. This time it was *him* watching me. Only it wasn't. I felt light headed.

"I have to…I really must…"

I turned and walked back into the pub. I pushed past several early drinkers and out the other side to the car park. It was almost dark, and I made my way across to a small pathway that wound along the side of the beer garden to join the main road.

I'd taken about three steps along the path when I heard footsteps coming quickly towards me.

"Phoebe, wait."

I didn't really want to wait. I wanted to go. Ferris would be wondering where I was. I needed a drink. I needed to laugh about this with someone. Only I wasn't sure who I could tell. But I didn't want to wait.

"Please, wait."

I turned slightly.

"Don't you see? That's why it wasn't fair. I had to tell you."

"No, it wasn't fair."

George frowned.

"It wasn't fair," I repeated.

"Hold on. I stopped it. I needed you to know the truth. But that's the point. I stopped something that had already begun."

I swallowed.

He took another step towards me. I wasn't sure what to do. It was as if there were no thoughts inside my head. He kept coming until we were face to face, almost as close as we were in the stairwell. I could smell his thick, warm aftershave.

Very slowly, I reached out and took the edge of his tie. Italian silk. I rubbed it between my thumb and finger, then let it fall back against his chest as if letting go of the last evidence that I could believe in.

I raised my hand to his neck and ran the back of my knuckles up and down his throat.

"Rookie mistake," I said, hardly believing that I was capable of making a joke.

He let out a short, humourless laugh, but there was no adam's apple there to bob.

"George?"

"Georgiana McCally."

I bit my lower lip and nodded. "Right."

She hung her head for a moment, expression obscured by the rim of her hat.

"Look, it's alright. I just – I wanted you to know that I'm sorry," she said, raising her eyes to mine. "Really, I am. It shouldn't have happened."

I wasn't sure what I was about to say, but I never got the chance to find out. My phone rang.

"Yeah?"

"Hey, Phoebe, I'm on the bus now."

"Oh, great," I said hollowly. "I'm on my way."

We stood facing each other for a moment. I couldn't help myself. I stepped forward, reached down and felt the crotch of her trousers. It was completely smooth.

She just stood there and let me do it.

"Hmm," I said, drawing back. "No sock?"

But she wasn't smiling.

I'd broken the illusion.

CHAPTER ELEVEN

Ferris was later than I'd expected. I beat him to Henry's and ordered a large G&T. My mind was still utterly blank. I couldn't think of anything to think about, so I drank. The last thing I felt like was a date, but I knew that I had to go through with it.

"Hey, good lookin'," he said, sliding onto the bar stool next to me.

He ordered me a second G&T and a whisky mac for himself.

"How's your day been?"

"Yeah, busy. Yours?"

He gave me a funny look. "Thought it was your day off?"

"Oh, I got called in."

"Hey, if you want to go home just say. I didn't mean to be this late, and you've got to be in tomorrow, right?"

"I might skip food if that's okay? It has been a long day."

He nodded, strangely understanding for such a model of masculinity.

We chose a window seat and kept to light subjects. It turned out that he was a fan of reality TV shows, so we picked random people on the street outside and tried to think of scenarios for them, making up what they were saying to each other. It was fun for a while.

I drew the line after my third drink, and we paused at the door.

"Taking a taxi again?"

"No, there's still a bus going. Number sixty-two."

"I'm catching one from the other end of the street. I'll walk with you."

We saw my bus pull off as we rounded the corner. There was another one in fifteen minutes, so he stayed with me, and we huddled together for warmth. He wrapped one side of his coat around me.

"There it is," I said, eventually spotting it coming down the road. "I'm sorry I wasn't much fun tonight. Really, I'm so tired."

"Don't worry, I totally understand. Monday nights aren't great for going out, are they?"

I agreed and was just about to turn away when he leant down and kissed me. It was a long, lingering kiss, or at least it felt like it. I was too stunned to respond. When he drew back he apologised. "I don't know what came over me," he said.

"That's...fine," I managed to say.

"Have I blown it?"

"No, not at all," I lied. "Really. It was nice." I stood on tiptoes to give him a reassuring peck on the cheek. "Really." I gave him my best smile and got on the bus, waving as it drove off.

In all honesty, I don't think that I'd had a day more confusing in my entire life. Holding it together until I got through the front door, I hurried upstairs and ran myself a steaming bath: candles, incense – the works. Dad had already gone out, and I sank beneath the bubbles as though burying myself alive in the world's biggest feather duvet.

When I surfaced, I wiped my eyes clear and took a sip from my mug of hot chocolate. The marshmallows had melted into thick, sweet gloop on the surface.

Finally, space to think.

To my astonishment, I felt like laughing. What a mixed up world! The perfect, blue-eyed muscle man walks into my life and snogs the pants off me, and yet I feel absolutely nothing for him. I couldn't hear wedding bells if Quasimodo himself were ringing them. Instead, I pass him over for one of the sexiest men I've ever set eyes on, only to discover that *he* is a *she*!

I sank back under the water again and blew bubbles at the surface. Lying there, I allowed the image of George to float across my mind.

Orla and I had an expression. There are certain moments in a person's life when they look like the King of Cool. We all have those moments now and then, when we just look so damn hot. You see it in pictures of great leaders and rock musicians. They strike a pose, oozing supreme confidence, dressed in a snappy suit or a killer dress. Orla and I term it 'packing'. It comes from the term 'packing heat', which means you're carrying a weapon. Only, when someone looks that damn good, they are their own lethal weapon. So we say 'they're packing'. If you look at a T-shirt of Che Guevara, he was packing. James Dean in his leather jacket, he was seriously packing. Johnny Depp is packing in almost every picture ever taken of him.

George, up on stage at that conference. My God, was he packing. I'd never seen a guy wear a suit that well. He was in his moment. He controlled the room. Everyone wanted to know what he had to say. They couldn't take their eyes off him. Or at least, I couldn't.

The way he walked, the way he smoked his cigarette. The way he kissed…

I allowed my hand to slide down beneath the surface and rested my head against the rim of the bath. Slowly, I parted my knees.

Christ, I wanted him.

CHAPTER TWELVE

I felt so embarrassed. As the sudden thrill of my orgasm melted away it was replaced by a cold chill, as though the bath water were filled with ice. I couldn't believe I had brought myself to climax over a fantasy of George. Georgiana.

In my mind he was male, but I knew he was not. He smelled male, his voice had a rough lilt that passed for male, and he looked so believably male in his hat and tie. But it was all an illusion. It was all what I wanted to see, what *she* wanted me to see. It wasn't real.

And the part that twisted me inside, is that I think I knew. That time we met at Henry's, when he recognised me and came over. I think some part of me guessed it right there and then, but chose to look the other way.

I felt so foolish.

Pulling the plug chain with my toe, I let the water drain half away before climbing out of the tub and reaching for a fresh towel.

The next day, in work, I found Miriam updating her Facebook status to: *It's complicated*.

"What happened?" I asked.

"Oh, nothing. I just do that occasionally to keep him on his toes." She twisted her hair playfully.

"You're sick."

"Hey," she said, with a mild trace of offence. "I have to mess with something. It may as well be his mind."

I rolled my eyes and went to get coffee.

"Still up for drinkypoos?" Eddie accosted me by the machine.

"Sure, I could start now."

He laughed. "I'll pick you up around ten past, just the two of us." He winked and disappeared behind the filing cabinet. Ten past would give Miriam a chance to pack up and head home. I had no problem with her, but she could be a bit airy sometimes, and I think Eddie found her hard going.

By the time we got to The Cambria, I was gagging for a G&T. The place was a mood-lightingly drenched pub at the end of Holloway Road. It flew the rainbow flag proudly above the door, and both the bar and the mustard-tiled floor were polished to within an inch of their lives.

We took green a leather snug in a quiet corner, and I fought an inner sense of wrong as Eddie swigged bright blue vodka pop from a bottle.

"Oh, it's one little vice," he said, seeing me grimace. "Reminds me of my clubbing youth when I could keep it up all night. Gone are the days."

It was maybe my second time in a gay bar. I think I ended up in one with Orla once, when we were teenagers. We bumped into some people dressed in PVC outside a club and somehow followed them in. I didn't remember much about it. But The Cambria wasn't what I'd expected. It was clean, mellow, and quiet.

"How are you?" I asked.

He shrugged and sat back against the seat. "Heartbroken. But what can I do?"

"Is he still seeing that woman?"

"He's moving in with her."

"I'm so sorry."

"These things happen." He took another swig of his drink. "You know," he continued, "it could be the right thing. Might push me to do something different with my life."

"Different like what?"

"Well, I don't know. Maybe get involved in things more. Meet people. I was thinking about offering to help with the

Mardi Gras committee this year. Usually all I do when I get home is curl up on the sofa with…" He paused and then skipped over the name. "Maybe that's why he left. Maybe I'm a boring old fart already."

"Don't say that!"

"But I could help out more, maybe get involved in some campaigning. Might even try for a different job. I quite fancy Stonewall."

The name jolted me. "You know the manager of VAC used to work for Stonewall?" It was out before I even heard myself saying it.

"Who, Georgie boy? He's worked there forever. Bit of a living legend."

I felt a tingling sensation in my stomach. "You know George McCally?"

"Everyone knows George." He was looking at me carefully, probably wondering why I had leapt up like a rabbit at the mention of his name. "He was instrumental in starting the campaign against workplace discrimination. He headed an amazing team for a couple of years, then they promoted him to Director of Public Affairs. Wasn't long after that he got offered the VAC position."

"Bit of a step sideways, wasn't it?"

"Well, maybe. I think he just wanted to try something different. Just because you're a tranny doesn't necessarily mean you want to talk about it all day every day."

"I saw him talk at the conference last week. I honestly thought he was a man," I confided.

"Convincing, isn't she," he grinned. "I don't know anyone who does it better."

"Yeah." I couldn't understand why my mouth had gone dry. "Want another drink?"

I went to the bar and, against my screaming conscience, bought him blue vodka whilst I ordered a double G&T. I stared at myself in the mirror behind the bar. I looked tired, and I needed to touch up my hair. The woman passed me my drinks with a smile, and I put the change in my pocket. As I reached to pick up the glasses, a burst of high-pitched laughter made me turn.

In an alcove in the adjoining room, a group of three men were talking animatedly over their drinks. They must have laughed at a funny story someone was telling.

"She was sick *all over my shoe!*" I heard one of them say, and they laughed again. "Well, I said, you can take her home if you like, but call me if she tries to attack you!"

They creased up double. If the voice and the vaguely familiar profile hadn't alerted me, what I had just heard left me in no doubt who the comedian was: the other guy from the alley. I turned back to my drinks and slipped away as quietly as I could.

"Thanks," Eddie said, reaching for the bottle. "What's going on through there? Sounds like a riot."

"Oh, some friends having a laugh."

Just as I said this, I heard someone walk behind me, still laughing, towards the toilets.

"I thought that was Sebastian," Eddie nodded, his eyes following the person behind me.

"Sebastian?"

"Vicious queen. Laughs like a mule."

"Blond, slightly chubby?"

"Fake, fat and easy to forget." He waved a hand, and we returned to the subject of work.

"You don't like Miriam, do you?" I ventured.

"I have absolutely nothing against Miriam at all. There are just some people you wouldn't want to get stuck in a lift with."

I laughed. "That's cruel."

"Not at all. I just recognise that we both need different things from a conversation. I, for instance, need intellect."

Talking to Eddie was like being the sole female member on a comedy panel. Everything you said was a run-up to his punch line. It was hugely entertaining, but somehow you never really scratched the surface of who he really was. He fascinated me. Was all of the bravado a cover for something deep and insecure? Maybe not. Maybe it was a double bluff: look how extrovert I am, masking a mysteriously reclusive inner self, masking a totally together, down-to-earth, normal bloke. But there was never an opportunity to prove that hunch.

We sat, getting gradually drunker. We dissected the inner workings of our boss' scheming mind and lamented our overworked, under-paid hours. We even touched on world politics and the impact of the financial crisis on Individual Giving to charity; how, oddly, in times of great financial decline, people often reach further into their pockets to give to those less fortunate, because they start to empathise that little bit more.

"Thanks," I said, as we stumbled towards the door. "I had a really good night."

"Me too, darling. Who would have thought, you and me – drinking buddies!"

I tripped on the step and giggled. "Beats working for a living."

He laughed and gave me a big hug. "We should do this again. You'll have to come to Weavers some night."

"Weavers?"

"It's a club by the river. Every Friday there's live jazz. You'd love it. George always goes, and sadly the lesser crested Seb, but it's fun."

"Am I sensing a history there?"

"*Moi*?" he said with mock innocence, raising his hand to his chest. Like Ferris' accent, Eddie's campness became more pronounced the more he drank. "It was a *very* long time ago, and completely unmemorable."

He wobbled for a moment on the spot, hand still raised to his chest and a look of boozy vacancy on his face.

"Hey, really, are you going to be okay about Tim?"

"Absolutely fine. I actually feel a little sorry for him. I'm gay, you're straight, but he gets the worst of both worlds."

"How do you mean?"

"Well, he went through all of that with his straight family – the coming out, the big secret bursting onto the scene. It was hard to do, telling them he was in love with a man, especially one like me," he chuckled. "Now he's got to go back and tell them that he made a mistake. But it'll never be the same for him.

He can't ever take back what he said before. To them he'll always be a little bit special." He gave the word 'special' an edge that made it sound cold and unforgiving. "They'll always look at him a little funny. See, straight people can cope with gay people, because they know what they are. But straight people don't like bi people, because they're never too sure what the hell's going on there."

Poor Eddie; he was drunk and hurting. I simply listened.

"Straight people have this opinion of bi people, that they're all promiscuous, all looking for the next lay. Keeping their options open. And the gay community aren't much better. He's a bum bandit, she's a lezer, but that one over there - they're after the best of both. They're not serious." He wavered again, that same, unblinking look in his eyes.

"I thought sexuality was a sliding scale?"

"Hah," he said harshly. "Maybe, but I've never once in my life wanted to sleep with a woman. It'd be a bit presumptuous of me to say that all straight people want to test the water. Sure, maybe more of us are adaptable than aren't, but I know what I like, and I'm sticking to it."

I took that on board. It made sense. I'd never in my life wanted to sleep with a woman either.

"Come on, time for peepee bye byes," I said, taking his arm and turning for the taxi rank.

CHAPTER THIRTEEN

I was lucky. Thanks to Sheila's emergency, Wednesday was a day off for me. I peeled my face from my pillow around eleven o'clock and rolled into the bathroom. I spared a fleeting thought for Eddie, who was full-time and in the office first thing. But really, this whole hangover was entirely his fault, so he deserved it more than I did.

As I sat, digesting the dregs of daytime TV with a cup of strong coffee, I started to wonder what had happened to Orla. I'd heard practically nothing from her all week.

Reaching for my phone, I sent her a text. Ten minutes later she called me back.

"Phoebe! God, where have you been?"

"Where have I been? Err, hello, Ms. Breast Stroke."

"Oh, have I been naughty? I don't know how you put up with me sometimes. He's just, well, delicious!"

"So long as you're keeping safe and staying out of trouble."

"Yes, and sort of. Only the fun kind of trouble."

"That's alright then."

"Let's meet for ice-cream at lunch. I've got so much to tell you."

"It's almost lunch now," I said, glancing at the VCR clock.

"Late lunch, say two-ish?"

So that's when we met, at our usual haunt in the shopping centre.

"...in the pool, after everybody else had gone. It was so romantic."

I listened, astonished, as Orla gave her reply to my question as to whether or not she had bedded the beautiful Andrew Ashbourn.

"Weren't you worried about CCTV or anything?"

"No, they don't have it. We did look."

"People walking in?"

"He had the key! That was the beauty of it. As a swimming coach he gets to keep it to lock up afterwards."

I shook my head in mild disbelief. "So, was he worth it?"

"*Completely* worth it. Worth it in a way no one has ever been before." She was practically glowing. "So, how was your week?"

"Strange. I went for a drink with Eddie last night."

"Eddie? Eddie, Eddie..."

"Gay guy, works at my office."

"Oh, Eddie! Where did you go? He didn't take you to The Cambria or anywhere like that, did he?"

I was about to say 'yes', but something in her tone made me cautious. "The Cambria?"

"It's positively yucky. Really seedy, full of homos. Best avoided."

"I thought you loved Mardi Gras?"

"Well, yeah, but that's a street carnival. Everyone goes."

"Yeah, well, everyone can go to a gay bar." I know it wasn't a strong argument, but I was finding it hard to say what I meant. I never knew that Orla had a thing against gay bars. But just as I was recovering from that surprise, she landed another one that knocked me sideways.

"Oh, look, I wanted to show you these. Jess at work was throwing them out, and I said I'd have them. They fit perfectly. Aren't they gorgeous? It would have been such a waste." She reached under the table and lifted up a plastic bag. Inside were a pair of mint green wedge-heeled shoes.

I tried to swallow. "Who did you say gave you these?"

"Jess. Jessica Coleman. You know, you met her at my Christmas party. Big boobs, red falls?"

A vague recollection surfaced of talking to a girl in a tight yellow dress with a nose stud and bright red hair extensions. She was drinking beer from a freshly opened bottle. The bubbles kept overflowing at the neck, and she was licking them flirtatiously as she spoke. At the time I remember thinking that she had enough sex drive to power a third world country.

I looked down at the shoes again, slowly reaching out and turning one over in my hand. The material was shiny, probably satin, and the heel was heavy enough to bludgeon somebody with. The thought did cross my mind for a split second.

"Fee, what's wrong? You've almost gone as green as those shoes."

"No, that's just it. These *are* the shoes."

She stared at me blankly.

"These are the shoes I saw underneath the toilet door. With the red trainers. With Mark's red trainers."

Her mouth dropped slightly as she understood what I was saying. "How can you be sure?"

"Look at them. These aren't mass produced. These are one-offs. More than that, I just know these are the ones. The shape, the size, everything about them is the same."

Orla stared hard at them, as if they might confess under interrogation.

"Awww," she eventually pouted. "Now I can't wear them. Not now that I know where they've been! And I gave her a tenner for those!"

"I thought she was throwing them out?"

"Like you said, they're not mass produced. She would have eBayed them. Christ, now I feel like I've financially contributed to your misery." She went suddenly quiet, and I watched her eyes widen. "Oh, no."

"What?"

"The Christmas party! She was helping me with finger food, and you guys arrived early. You went to the bathroom to change, and we were in the kitchen together. Fee, I was the one that introduced them!"

I bit my lip and tried to repress the memory. That was exactly it. I'd changed into my party frock, came downstairs, and Mark and Jessica were talking in the kitchen. Mark gave me a brief peck on the cheek and went to take his turn in the bathroom. That's when Jess passed me a bottle of beer and opened her own. We stood chatting until the doorbell went and other guests arrived.

"How can you ever forgive me?"

"It wasn't your fault. You had no idea what would happen."

"That girl's a firecracker. She makes men explode like it were bonfire night."

I smiled and put my hand reassuringly over hers. "I never wanted to marry a firework, honey. You did me a favour. Better he fall to temptation whilst there's still time for me to move on, than find out on our wedding anniversary."

"Still, I feel shitty about it."

"Only one cure for that."

"What?"

"Ice-cream."

We ordered a second scoop.

CHAPTER FOURTEEN

It shouldn't have bothered me. It really shouldn't have bothered me. But it did.

I lay beneath the covers, kicking myself. Fucking Jessica! Of course I remembered her now. Tits like watermelons, lips like an octopus' sucker pad, and the most fake, synthetically manufactured hair ever seen since Bimbo Barbie fell off the production line.

Jezebel Jess. Mark left me for *that*?

It's stupid, and it's irrational, and it's one-hundred per cent counterproductive, but I just couldn't stop thinking about it.

I tossed and turned and watched the neon numbers of my bedside clock slowly tick up past one o'clock, two o'clock, three o'clock. Eventually I passed out, and when the alarm went off I felt like I'd only blinked. Hardly any sleep, combined with a heavy night the night before, was a serious recipe for disaster. I had bags that you could carry your shopping in, and hair that the RSPB would probably designate a nationally protected wilderness zone.

I fell into the office only to discover that it was monthly staff meeting time. Two hours of 'Sooo, what have you been doing?' Doubly dreadful due to the absence of any form of Jaffa cake or chocolate Hobnob. Only plain old digestive biscuits, keeping the budget in balance.

Afterwards, Eddie and I escaped to the baguette shop two streets up. Everyone else went to the café over the road, but after spending the whole morning together, we needed a break from the crowd.

"Did I ramble like a complete twonk the other night?"

I toyed with making him suffer, but decided he'd suffered enough. "No, just like a regular twonk."

He laughed.

"Were you still alive on Wednesday morning?"

"Barely. It was fun though."

I smiled. "Yeah."

"He's filing for dissolution, you know. Tim."

"Are you giving in without a fight?"

"Yeah. Might as well. We're not arguing over money. Neither of us have any."

I nodded. "Well, at least it'll be over quickly."

He took a sip of his coffee. "He doesn't love me."

"Sorry?"

"On the forms. There's a part where you have to explain why the marriage has 'broken down irretrievably'. He said he simply doesn't love me. That he did once, but now he doesn't, and he can't get that back." Eddie's bottom lip quivered for a second. He pinched the bridge of his nose, took a deep breath and sat upright. "No point fighting that."

"Oh, Eddie-"

"Don't! I don't want your pity." He slammed his hands against the table as he stood up. "Let's go. No rest for the wicked."

I'd been back in the office two minutes when my phone rang.

"Phoebe?"

"Yes?" I said, uncertainly.

"It's me – Ferris. It's Friday tomorrow. I was wondering what you're doing after work?"

My mind raced ahead. I had absolutely no idea what I was doing tomorrow, and I couldn't invent an excuse on the spot. "Seeing you?"

"I hoped you'd say that." His twangy accent laughed down the line. "This sounds so lame, but I have to go to Birmingham on Saturday for a conference. Would you mind making it an early one?"

"Not at all!" I was fairly relieved. Start early, finish early.

We arranged to meet at The Millers for a change of scenery, plus the food was good there.

I went home after work to change. It was a tough decision again, now that Ferris had seen me in my fancy best and casual chic. I fished through the back of my wardrobe in case something fabulous had magically been knitted by elves and left as a present behind the shoe stacker. Or in case something had fallen off a hanger and been forgotten about.

As I crouched down to reach the back, I accidentally knocked the lid off my memento box. Mum's photo beamed up at me, and I sat on the floor for a moment, holding her.

"Mum, you wouldn't believe the fella I'm seeing tonight. Sweet as maple syrup. A complete gentleman. You'd be proud."

A small sense of panic washed over me.

"I love you, Mum. Wish me luck," I said and hurriedly put her back in the box, replacing the lid. I took a couple of deep breaths and busied myself with the back of the wardrobe again.

I had just touched the very edge of a panic attack. I hadn't had one in years, not since a few months after Mum died. Seeing her dead like that, being so close to her and yet knowing that she wasn't there…

It wasn't seeing her dead body, or even so much the fact that she was dead; it was knowing that I had so much that I wanted to say to her, and no one there to hear my words. All of these unsaid things built up inside me without any release. They filled me up entirely, to the point where I could physically feel them pressing against my bones and thought that I might actually burst. All of the things that I needed to say, every sentence from every conversation I couldn't have, felt like it was taking me over. As though there was no room left inside for me.

That's when I'd have an attack. I couldn't breathe. My lungs were screaming for air, but no amount of sucking or gasping seemed to fill them. They lasted several minutes, and my face and hands would go deathly cold, prickling with numbness.

Afterwards, I'd feel a bit better. Like I'd managed to clear some space and there was a little room for me again. Eventually they stopped altogether, and I even forgot about them. But just then, as I was looking at her photo, some strange recollection waved to me from across a crowded room.

You'd be proud, Mum.

But that was just it. Would she be?

I couldn't ask her.

CHAPTER FIFTEEN

I decided on a cute green dolly dress, patterned tights and matching low sling-backs. When I arrived at The Millers, Ferris was waiting for me outside the door, above and beyond the call of duty.

"You look really beautiful," he said.

As we turned to walk inside, I glanced over my shoulder towards the car park. I could almost see my former self and George over by the path, my hand between her legs.

The thought left as soon as it arrived, and I ordered a large glass of red wine. Ferris didn't smoke, so we sat in the warmth of the dining area and looked through the menu.

"A little bird told me that it's your birthday next week," he said, after the waitress left with our order.

"Oh, God, keep it to yourself."

"You don't like birthdays?"

"I love other people's, but I don't really like my own. There's always such pressure to do something spectacular."

"There must be something you'd like to do though?"

I thought about it for a moment. "I'd like to go away maybe. I haven't been abroad since I was very little, before my mum died. Maybe I'll think about a beach holiday with Orla."

"Or me," he suggested.

"I can't picture you in a bikini."

"Well," he laughed, "surely a romantic holiday with your boyfriend tops a weekend away with the girls?"

Our plates arrived. I was ridiculously grateful for the distraction. The thought of going on holiday with Ferris hadn't even crossed my mind, yet his was already racing so far ahead that he'd proclaimed us boyfriend and girlfriend. I struggled to think of a tactful way of downplaying our relationship.

"Perhaps we could make it a double date? You, me, Andrew and Orla?"

My heart sank.

"Sure," I said. "Sounds like fun. Would you excuse me for a moment?"

I headed for the bathroom. Standing there, staring at myself in the mirror, I felt seriously distressed. What was wrong with me? Ferris was gorgeous. He looked like every hot-blooded heterosexual girl's fantasy.

I remembered a documentary I'd seen once, in which a scientist asked girls to sleep in the same T-shirts for a week. Then they extracted the women's scent, and the scientist had to sniff each one and place them in order of which smell he found to be most attractive.

Afterwards, they analysed DNA from each woman. It transpired that, without fail, the scientist had placed each bottle in order of which woman was biologically most compatible with him. He'd done that entirely by smell.

It had to be something like that, right? There had to be a biological reason for it, because there certainly wasn't any other obvious one. He was very handsome, educated, funny, well travelled, financially secure. But I just felt nothing.

Then again, if it was all about biology and smells, how could he have decided that I was the perfect mate, when I wasn't flaring my nostrils and thinking the same?

I was starting to get a headache. I popped a painkiller and washed it down with water from the tap. I had to get back out there before he came looking for me, but I didn't want to leave without a game plan. It was getting too serious. He was talking about going away together. He was talking about boyfriends and girlfriends.

Was I a girlfriend? We'd kissed. Or rather, he'd kissed me. Did that count? Is that all it took to make a relationship? Then again, Mark and I were in a relationship, and he hardly ever kissed me properly towards the end.

I focused on my eyes in the mirror to try and shut my brain up. Still, a rising sense of panic was building. I wasn't kidding when I told him that I didn't like my birthday. I really didn't. I hate all that attention and the weight of expectation that you are going to do something outstanding, that no one will forget, and that future generations will still laugh about in their rocking chairs whilst telling their own children of the wild and heady days of their grandparents' youth.

Fuck. If someone invented a time machine, I wouldn't use it to go back and see the wonders of the world being built. I'd simply use it to skip forwards two weeks so that all of this would be over.

"Phoebe, you're an idiot," I said to myself, just as another woman entered the toilets. She gave me a sympathetic smile. Every girl knows what it's like to tell herself off in the mirror for doing something lamentably stupid.

It was time to give myself a very stern talking to.

Look, he is *handsome. He is very, very attractive. He has money, and he treats you like a lady. Orla is crazy about him. You should be too. Okay?*

"Okay."

I heard the toilet flush behind me. Straightening up, I applied my lippy and returned to the table.

"I ordered us baked cheesecake for after, is that alright?"

"Yummy," I said with genuine enthusiasm.

We were more than halfway through a bottle of red. I took a large gulp and studied his face over the rim of my glass. I focused on his chiselled jaw with its hint of stubble. He had thick, sandy lashes and alert, interested eyes that made you feel like you were under a spotlight when they focused on you.

By the time we got to coffee we'd finished the bottle and had drunk two more glasses each. I was definitely feeling mellow.

He paid the bill and, instead of leaving through the car park, we went out through the back door and down to the river. There was a path leading under an old red-brick bridge. We were quite a way from the centre of town, but not that far from the main road. Even so, noise from the traffic seemed to melt away as we walked.

"It's like we're in the middle of the countryside," I smiled, taking his arm.

"Well, you know what these British country people are like."

"No, what are they like?"

"They're all up for a roll in the hay," he said, reaching down and tickling my sides.

I screeched and tried to twist away, but he wrapped me up from behind in a big bear hug and I had to turn back to him. We were coming up to the bridge and he pushed me against the side of it, kissing me.

Don't worry about it, I told myself. *Just relax.* So I did. I kissed him back and allowed him to fondle my breast in his hand. We stood there for what felt like ages, kissing. He was really getting into it, and I twisted my head from side to side and opened my mouth to allow his tongue inside. But it wasn't working. It was almost dark. I was getting cold, and it just felt so wrong. It felt more like being licked by an Alsatian than kissed by a Canadian. Not that I could honestly draw that comparison from my own experience, but it was just a big wet tong mashing against my lips, interrupted by the occasional grunt of hot air as he surfaced for breath. Occasionally I felt as though I would gag, but he just kept going, and I didn't stop him.

Before I knew it, he'd slipped his hand under my dress and up behind my under-wired bra, squeezing my naked boob almost painfully.

"Uh-" I tried to tell him, but his mouth kept squishing against mine, so I reached up and pulled his wrist down. He took this completely the wrong way. Instead of withdrawing his hand, or squeezing more gently, he took it all the way down and into my knickers!

I gasped in surprise. Before I could complain, he started rubbing me between my legs.

"Ferris-" I tried to say, but he pushed his fingers up inside me, and I gasped again. "No-"

His lips were crushing against mine. "Shhh," he whispered in my ear. "It's your birthday."

My stomach gave a lurch. Had I encouraged this? Is this what he thought I wanted for my birthday?

He bit down on my neck heavily, and began sucking. Pinching my flesh between his teeth, he pushed a third finger up inside me and rubbed furiously with his thumb.

He was too fast, too brutal. All of the sexual sensation that could have been teased out of me was spent. He'd taken a sledge hammer to cut wild flowers. It just felt like someone was bashing their hand against my genitals – because he was.

I reached down again and forcefully pushed his hand away, feeling the sudden emptiness inside as his fingers slid out of me.

I watched as he put them in his mouth and sucked. My whole body felt cold.

"Let's not do this," I said.

"It's okay. Nobody's coming. I promise."

His concern stopped me for a moment. He really didn't understand. He had no notion what so ever that I wasn't enjoying this. To him, it was all a question of my modesty, of avoiding getting caught. Not whether or not I fancied him; that was just a given.

And I don't know why, but I stood there and let him pull my tights down. He parted my legs and, before I knew it, he pushed himself inside me. I hadn't even realised he'd unzipped himself.

"Oh!" That involuntary sound which, to my ears, expressed my shock and dismay. To him, it expressed my pleasure and longing. So he thrust himself again, harder this time. It hurt as though someone had bruised me deep inside.

I grabbed hold of his shoulders simply to stop myself from falling over as he upped the urgency of his bullish throws.

"Ah-" I cried out in pain. Once again I felt his teeth bite down against my neck, sucking up a bloody welt. Marking his territory.

I was silent after that. I realised that any sound I made would only encourage him, unless I screamed, and that would drive him into a panic. He wouldn't understand what he had done wrong. And, despite the pain and discomfort, despite the humiliation, I didn't want to wound him. It wasn't his fault. He just didn't know. I hadn't told him. So it was my fault.

One final plunge and he lifted his head back, teeth clamped together in an ecstatic grimace.

He withdrew with a squelch, and I could feel the hot wet cum start to drip down my legs. Hurriedly, I pulled my underwear back into place. My tights were laddered. I slipped them off and held them inside my knickers for a moment before wiping and throwing them into the scrub. All the while I was doing this, he leaned half against me, half against the bricks, panting.

"Oh, God," he said finally, "that was amazing. You were amazing." He kissed my neck gently. "You were."

With every ounce of restraint in me, I turned my head, kissed his cheek and whispered: "So were you."

"Good birthday present, huh?" he said with a chuckle.

But that was too much for me. I simply nodded.

CHAPTER SIXTEEN

We continued to walk along the river for a while until we came to a path leading up to the main road. It came out next to a bus stop. I think someone was watching over me because, as we reached it, a town-bound number fourteen appeared from nowhere.

Ferris took my hand and went to get onboard.

"Hold on," I pulled him back. "Babe, I'm *so* sorry. I promised to meet a friend from work. She lives round here."

"Oh," he said, surprised. "You didn't tell me earlier."

"I know, I know. I'm an idiot. I didn't think we'd get so carried away."

He grinned. "Okay. You don't want me to come, I gather?"

"It's a girl thing," I nodded. "Sure you don't mind?"

"Only if you're sure."

"Absolutely. But I'll call you tomorrow, yeah?"

"Text me when you get home safe."

"Promise." I drew a cross over my heart.

He planted a kiss on my cheek. "You might want to get a scarf," he said, winking as he stepped onto the bus.

I could already feel my neck starting to throb.

I stood and waved as the door closed and the bus pulled away. Then I turned and walked back down to the edge of the river. Curling up in a ball, I started to sob.

It wasn't rape. I hadn't protested. I hadn't told him to stop. I hadn't really put up much resistance at all. If I had, he would have stopped. I know he would have. The simple truth was that I let it happen. I let him inside of me because I couldn't think of any reason why not. I couldn't think of an excuse good enough. He was handsome. He was good looking. He was everything any mother would want for her daughter.

I cried and cried and cried, until my throat hurt and my eyes were red and sore. When I finished, I sat there on the cold ground, swimming in dazed silence until the pungent, warm aroma of sex made me feel sick.

Scrambling to my feet, I made my way back to the main road. A few cars went past, but otherwise it was deserted. Not entirely sure where I was, I turned back in the direction of The Millers and started walking. Actually, it was more like floating. My entire body felt numb.

Ten minutes later, I passed the pub on my right. I didn't feel like getting on a bus. I felt unclean. If people could smell me, they would know what had happened. If I'd been with my lover, someone that I really wanted to have sex with, then I would have worn that smell with pride. I would have held my head high and smiled at everyone I met. But now, all I felt like doing was taking a long, hot shower and scrubbing myself clean. I needed to find a taxi.

Opening my bag, I reached in and felt for my phone. As seconds passed, my searching became more frantic. I stood on one leg, resting the bag on my knee, pulling larger items out. I dropped my hairbrush and lipstick. When I bent down to pick them up, I decided just to empty everything onto the pavement.

No phone.

I considered going into The Millers in case I'd left it there, but it was brightly lit and full of people. I couldn't bring myself to do it. I just wanted to go home.

I walked on for five or six minutes and came to another dark car park set back from the road. A group of people walking towards me veered off across the enclosure and entered the pub. The thought hit me that perhaps the pub could call me a taxi.

I glanced over at it. The giant bay windows were blackened, and a sign swung from the first floor with a top hat and cane painted on it. It read: *Weavers*.

I stood there, shivering. I could hear the faint, erratic beat of a jazz band, which grew suddenly louder each time someone went in or out. There was a steady stream of individuals, couples and groups coming and going. I suppose I must have been mesmerised.

A car went past and beeped at me, its teenage occupants jeering out of the window and shouting that they wanted some cunt. It shattered my momentary peace, and I felt hot tears against my cheeks once again. Panic was starting to rise. I needed to go home, *now*.

I began to walk towards the club. As I opened the door, live music enveloped me. I found myself in a short passageway with a counter to my right. The Perspex screen was blanked out with corkboard, leaving only a little space at the bottom through which to pass money.

"Hey," a voice called out. "Three quid."

I stepped over to the board.

"Please," I said, my voice fluttery and insubstantial. "I just need to use the telephone."

"Three quid." A disembodied finger tapped the counter behind the screen.

"Please-" my voice broke, and I began to cry.

A pair of eyes peeped underneath the screen and stared at me.

"You poor thing!" they exclaimed. "It's okay, go on through. The phone's behind the door on the other side of the room."

"Thank you," I breathed, never having felt more grateful for anything in my life.

"Are you sure you're alright?"

I nodded and turned hurriedly along the hall. I paused for a moment at the end. My hand pressed against the door, trying to muster the strength to push it open. I didn't want to be around people. I didn't want to see or talk to anyone. I just wanted to go home.

I pushed forward and stepped inside.

Despite all of the people I had watched coming and going, the main room of the club seemed more or less empty. It was dark and the lighting was slightly blue. On the left was a stage with a drum kit, but no band. To the right was a long bar without a bartender. Three or four people sat at a table at the far end, though it was too dark to make out who they were. In the middle stood a wide, square pillar supporting the roof. The music was definitely a lot louder in here, though it seemed to be coming from upstairs.

The room had a faintly hazy quality, as though the ghosts of long dead smoke machines lingered in the ether. I stepped further into the room and saw that the pillar had been obscuring another swing door on the opposite side. That must be where the phone was.

I took a step towards it.

The door opened.

I stared at George, and he stared at me. His face was a perfect expression of the surprise that I felt.

The woman standing next to him was gaunt, almost skeletal. Her hair was so short and fine that it looked as though it had been plastered to her head. She had pixie-pointed ears and, even in the half-light, she looked too old to be wearing a figure-hugging crop top and mini skirt. In her midriff sat a glass bellybutton jewel, and her legs ended in a pair of big, furry boots.

My eyes quickly returned to his. The woman next to him looked from me to George and back again. Neither of them moved.

I suddenly felt very intimidated as my surprise turned to panic.

I didn't know what the protocol was for talking to someone you had kissed who you thought was a man but was actually a woman and you were now standing in front of but they probably thought you were a stalker and anyway they were in a gay club where you had never been before with their friend or maybe lover who you didn't know and you hadn't paid to get in because you only needed to use the telephone because you had lost your mobile phone because you'd been on a date with a man who had sex with you that you didn't want because you thought you should and you didn't know how to tell him that you didn't want to and you needed so very very badly to find a taxi because you really wanted to go home now more than anything in the entire world that money or all the tea in China could buy.

My chin crumpled. I was trembling with exhaustion. I felt my lips tighten in the way that they do before you let out a long whine, followed by wrenching sobs.

I turned and ran out of the building.

CHAPTER SEVENTEEN

When I reached the middle of the car park, I stopped and buried my face in my hands. My shoulders shook up and down with each pathetic hiccup of emotion.

I just needed to get home.

"Phoebe?" I heard George's puzzled voice behind me, but I was so embarrassed that I couldn't bring myself to lower my hands. "Phoebe, what happened?"

I could feel the heat of him as he came and stood in front of me. I was trembling all over. My muscles felt like iron, and I couldn't move.

He reached out and gently placed his own hands around my wrists, teasing them away from my face.

"I wasn't looking for you," I blurted.

He let go of me and took a step back.

"I-I-" I faltered, eyes fixed at the concrete. I couldn't think of any way of explaining myself.

"You need a lift?"

I looked up at him. He was wearing his suit and tie, his trademark trilby set at a slight angle. I couldn't read his expression, so I nodded dumbly.

"I'll be right back," he said, turning towards the club.

As I stood there, alone in the car park, irrational thoughts sped through my mind. I could run for it. I could just leave, now. I'd find a taxi. I could get home, crawl into bed and pretend none of this had ever happened.

But George was a colleague. He knew where I worked, he knew my boss and he even knew where I lived. He'd remember. He'd think I was even more nuts than I was.

I could say I was mugged. That would explain it. I was mugged – they took my phone. That's why I needed to use the one in the club, and that's why I was such a mess. If I told that story enough times, even I could believe it.

He was back before I knew it. I heard the clink of his car keys in his pocket as he approached.

"It's this way," he said, gently, so as not to startle the already traumatised rabbit in front of him.

I followed meekly behind. He pressed his keys and the lights of a red Chrysler Crossfire flashed in the dark.

"That's your car?" I asked.

"Impressed?"

I was impressed enough to relax my shoulders slightly, feeling the stiff ache of emotional meltdown thump against my spinal column.

We slid in. I pulled my seatbelt across, suddenly feeling incredibly tired.

"Home?"

I leaned my head back against the rest and nodded. The engine sparked into life, and George began reversing into the lot, arm stretched behind my seat as he turned to look where he was going. I caught a waft of his warm scent. That familiar aftershave mingled with sweet sweat. He must have been dancing.

"We're here," he said.

I'd fallen asleep. Blearily, I sat up and peered out of the window. This was my street, and there was my house. I swallowed, my mouth dry. The low hush of the car heater blew an arid wind across the furnished tundra.

I was aware that he was watching me.

"Is anybody home?" he asked.

I shook my head.

"You live by yourself?"

I shook my head again. "I live with my dad, but he works nights."

"You want me to come in with you?"

"No." I continued to stare out of the window at the dark, empty house. The warmth of the car seemed so friendly and comfortable that I didn't want to step out into the cold. "I'm building up to it," I said.

He didn't rush me, but after a few moments of silence he made another offer.

"Do you want to come back to mine?"

My reflection nodded.

Without another word, he twisted the key in the ignition. The relief that I felt was almost as strong as the relief of being told by the bodiless bouncer that yes, I could use the telephone. Minor miracles in the midst of mayhem.

It seemed to take quite a while to reach George's place. We passed through back streets and suburbs I didn't know very well, and some that I had never seen before. It was strangely comforting. Like being whisked away to a different dimension, far from all your problems, to a safe house where nobody could find you.

We finally pulled into a brick-paved driveway outside a semi-detached house. It was a quiet street, middle-class residential. Much more spacious than the row of Victorian terrace houses on my side of town. These were modern. The hedges were immaculately trimmed, and the car didn't look out of place.

George got out, walked around, and opened the door for me. The chilly night air, which I had desperately hoped to avoid, suddenly assaulted me. Unfastening my seatbelt, I climbed out.

A rapidly growing sense of curiosity blossomed. So this was where George McCally lived. Manager of VAC. Gay rights crusader, snappy cross-dresser, and mystery owner of the crimson bat mobile. Everybody has to live somewhere, but usually we never get to see where. And if we try to imagine it, we're usually wrong.

"I thought you were more of a townie," I said as he opened the door and let me walk in front of him.

He laughed but declined to comment.

The front room was surprisingly conformative. Neutral, beige décor and net curtains. I was more than a little surprised. Given the flashy car and his other alternative attributes, I guess I was expecting something more flamboyant, or at least a statement of some kind. At the other end of the room two steps led up to an open-plan kitchen. Again, nothing out of the ordinary, though red kitchenware seemed to compliment black granite surfaces. A large French window, like a science-fiction portal, gaped across the back wall.

"Would you like a drink?" he offered.

"Please," I replied, still taking in my surroundings. "Would you mind if I took a shower?"

He tilted his head slightly as if considering my request. "Sure, it's upstairs, straight along to the end of the corridor. There's a fresh towel on the rail. I'll leave a T-shirt outside the door for you."

"Thanks," I said, turning and making my way up the stairs. A normal, white wooden banister led up to a normal, beige coloured landing and along to an equally normal and nondescript bathroom. It was almost as though George didn't live there. The house didn't feel like him at all.

I turned on the hot water and watched it swirl down the drain until it heated up to the right temperature. Then I pulled off my clothes and left them in a heap on the floor. As I removed my knickers, a pungent, salty smell rose from between my legs, and I felt my emotions boil.

I wrapped them up in my dress and sat down under the shower, legs pulled up to my chest. The drumming of water against my ears helped to drown out my thoughts. Despite the soothing heat, I felt cold and shivery. I started to cry softly again until I heard a creak on the landing outside. Swallowing my anguish, I opened my mouth, let it fill with water and spat it out.

Perhaps half an hour passed before I got to my feet and reached for the shower gel. It was a heady, African spice mix, and I poured more of it than was necessary into my hand. No matter how hard I scrubbed, I couldn't seem to clean myself properly between my legs. What I really wanted to do was to clean inside me. Was there a number you could call to get your plumbing replaced? A fresh set of untouched pipes?

I forced myself to put the gel down before I finished the bottle. What was I doing? This wasn't rape, yet I was behaving as if it were. I had let him do it. I hadn't put up much of a protest. I hadn't said *NO!* He was a good guy; there was no reason I shouldn't have enjoyed it. He was trying to make me happy.

The problem was me.

My fingers were like prunes by the time I turned off the water. Wrapping myself in the big white towel from the rail, I opened the door and found a long T-shirt and a clean pair of boxer briefs. I pulled them on and rubbed my hair dry. Devoid of makeup, my face looked even blotchier and tear-stained than it had before. I didn't look well. The thought of going to the chemist for the morning after pill made me feel even sicker. But I didn't need to think about that now. All I had to do was sleep. Tomorrow would be a brand new day. Everything would start afresh.

CHAPTER EIGHTEEN

Feeling conspicuous in a T-shirt that ended just above my knees, I made my way downstairs with my bundle of clothes.

The main lights were off, and the room was lit by two lamps at opposite ends. It was a softer, more relaxing light. Mellow jazz piano, like they play at Henry's, was drifting quietly from the speakers. George sat on the cream sofa with his head resting back and his eyes closed. He held a tumbler of whisky along the arm, but I wasn't sure whether he was awake or not.

I cleared my throat.

He rolled his head to look at me. "Feeling better?"

"Much." I raised my hands a little. "Do you have a bag?"

In the kitchen he passed me a plastic carrier bag from a collection under the sink. I put the clothes inside and half considered throwing them away, but thought that was a little over dramatic.

"You must be tired," he said.

"Yeah, a little."

"Let me show you where the bedroom is."

He led me back upstairs and into another mundane beige room with a queen-sized bed in the middle. The bedspread was black and white, matching his suit and shirt. It looked a little harsh against the rest of the colour scheme.

"Sorry," he said. "It's technically a three bedroom house, but I turned one into an office and the other is a storage room. Hope you don't mind. The sheets are fairly fresh."

"Where will you sleep?"

"I'll take the couch."

"I can't do that to you!"

"Really, it's no problem. I do it all the time."

I stared at the bed and then back at him. "I can't make you sleep downstairs."

"Well, there isn't much of a choice," he laughed.

"You could sleep with me."

His laugh evaporated. "I don't think that would be such a good idea."

"No, really, I don't mind. We're both women."

His jaw flexed. Had I said the wrong thing?

"I don't really want to be alone," I added. It was the truth.

He considered me for a moment. "Okay."

He went to use the bathroom, and I pulled back the covers and nestled down beneath them. It was a soft bed and the eiderdown was real. I heard him go downstairs to switch off the lights and lock up. I was drifting on the edge of slumber when he finally slid beneath the covers next to me. He switched off the bedside light and lay there on his back, on the opposite side of the bed.

I listened to him breathing, wondering whether he was as keenly awake as I now was. I wriggled slightly, to let him know that I was still awake, but he didn't move or speak.

"George…"

"Yeah?" He was awake.

"I meant it, you know. I wasn't looking for you tonight. I'm not stalking you."

"Stalking me?" he laughed.

"You know what I mean. I don't plan to turn up and make your life difficult. Every time you see me I'm doing something stupid."

He didn't reply. I didn't know what to make of his silence. Orla would have said: "Don't be silly, you're perfect the way you are," or something like that. Told me not to worry. Told me to relax – to chill out. But I couldn't tell what George was thinking. Maybe he wasn't replying because he was agreeing with me, that I was a totally dipsy pain in the arse.

"But thank you," I continued, "for everything. This is the second time you've saved me."

Another moment of silence passed.

"What was I saving you from?"

"Myself." I suddenly felt a wash of sadness. My emotions were all over the place.

"Hey, Phoebe, it's okay."

"I'm such an idiot. The reason I'm always doing stupid things is because I am stupid. I just get into these situations, and I don't know how to get out of them." I buried my face in the pillow and took several deep breaths.

George rolled onto his side, facing my back. He reached out a hand to my shoulder.

"Phoebe, wow, slow down."

I sniffed and tried to control myself.

"Nothing's ever as bad as all that. What happened?"

"I just can't seem to get anything right anymore."

"Like?"

"Well, my ex."

"That's hardly your fault."

"It's my fault that I knew how shit our relationship was long before that happened, but I didn't have the guts to say so."

"Everybody's guilty of that, though. We all bump along the bottom of relationships from time to time. It just makes you normal."

"Yeah, well, not everyone sleeps with someone just to feel normal, then schizes out over it."

He paused for a moment, just long enough for me to steam on regardless.

"This guy I was seeing-"

"The Canadian?"

"Yeah, the Canadian. He decided to give me a 'birthday treat', down by the river." My eyes overflowed. I felt wretched.

"I didn't realise it was your birthday. Congratulations." There was coolness in his tone.

"I didn't want to do it. But I did. And I don't know why."

"He didn't-?"

"No. But it was so awful. I just wanted to go home, but I lost my phone. I was walking to find a taxi and thought that I could use the one in the club, and…" As I turned my face back into the pillow, George's arm slid beneath my neck and his other one moved across mine, cradling me up against him. He rocked me gently until I fell quiet.

"And instead, you found me." He let out a slow breath and loosened his warm grip a little.

"I don't know why I'm acting like this."

"You're tired. You've had a shitty month. Things got on top of you. It happens."

"Could you stop being so nice about it!"

He laughed. "You'd prefer to walk home? I could kick you out if you like."

"No, thanks."

"Cover your eyes," he warned, switching on the lamp. I heard him rummaging in the bedside draw. There was a brief moment of silence, then I felt his hand lightly brush against my neck. "Christ!"

I parted my fingers and squinted up at him.

"What?"

"Have you seen yourself?"

I scrambled to sit up, suddenly worried. "What is it?"

"Your neck, Phoebe. It's, uh…impressive."

I frowned and pulled back the covers. In the bathroom, I stood, open-mouthed, holding my hair back with one hand. I knew that I had a love bite, but I had no idea how bad it would be. At least three separate welts glared back at me in the mirror, absolutely purple-black.

George appeared behind me and gently touched the skin above one of them, examining it. "He really did a number on you. Does it hurt?"

"Actually, yes. It really does," I managed to smile.

He continued shaking his head and checking my injuries. Eventually he stood back with a whistle. "Well, I was just about to offer you a pick-me-up, but it's a great analgesic too."

"A what?"

"Painkiller," he smiled. "Come on."

We went back into the bedroom, and I re-settled myself beneath the sheets. He slid in the other side and propped himself up against the pillows, readjusting his T-shirt. I watched in astonishment as he reached back into the bedside draw and pulled out a bundle of king-sized Rizlas and a thumb-sized lump of hash.

"You've had a shock," he said. "This'll help. Medicinal, of course."

He finished skinning up and licked along the paper. Pulling a cheap plastic lighter from the draw, he lit it and placed a tinfoil ashtray on the sheets between us. I pulled myself upright and took the joint from him.

A couple of tokes later and I really did feel a lot better. I felt light hearted, giggly, and a little bit silly. I passed it back.

"Better?" he asked.

I nodded and grinned.

"Good. Don't ever let the fuckers get you down. Life is a beautiful thing, you know? And even if it isn't, it's short. So really, the only thing that matters is you. What you think. What you feel. What you want to do."

"That sounds like a spliffingly good philosophy to me," I said, taking possession once again.

He let out a short laugh as he exhaled. "The only reason we think it isn't that way is because we place our happiness in the hands of other people. We say 'in order to be happy, I need him to do this,' or 'her to act in such and such a way.' We forget that we can't control other people; we can only control ourselves. So, by doing this, we constantly set ourselves up for a kick in the guts."

I was listening.

"If you think about your life – all your hopes and dream – it's like a swingometer. All the things you can't control down one end, and all the things you can control at the other. All that stuff we can't control – like the actions and reactions of other people – well, you may as well forget it. Just forget all about it, because trying to control them will only ever end in failure. It's a waste of your precious lifetime. All the stuff at the other end, the stuff you can control, like your own actions and reactions – those are your gifts. You can use those things to make your life better. To deal with the shit and achieve your goals."

I was listening so hard that the joint was turning to ash in my hand. He tucked the foil tray under it just in time, taking it from me.

"So what about earlier?"

"Before you can get what you want, it helps to have a rough idea of what it is that you want." He blew a cloud of blue smoke up toward the ceiling. "Sounds like you only figured out what you wanted after it was all over. Once the decision had been made for you."

My brow furrowed in contemplation, and he eventually stirred me by pushing the reefer back between my fingers.

"Okay," I said slowly. "I thought I knew what I wanted. I thought I wanted to sleep with him."

"Bullshit. You knew that you didn't *want* to sleep with him. What you actually thought was that you *should*."

"Okay," I said, trying hard to grasp what he was saying. This was becoming complicated. I wasn't sure that I could keep up.

"The question is, why did you think that sleeping with him would make you happy?"

"Because he wanted to, I guess. And because..."

"And because?" His green eyes focused on me.

"Because I thought it would make my mum proud, to be with such a nice man."

George frowned. "Your mum?"

I nodded. "She died when I was little."

Now it was his turn to sit quietly whilst the ash burned along the Rizla. "Oh," he said eventually.

"I'm sorry," I said.

"What for?"

"I spoiled the mood."

"No, you didn't. I just didn't know. I'm sorry she died."

"Yeah, me too."

"But you see what I'm saying? You placed your happiness on somebody else's shoulders. You thought that what you were doing would make other people happy. You have no control over what other people think, only what you think and do for yourself. Don't judge yourself by other people's standards, and don't give your happiness away again. It's too important."

CHAPTER NINETEEN

I woke with the mighty mouth of death. My tongue was as dry as match paper. Small, jagged pieces of peanut protruded from between my teeth.

That conversation had been the only low point of the night. After that, we moved on to talking about TV programmes we used to watch as kids. How, once you grew up, it seemed blatantly obvious that *The Magic Roundabout* was all about psychedelic drugs and that whoever wrote *Whizbit*, about a six foot white rabbit and a giant yellow triangle, must also have taken their fair share.

We ended up in hysterics at the thought of the Cookie Monster having a threesome with Bert and Ernie and whether, in the end, they ever did catch the pigeon.

It was stuff that only made sense when you were stoned, but for the first time I was crying with laughter instead of unhappiness. George was right; it was incredibly medicinal.

Then we got the munchies. He went downstairs and came back with a packet of dry roast peanuts, a tray of pre-packed supermarket sushi, and a big bag of Kettle Chips. We pretty much ate the lot, then passed out cold.

I groaned as I rolled over in the covers. All of the pain that marijuana had taken away the night before, suddenly caught up with me. My neck felt like I'd been mauled by a blunt-toothed vampire, my throat had been sandpapered and my stomach pleaded to be pumped of junk food.

I crawled out of bed and along the landing to the bathroom. I could hear George downstairs in the kitchen, clattering pots. After a shower, I borrowed floss and mouth wash and did the best I could without a toothbrush. Humanity was slowly seeping back.

With one towel around my body and a hand towel around my head, I walked back into the bedroom.

"Oh, sorry," George said. "I thought you'd be in there a bit longer."

"It's okay," I assured.

He was half dressed. Dark, slightly loose trousers with a CK band peeking over the waistline. A deep spinal groove ran from the base of his neck all the way down his smooth, pale skin. He turned to face me, plucking his shirt from the bed.

"I'll go next door," he said.

I couldn't help it. I stared.

As he drew level with me, I reached out my hand and he stopped. I couldn't find any words, so I tentatively raised my fingers and drew them along the contour of his chest.

"My God," I murmured.

He didn't move. Like before, at The Millers, he simply stood and allowed me to touch him in the most intimate of places.

Although I knew that George made a convincing guy, if I really thought about it, I still knew that he wasn't. Even Eddie had confirmed that. I think that's why it struck me speechless.

He had no breasts.

I drew my thumb along the thin silver scar that ran from the left side of his body to the right, interrupted for a couple of centimetres in the middle. It was noticeable, but well healed. His chest was flat; two dark nipples carried high on either side of his sternum.

As I looked further, I saw a dark lick of hair beneath his navel which tapered down below the waistband of his briefs. I was stunned. For all the world, George had the torso of a man. I doubted myself so much that it was all I could do not to place my hand back between his legs.

"I'll give you some privacy," he said, avoiding my eyes. He stepped away and closed the door behind him.

I rubbed my fingers together as though I could still feel his body beneath them. How was that possible? Obviously he'd had surgery of some kind, but the hair, and his voice… The more I thought about it, the more I found it impossible to imagine him ever looking like a girl. Had he ever looked like a girl? When had he stopped?

My contemplations were interrupted by the sudden realisation that I didn't have anything to wear. The plastic bag of clothes sat in the corner of the room, accusatorily. There was no way that I could put those on again. I opened the door and stepped out onto the landing at exactly the same time George emerged from the room next door, fully dressed in a casual, striped shirt.

"I don't have anything to wear," I confided.

He smiled. "Check the cupboard. There's some jeans and T-shirts – help yourself."

I retreated back inside and opened the pinewood flat-pack in the corner. His jeans were ever so slightly loose on me, but then he seemed to wear everything loose anyway, perhaps it was just his style. The one concession I made from the plastic bag was my bra. I hooked it on and found an open pack of new briefs in his underwear draw.

At the bottom of a pile of plain T-shirts, I found a black one with the Rolling Stones' tongue sewn on in sequins. It was baggy but kind of hip, so I pulled it over my head and ruffled my hair in the mirror to make it dry curly.

I couldn't remember the last time that I wore such loose, unfeminine clothes. Not that I never did, just that it felt unfamiliar, like I hadn't in a long time.

I smoothed myself down in the mirror on the back of the wardrobe door, noticing how the T-shirt swamped my breasts. But they were still there, their plump little selves pushing against the thick, dark material. There was no denying my gender.

In the kitchen I found the table laid with croissants, fruit salad, and yoghurt. Quite a contrast to Dad's Full English. I took a seat and waited whilst George brought a fresh cafetiere of coffee over.

"Did you sleep okay?" he asked, moving a copy of *The Guardian* to one side to make room for his cup.

"Eventually." I smiled, and so did he, lifting the awkward reserve of morning in a stranger's house.

"So, it's your birthday next week," he said, pushing the butter towards me. The smell of freshly heated croissant filled the room, warm and comforting. "What are you doing?"

"I have no idea."

"I love other people's birthdays," he said. "I could just do without my own. I can't stand all that attention."

"Me too!"

"Why don't you get away somewhere quiet? Leave everything behind you for a weekend. There's some good deals on package holidays at the moment."

"Yeah, I thought about that. But I'm not sure where I'd go. I haven't been abroad in a long time."

"Majorca's nice. They have these big underground lakes. They inspired Jules Verne to write *Journey to the Centre of the Earth*."

"Really? In Majorca?"

"Now they've got a whole light show extravaganza projected onto the wall of the caves, and these people in costumes row out into the middle of the underground lakes and sing opera."

I laughed. "Sounds tacky."

"It's entertaining," he shrugged. "So what do you like?"

"I don't know. Somewhere with a beach, I suppose. Pretty. Warm. That kind of thing."

He tore into a steaming croissant, and I reached for one myself.

"Who would you take?"

"Orla, I guess. My best friend."

"Sounds like a plan."

"What about you? Who would you take to Majorca?"

"Oh, I don't get holidays. Slave to the machine."

"Come on, you must go on holiday sometime?"

"Not for a long time."

I frowned. He seemed to be concentrating very hard on spreading jam. He hadn't looked up once as we spoke.

"Well, who would you go with if you ever did get a holiday?"

He touched the croissant to see whether it had cooled down, then sucked butter from his thumb and smiled. "James Brown, Dolly Parton and the Queen of Sheba," he grinned.

"Seriously, there isn't anyone special?"

He kept grinning, but somehow it seemed forced. "You're nosey, aren't you?"

I realised that I'd overstepped the mark and felt a flush of embarrassment. "I'm sorry, I just-"

"Wanted to know more about me."

I nodded. "You wouldn't happen to have any concealer, would you? My neck's a mess."

"Funnily enough, no, it's not something I keep handy. But there's a scarf in the wardrobe. You're welcome to borrow it."

"Thanks."

After breakfast, I wrapped the scarf carefully around my horrible bruises, and George drove me home.

"Christ, you need a zoot suit just to drive this thing," I joked as he pulled up opposite my house. I reached into the back for my bag before opening the door. Pausing, I turned back. "Thanks again. You have no idea how much I appreciate what you did."

"Rough night. Everybody has them."

"But really, you didn't have to do any of that for me."

"Shush. Get gone." He flashed me a wink as I stepped out gingerly onto the pavement. He waited until I was inside before pulling off. I stood in the window, watching the space where his car had been.

It felt as though I'd been standing there all along. Maybe last night had never happened. Maybe I just got out of bed, came downstairs and decided to look out of the window. And maybe someone had been parked in that space over the road. But they weren't there anymore.

CHAPTER TWENTY

I listened to the sound of my father snoring upstairs, then went to the kettle and made myself a coffee. Around ten o'clock, Orla called on the home phone.

"Why aren't you answering your mobile? We so need to talk! Meet you at the Centre in an hour."

A directive, not a discussion. I went upstairs and changed into something more me, folding George's borrowed clothes neatly at the end of my bed.

It was an overcast day, for which I was grateful because it meant that I could continue to wear his scarf without drawing attention. I slathered on some Max Factor just for good measure.

"Get you!" Orla chirped as we sat with our double scoops of Chunky Monkey. "I'm so *completely* stoked!"

I had absolutely no idea what she was talking about.

"You and Ferris! That's amazing. I just *knew* you two would hit it off. He's quite a dish, isn't he?"

My heart did a little summersault, like the last leaf falling off an autumn tree.

"He told you?"

She frowned and sucked the end of her spoon. "Well, not in so many words. Actually, sort of yes. Well, he told Andrew, and Andrew told me."

Someone was grinding mince meat in my stomach.

"Oh," I said, very quietly.

"But I knew you wouldn't mind," she steamed on. "So, how was he? As good as he looks?"

"Yeah, great," I smiled, thinking that if she really was my best friend, the one I'd known since nursery school, then she should be able to see straight through my false bravado to the utter unhappiness beneath. But she didn't.

"Great work, girlfriend. This one's a keeper. Oh, and some really juicy gossip. You'll never guess what."

"What?"

"Well, me and Jessica had a little chat the other day."

"You *what*?"

"No, it's okay, really." She put her hand out to calm me. "I was very discrete. Just asked whether she was seeing anyone. Anyway, you won't believe this, but she's a total dyke! She only does men in between. So maybe I wasn't so discrete. I did ask if she'd done Mark, and she confessed, it was her. But she did it because her girlfriend, Jodie, dumped her that night. She had absolutely no idea you two were still going out, and I believe her – she really was mortified when I told her. She wants to make it up to you, but reckons you're better off without him, which we all knew anyway…"

I started to drift out of the conversation. Orla had been my best mate for as long as I could remember. We'd done just about everything together: smoked our first cigarette, smoked our first joint, got drunk, sobered up, kissed our first boys, did other things with them. We were sisters. But at that moment, all I wanted was for her to shut the fuck up. Just for two minutes.

I reached into my bag and took out my Paracetamol.

"Have you got a headache?"

"I'm getting one," I replied.

"So, when are you seeing Ferris next?"

"I'm not sure."

"Well, I think he's planning something special for your birthday."

I groaned inwardly.

By the time I got home, I felt as though my ear had been chewed clean off. I'd managed to stop her planning my love life by asking about her own, and for the next forty minutes she had barely stopped for breath. It was painful.

I checked my neck again in the mirror and winced. It was still throbbing, and I was deeply resentful of what Ferris had done to my body. It wasn't cute, and it wasn't sexy.

By eight o'clock I was shattered. The trauma of the night before had caught up with me, and my body was screaming for sleep. Obligingly, I made a mug of hot chocolate and took myself to bed with a little pill that had cost me twenty-five pounds from the chemist. Expensive fuck.

I don't remember anything after that, but morning delivered a little daydream in that blissful half-haze of consciousness.

I was surrounded by heaving bodies. Male or female, I couldn't tell. They were all around me, skin pressed against skin, black, white, brown...

I could feel a hand caressing my breast, and another caressing between my legs. It was incredibly erotic.

Someone moved against my stomach, kneading the area around my belly button, slowly stroking up towards my other breast. Lips met mine, and everything felt warm and wonderful. They gently moved up, kissing my eyelids and then my forehead. I opened my mouth to kiss theirs, yummy and seductive. I reached a hand to touch their face and, slowly, George's raven black hair and sea green eyes melted into view. The hottest, deepest tingling sensation spread between my legs. I drew in a sharp breath and kissed him. I felt his chest press against mine, and looked down to see that he had breasts! But it seemed natural somehow, and I slowly drew my fingers around his nipple, causing it to harden.

I raised one breast to my mouth and sucked. As I sucked, I felt someone's lips closing between my legs. Reluctantly, I pulled my mouth away and looked down.

Orla was there, between my legs. Her bright red curly hair covered my thighs. She looked up at me and grinned, devilishly.

I snapped awake, every trace of sexual lustre irrevocably dulled. I'm sure that my dream had been deeply Freudian, but I had absolutely no desire to know what it meant. Yet, as I stood beneath the hot water of the shower, it was George's face that came back to me. His lips against mine, his hand against my breast. I was consumed by an aching inside. I rested my head against the cool tiles and reached down to finish what he had started.

It was completely innocent. That's what I told myself afterwards. It was just a silly fantasy. We all get crushes, right? Everybody, at least once in their life, probably dozens of times, has had a dumb fantasy about somebody they will never actually shag. Be it a pin-up movie star or your best friend's boyfriend. Whatever. There's no harm in a little imagination. Even if it stretches the boundaries of gender and belief.

Monday rolled around much like Sunday. Every week was like a bank holiday weekend for me, both in the sense that I wasn't working and that my bank account was suffering. Eventually I made the brave decision to admit on Facebook that I had lost my phone. I told everyone to e-mail me if it was important, or call the home phone. I'd let them know when I replaced it.

It's funny how something bad can sometimes become something good. Losing my phone was awful. At the time it meant that I couldn't call a taxi, get home, or phone anyone for help. But now it also meant that nobody could call me. Not even Ferris. Especially not Ferris. And there was something really quite nice about that.

I started the week with a jog around the park. It was still bitterly cold but signs of spring were popping up everywhere. Snowdrops had long given way to crocuses. Soon the sap would be rising, although my libido already seemed to have taken a head start.

After I'd jogged home, I sat trying to focus on a daytime chat show. It was something totally ridiculous about a girl who didn't think that her mother was genetically her mother. I felt for the mum. I was fairly sure she remembered giving birth. But then, there was something a little strange about her too, and maybe it was the daughter's wishful thinking to have a different biological mum out there somewhere.

I made myself a sandwich. Then I went to the shop and bought a newspaper, browsed through the job ads – nothing, as ever. Half an hour later I decided to bake banana bread as the fruit in the bowl was looking a little ripe. The smell was wonderful but I wasn't really hungry, so I made another cup of tea.

I was fidgeting. Sign of a restless mind. For some reason I just couldn't seem to sit still. As well as fidgety, I found myself becoming irritable. I snapped at the television, even though the cloned offspring of an antelope couldn't hear a word of my distain over the jeering of the studio audience. So, instead, I pummelled my anger into a cushion and blew on a cup of coffee, just for variety.

When I could take it no more, I pulled up the internet search engine and typed in VAC. Reaching for the phone, I dialled the number.

"Hello, Voluntary Action, how may I help?" asked a prim, female administrator.

"I'd like to speak with George McCally, please."

"One moment, I'll just transfer you."

With each brrrp of the phone, my heart thumped against my chest.

"Hello?" That soft baritone.

"Hi, George, it's Phoebe."

"Hey. How are you?"

"I'm good. Really good."

"Great. What can I do for you?"

Oh, God, was I really about to do this? "I, uh, wondered if you'd like to go for a drink later? I wanted to thank you for the other night. I thought you might take payment in kind?" Payment in kind was a fundraising joke. It meant 'I don't have any money, but I'll buy you a beer'.

There was a horrible pause. I could hear his office in the background: people typing, phones ringing, paper being shuffled. It dawned on me that I may as well be calling from Mars. I had nothing to do with my day except sit around, infatuated. He, on the other hand, was probably scrutinising next quarter's spending budget, reviewing multiple funding applications, and organising team supervision meetings. He was probably wondering who the hell this weirdo was, calling him up in the middle of the day with enough time on her hands to discuss a social life. I'd done it again, proved myself a total ditz.

"Tonight?"

I breathed out. "Only if you're not busy. It was just a thought. We can make it another night -"

"That would be fine."

"Are you sure?"

"It's nice to have something to look forward to on a Monday."

"Great. I mean – yeah, great. How about The Almond Tree? I think they have a new chef. The food's supposed to be good."

"Sure."

"Oh, but I still haven't found my phone. If you need to cancel or anything, just send me an e-mail. I'll check before I leave. What time's good?"

"I finish at five. I'll take the car home and get a taxi in. Say half-six?"

"Absolutely. See you then."

We hung up.

What the hell was I doing? I was caught between wanting to squeal with absurd delight, and wanting to curl up in the foetal position and implode. What an idiotic sensation. It was just like first date nerves.

Only this wasn't a date. It was just a drink. To say 'thank you.'

CHAPTER TWENTY-ONE

The Almond Tree was a spacious pub towards the centre of town. Easy to find, and easy to find a table. One half was a restaurant, the other half a dance floor. It was usually quiet until after eight o'clock.

I was running late. I'd been so sure that George was going to cancel on me that I'd sat refreshing my e-mail page until the very last minute. I was positive that he would already be there, but when I walked in, I couldn't see him.

About a dozen people sat at different stages of their meals. There were a few couples leaning intimately in towards one another, a few older couples leaning conspicuously away from one another, and two or three groups of friends in fully animated conversation.

I chose a table for two in a quiet corner, within sight of the entrance. When the waitress came, I ordered a large glass of red, then settled back in my chair to worry. Before I left, I worried that he would cancel. Now that I was here, I worried that he wouldn't show. Yet, before my drink had even arrived, there was George. Suit, tie, hat and confident swagger. I took a deep breath.

He saw me immediately but paused to place an order at the bar.

"Have you been waiting long?" he greeted me. At that moment, the other waitress arrived with my drink. "Guess not," he grinned.

Placing his jacket on the back of the chair, he sat down. "Sorry I'm late, the traffic was dreadful."

"Oh, you're not," I said, a little too effusively. "I've only just got here myself."

He picked up the menu and glanced through. "This has changed," he said. "Last time I was here you could only get burgers."

"My colleague, Miriam, was raving about this place. It's supposed to be some *cordon bleu* chef or something."

George raised his eyebrows as he scanned the selection. When the waitress delivered his beer, we ordered. I opted for salmon and he chose lamb.

"So," he said, handing the menu over. "How are you feeling?"

Cringing slightly at the memory of the other night, I replied: "A lot better. Really, I'm-"

"Sorry about that? I know. Let's forget it."

I smiled.

"How is work, by the way? I saw your boss today."

"Oh, what a pity," I said.

He laughed. "She's an," he paused to think of a suitable word, "*interesting* person."

"If by interesting you mean a three-headed fire-breathing witch then, yeah, sure. Interesting."

"Ouch." He looked amused. "I said it before. You should leave."

"Maybe. I did see a position going, but I don't think it's the right time." I held his gaze for a moment.

He nodded. "Well, whatever you decide."

"Also, there's a friend who kind of needs me. He'd be on his own if I left, and he's going through a rough patch."

"Paying it forward?"

"Yeah, kind of. He's lovely."

"Sounds serious."

"No! Oh no, not like that. He's gay."

"Anyone I know?"

"Maybe. Eddie Beal?"

"I know him. Good guy. Got married last year." He raised his eyebrows. "Oh. A rough patch, huh?"

"Yeah, I think most people know now anyway."

"Shame, they were a nice couple."

Our food arrived.

"George, do you mind if I ask you something?"

"Everyone's entitled to ask," he said, with a twitch of his lip.

"Your chest," I struggled to phrase my question. "What happened?"

He took a sip of his beer. "I had them removed. It's called a bi-lateral mastectomy."

"How long ago?"

"Eight years. I was twenty-three."

I stopped myself from asking 'did it hurt.' That seemed like a particularly stupid question, and one that you would only ask if you were considering the procedure yourself.

He took another forkful of food and chewed slowly, watching me frown.

"Not the best dinner conversation, huh?"

I reached for my drink. "God, sorry."

"You do that a lot."

"What?"

"Apologise."

"I just – I wanted to-"

"Ask. That's fine. Go ahead. But keep eating or it'll get cold," he winked.

I smiled and picked up my fork.

"You have a nice body," I said.

"Do you tell that to all your friends?"

"Only the ones I've spent the night with."

Were we flirting? I took a bite of salmon.

"You have some hair, down there." I pointed just below my belly. "That's, um, very manly."

He took another bite of his food. "Yeah, that's testosterone for you."

I looked blank.

"This is really new to you, isn't it?"

I nodded. "I have to say, it's not something I'm totally *au fait* with."

"Well, I used to take injections. Once every two weeks at my clinic. It turns your hormones around, makes your body behave differently."

"So you grow hair like a man?"

"Amongst other things, yeah."

"And your voice drops?"

He nodded.

"But you didn't grow a dick?"

He almost choked on his drink. "Uh, no. Not for lack of trying though."

I smiled. "You don't have a beard either."

"I used to. I used to have to shave."

"What happened?" I scrutinised his chin, trying to make out the telltale marks of a past skincare regime I could only wonder at.

"I stopped taking the injections. Some things changed back, some didn't. It affects everybody differently. You can't predict what will change and what won't. I lost my facial hair, but not my landing strip. My voice stayed low, but my muscle distribution shifted."

I was frowning. "Why did you stop taking the injections?"

He paused for a moment, weighing up his answer. "It just seemed like the right thing to do at the time."

A thought struck me. "You didn't regret it, did you? You didn't want to be a girl again?"

His laugh bordered on scorn. "No, nothing like that."

I felt a little foolish. I knew George was humouring me by answering my stupid questions. I hadn't even done any Google research. I knew nothing about the subject of sex change. Perhaps, as long as I didn't know the technicalities of it, I wouldn't have to address any of the underlying issues that came with it.

"Would you like another drink?" he asked, catching the waitress' eye.

"Sure."

After that, we changed the subject. Or rather, he somehow changed it so tactfully that I didn't even notice. We touched on work, how all the smart charities were grouping together to form 'joint ventures', sort of like private companies bidding for larger government tenders. It was clever because it made charities competitive. They could share out their individual talents and resources to compete for work on a much larger scale than they could as individuals. Even though economics were slipping at an alarming rate, it was still cheaper for local authorities to outsource services than to deliver them in-house.

But work is boring, and we soon moved on to books, films and holidays.

"Have you thought any more about your-"

"Don't mention the 'B' word!" I said. "Just don't."

He smiled sympathetically. "What about this Canadian guy?"

"Ferris?"

"That's his name?"

"I know," I said, rolling my eyes. "That's one good thing about losing my phone, at least he can't call me."

"You should tell him, if that's how you feel."

"I should, and I will. It's just timing. Firstly, I have to make time to see him. Then I have to do damage limitation on my friend Orla. She thinks he's the best thing since panty liners."

"Have you shown her your neck?"

"No, she'd probably think it was kinky."

The plates were gone. We sat, fiddling with our beer mats.

"You'll work it out."

"Yeah." I nodded.

His phone went. "Sorry," he mouthed as he answered it, glancing at the screen. "Alright, sweetheart? How's it going?"

Sweetheart? I smiled. It sounded so natural and yet so strange coming from him. I wondered who he was talking to.

"Yeah, probably...uh-huh...maybe...yeah, I can do Wednesday...alright, stay out of trouble." He hung up. "Sorry," he said again, turning back to me.

"Hot date?" I asked, surprised at how tight my voice sounded.

"What?"

"Sweetheart?"

He laughed. "Oh. No."

We ordered ice-cream and coffee. By the time the table was empty, I felt as though I wouldn't have to eat for a week. When the bill arrived, I took the card reader and pulled out my plastic.

"Are you buying me dinner?" he grinned.

"It's the least I can do. Seriously. I was in such a state the other night."

"Well, if the food's this good every time you trip, I hope you have a nervous breakdown."

We headed to the exit and once again found ourselves standing in a quiet, deserted car park. We walked along for a while, towards the road. Our pace naturally slowed the closer it got.

"It's funny," I said.

We stopped.

"I *really* thought you were a man."

"Yeah, I *really* noticed that. But most people do. I have colleagues who still aren't sure."

"But you like women, right? I mean, you're not a gay man?"

He frowned.

"Okay, stupid question." I took a breath and tried again. "I mean, you wouldn't have come out tonight if you didn't like women."

He laughed that confident, derisive laugh which made me feel small.

"Why, is this a date?"

I found that I couldn't answer.

He stopped laughing and stared at me. "Phoebe?"

"You remember when I tried to kiss you before, and you stopped me? That was a good thing to do. I didn't know then." I placed my hand gently on his chest, smoothing the thin material against his skin.

"And now?"

"And now I do know."

I could see him swimming in his own caution. Worried that he was misreading my blazing, neon signals.

As our lips met, I felt that same explosion that I had felt in my dream. Warmth shot up through the very core of my being.

I felt happy.

CHAPTER TWENTY-TWO

We stood there, nose to nose, grinning like naughty school children. It was ridiculous and wonderful and weird, all at the same time. I'd never had a kiss like it.

Eventually, we continued walking towards my bus stop. There was no one else there, and no bright, revealing light, so we kissed again. He pushed me up against the glass and cornered me with his outstretched arm. But I didn't want to escape.

My heart sank as the bus arrived. We didn't say anything, but I stood by the door as it pulled away, our eyes locked, neither one of us quite sure what had just happened. A bewitchment. A delicious, apple-biting bewitchment.

That feeling stayed with me all the way home. Cocooned in my own temple of butterflies.

The next morning, when I walked into work, I found a white cardboard box waiting for me.

"Thank God you're here," Miriam said as I took off my coat. "I'm dying of curiosity."

"When did this arrive?"

"Ten minutes ago. That Floral Tributes company again. She caught me getting out of the lift."

I frowned and ran my fingers along the lid.

"Should we wait for Eddie?" I asked.

"Oh, he isn't in today. Flu or something."

"Okay, well…" I lifted it.

Staring back at me was the biggest single bloom rose I had ever seen. Orange. With red tips.

"Well I never!" Miriam was standing over my shoulder by this point, her voice hushed in reverie. "It's just like Eddie said."

I plucked up the card and opened it.

Weavers, tomorrow 8pm? G.

"Who's 'G'?"

"Oh, no one." I felt a little light headed.

"Yeah, right."

I sat down heavily in my chair. "You know, I'd love a coffee if you're making one."

Miriam looked at me for a moment, then decided not to argue. "Semi-skimmed okay?"

I nodded.

It's something all gay men know. We brush up on these things. Eddie's words echoed around my mind. Well, of course. No straight boyfriend had ever made such a romantic gesture.

I stared at George's handwriting, wondering what I was missing. It was romantic, of course it was romantic. But I didn't understand. He must have sent the first rose, all that time ago on Valentine's Day. My one thorny sword, cutting back loneliness as I sat watching telly on my own. Slowly, it dawned on me. When we went for drinks in the rain, he had already known who I was! Had he seen my name on the post when he nursed me to bed? Remembered the e-mails? Seen my picture on the staff profiles of our website? Somehow put two and two together?

"Here you go," Miriam said, placing my coffee on the desk.

"Thanks."

On the bus on the way home, I almost missed my stop. Too busy staring out of the window at the world going by. When I don't know what to think, I generally don't think at all. I fall into a limbo of thoughtlessness. I don't think that I'm not thinking – I just think that thinking moves to the back room. Like there are little office workers in my brain who have to adjourn to a secret meeting where they bash out plans and blueprints. Then, when they're ready, they reappear in the main office to present their findings.

I let them get on with it.

When I got through the door, I could hear Dad snoring loudly upstairs. It would still be another two or three hours before he surfaced, so I put the rose in a vase by the TV, then started making myself a sandwich.

There was a knock at the door.

"Hi." Mark stood there, looking at me through his dishevelled fringe. He had thick stubble and a stale smell about him.

"Hi," I said slowly.

"Um, can I come in?"

"No." I shook my head. He blinked, unsure what to say next. He looked so pathetic that I took pity on him: "I feel like taking a walk."

He brightened at this, and I reached for my coat.

We headed in the direction of the park. It was clouding over, and only a few people were walking their dogs in the distance. A bleak landscape for a bleak reunion.

"I just thought I'd see how you are," he mumbled, after we'd walked in silence for a long while.

"That was thoughtful of you."

"I didn't know how you were."

"Uh-huh."

"So. How are you?"

I stopped and stared at him. "A lot better than you look."

He blinked and scratched the side of his chin. He'd lost weight, his hair was unwashed, and his T-shirt had food stains on it. I wanted to flatter myself that he was pining for me but, even to my subjective eyes, he didn't look well.

"What happened to you?"

He clasped his left elbow with his right hand and blinked at me a few more times. "What I did to you, Phoebs. I'm really sorry. You know that?"

I simply waited.

"It was unforgivable. I can't believe the way that I acted."

"Okay."

He shifted from foot to foot as though he was having difficulty standing still. Letting go of his elbow, he licked his lips and tried to look me in the eyes. "Can we keep walking?"

I couldn't object to that, so we started off along the path again. A dog barked in the distance, and a man's rough voice yelled out unintelligibly.

"So, how's your girlfriend? What was her name, Jessica?"

His head snapped round, eyes practically bulging.

"How did you know about Jessica?"

"Women's intuition. Don't you know that we're all psychically connected?" There, that would mess with his mind.

"I kind of suspected."

"Is she well?"

"She's not my girlfriend. Not any more. She never really was."

"But a good lay, right?"

He turned suddenly, making me jump. "I said I was sorry, alright?"

"I'm going home now, Mark."

"No, wait – no. Please don't go."

"The reason it didn't work out between us is because you're a complete and total tit, okay? I'm not going back there again. Sort your own life out."

As I turned, his arm shot out and grabbed me by the shoulder. He realised what he'd done and leapt back in apology. "Please, please wait."

There was a desperation in his voice that I had never heard before.

"I think I'm in trouble."

"What kind of trouble?"

His eyes looked everywhere but at me. For a moment I didn't think that he was going to say anything. "I lost my job," he confided, shoulders sagging in defeat.

"Why?"

"I wasn't well."

"Mumps? I've heard they can make you infertile."

He didn't even smile. He simply scratched the back of his head and looked at the ground.

"It's complicated. You know when we had that row? The way I was acting and everything?"

"Your rapid descent into cockdom?"

"Yeah, that too. Well, um, I might have been overdoing it."

This was like pulling teeth. "Overdoing what?" I asked, patiently.

"You know. The party fodder."

For a moment I didn't understand what he meant, then a light went on in my brain. "You're a junkie now?"

"Don't be like that. Of course I'm not. I'm not shooting up or anything. I wouldn't be that daft."

I raised an eyebrow.

"No, I wouldn't. It's not like that. I've just had a few too many lines is all."

"How many's a few too many?"

"Quite a few too many." He was still having trouble making eye contact. "I thought I had it under control, you know. I thought I could handle it. But it just got silly. I've spent almost everything I saved. My job's gone. I'm about to lose the flat."

I felt a sinking sensation. Yes, he could be an arrogant tosser at times, but I had loved him once. And was I slightly to blame? After all, we'd seen each other almost every day for over three years, and I hadn't even noticed that he was snowed under. I mean, I'd noticed he was getting a bit more bolshy than usual. I'd noticed his attention span, at least for me, was dropping. But I had no idea that he was snorting his own bodyweight in coke. I told him so.

"God, Phoebs, you can't blame yourself. That's what it does to you, isn't it? It gives you that sparkle. Makes you the man. I was on my own little power trip there, taking the world by storm." He smiled for the first time, almost a grimace.

"I see," I said, not really seeing. I'd only tried it once. Low-grade pub cocaine. It stung my nose, my eyes watered, and I got a headache. "So, what is it you think I can do?"

"Well," he said, scratching the side of his nose.

"I'm not giving you money."

"No! No – hell no, I don't want to take more of it. Really, I don't. I want to get off it. And you know people. You're in the whole charity world. You know organisations that can help me, don't you?"

"Have you been to your doctor?"

"Not a chance. I can't have this on my records."

"You mean nobody knows?"

He shook his head. "No way."

"You lost your job, you're about to lose your flat – and nobody knows?"

"Phoebs, please, you're the only one. I can't. Really, I can't."

I took a deep breath. "Okay. Well, try Action on Addiction. They have a helpline."

"Yeah?"

I nodded. "But you need support. You'll need somewhere to live. People to help you. You have to tell your family."

"I'd rather die."

"Wow, okay."

"Seriously. Nobody can ever find out."

CHAPTER TWENTY-THREE

I'd totally forgotten about the rose by the time I crawled into bed. Of all the people, why the hell had he come to me? What could I tell him that an internet search couldn't?

I had the horrible feeling that he was expecting me to help him through this. To be there for him. His 'buddy'. It made me feel cold-hearted, but I really didn't want to. At least now I understood his actions. I understood why he was behaving like such a child towards the end. But if I'd known back then what I know now, I'm not all that sure I would have cared. Maybe that's just hindsight. It's one punch to the jaw and a pair of green wedge heels too late. How could I ever really say what I would or wouldn't have done? But I was relieved in a way. He's not my problem anymore. Only if I choose to make him one.

Wednesday was a half-day afternoon. Eddie still wasn't in, and I made a mental note to call him and find out how he was doing. Someone said there was a bug going round. Apparently everyone was going down with it.

On the way into work I'd caved and bought myself a new mobile. I sent a mass e-mail to all my contacts, informing them of the change of number. On the way home, my phone beeped and I saw that it was a text message from George.

Are you coming?

For a moment, I couldn't think where, then I remembered the rose. I'd completely forgotten to answer.

Of course! x

A sudden surge of hope swelling inside me. Of course I was going to forget about Mark and his stupid problems. Of course I was heading home to get changed and go out for the night.

Then my phone rang.

"Hey, chick." It was Orla. "What are you doing on Friday? Say 'nothing'."

"Nothing," I groaned.

"Good, because it's not an option. Henry's, seven o'clock. Dress posh!"

She hung up. I had half a mind to throw the sodding thing in the nearest bin. I'd had it for all of five minutes, and already I was being harassed. I just hoped that it would take a little longer before someone passed my number on to Ferris.

I took a walk-through shower, pulled on a pair of figure hugging jeans and a top from the Monsoon sale.

I arrived at Weavers just as George's Chrysler pulled into the car park. A woman got out of the passenger side, and I realised it was the same woman that I had seen him with last time. She was skinny and wrinkled. Her mousy hair was gelled like cotton wisps to her head, and combed into thin grooves. She wasn't ugly, just odd. This time she was wearing a long, flowing gypsy skirt and a short, glittery crop top. It showed her midriff again, which was perfectly flat, but also wrinkled.

I tried not to stare as they approached. In contrast, George was in a dapper black suit and crisp, wide-collared shirt. His trilby was set at a rakish angle. I felt my heart skip a beat.

"Hey, toots," he smiled.

"Hi," I grinned back.

"I want you to meet June. She's my surrogate mother."

I added a puzzled frown to my smile as I shook her hand.

"Don't listen to him, deary. I'm his sister."

I was confused.

"Long story," George said, placing his arm around my shoulder as we walked towards the door.

Inside, there was no one at the payment booth, and we walked straight through into the main room. It had the air of a school gym the morning after a disco.

We continued through the far door, where there was indeed a telephone, and up the stairs into a stylish lounge with a smaller stage in one corner. We were the only ones there, and George set about pulling some of the seats around a large table.

June excused herself and went to the ladies.

"Your mother?"

"No," he smiled. "Just a really good friend. I've known her for years. She took me under her wing when I first came on the scene. Looked after me, helped me through the op."

"Oh."

"What happened to you yesterday? I didn't think you were coming."

"I just got caught up in work. Of course I was going to come. What are we doing though?"

"Well, you bought me dinner the other night, so I thought I should return the favour. Give you a taste of the underworld."

I didn't understand.

"It's the Mardi Gras planning committee," he elaborated. "But after this, we'll eat, promise. I just thought you might like to come along, maybe get involved."

"Orla loves Mardi Gras."

"You should bring her."

I knew that I never would. It dawned on me that I was developing two sets of friends. The ones I went for ice-cream and birthday drinks with, and the ones I frequented gay bars with. It was strange to think that, whereas the second group would probably be fine going for birthday drinks, the first lot would never understand what I was doing here.

Eddie appeared at the top of the stairs. When he turned and saw me, he stopped.

The awkwardness was broken by June coming back from the ladies'.

"Eddie! Fancy seeing you here," she chirped. "Pleasure, as always. Liking the stubble. Very rugged."

It was true, he had an impressive five o'clock shadow. What was it about men at the moment – they all seemed to be getting hairy.

"Hi, June," he said, taking a seat. "Bar not open yet?"

"Still waiting for Mitch with the keys. Won't be long now."

"Hi, Eddie," I said, smiling over at him in what I hoped was a friendly fashion.

"Hey, Phoebe. What are you doing here?"

George sat down next to me, thumbed his nose and leant forward, resting his elbow on his knee. I don't know if it was some sort of coded signal, but when Eddie looked back at me, he raised his eyebrows in surprise.

"Just helping out," I said. "I guess you decided to do the same?"

"Had to get out of the house," he nodded.

I almost joked that work was also a good way to get out of the house, but stopped myself short. I sensed the atmosphere wasn't quite right for a jibe like that.

A man arrived. I assumed it was Mitch with the keys. He wore a tight black T-shirt that showed off his bulging, tattooed muscles. His mouth was hidden by a long beard. He looked more like a Hell's Angel than the bar tender at a gay club.

The minute the shutter went up, June was at the counter. She bought a round: beer for George, red wine for me and Eddie, and a G&T for herself.

Two minutes later, a studious looking young woman arrived. She had thick, curly brown hair, a pinched nose and wire-rimmed glasses. She was dressed in a pleated grey skirt, black tights and an oversized cardigan that made her look a bit like a schoolgirl.

"This is Charlotte," June leaned over to explain. "Chair of the Mardi Gras committee."

She sat down at the head of the table and shuffled her papers.

"Is this everybody?" she asked, scanning the room.

"Well, Irvin and Mac said they might come later. I think they've got an am-dram thing on," June replied.

"Hold your horses! We're not late – we're fashionable," came another voice from the doorway.

My heart sank.

"Come along, darling," Sebastian called down the stairs. "They're about to start without us." Another man, taller and slimmer, with strawberry blond hair, appeared next to him. "Everyone, you know Ellis? We're joined at the hips, on a good day." His eyes fell on me. "Well, well," he said, "what a bunch of faces we have tonight."

"We need to start, so if you could take a seat please," the officious voice of Chairwoman Charlotte instructed.

"Just let us get a drink, darling." Sebastian went to the bar.

The meeting was called to attention as he placed his order, then he and Ellis came and sat at our end of the table.

"God, it's good to see you here," I heard him whisper to George. "It's dead as a dodo."

George smirked and took a sip of his beer. Maybe it was just my own insecurity, but it felt as though the temperature in the room had dropped ten degrees.

The meeting was fairly brief. Many of the people who had been involved in running the event in previous years were out of town or unavailable. It wasn't a major problem though. There was already a template for doing it. It was just a case of dishing out various tasks and drawing up an action plan to keep track of what had been completed.

George offered to contact last year's sponsors. Sebastian and Ellis volunteered to line up the guest speakers, and to research logistics such as portaloos and food trailers. June had contacts in the art world who might be willing to put forward some extra money. Charlotte was busy organising everybody else, which just left me and Eddie. I said that I'd help George, and Eddie said that he'd like to design the promotional flyers.

As meetings go, it was unusually swift and efficient.

When we broke for a refill, people fell into their own conversations.

"So," Sebastian said, resting his head lazily on one hand. "You're looking better. You probably don't remember me, do you?"

"Seb," George cautioned.

"Well, we've all been there," he shrugged.

It surprised me. A strangely lenient concession. I had thought that he was setting me up for a put-down. If I hadn't caught him laughing about me with his friends, I could almost have warmed to the guy.

"Just, next time, aim for Primark rather than designer couture."

That was the knife behind his back. I smiled, because that's all I could do, then turned and leaned into the conversation that June was having with Eddie.

"...so good together." I heard her say.

"Well, 'all good things'," Eddie shrugged. He looked pale, and I wondered whether he did in fact have a cold. Probably man flu. "Hey," he said, catching me listening. "Looks like things are good with you?"

I felt my cheeks burn. "Yeah, you could say that."

"Over Mark then?"

"So over. Mark who?"

He smiled.

"Eddie! Eddie, Eddie, Eddie." It was Sebastian. He and Ellis were walking towards the door. They paused behind me. "How was the honeymoon?"

"It's over," he replied, flatly.

"Oh, I am sorry to hear that. Did you get your money's worth?"

Silence descended. Everybody was listening.

"Well," Sebastian continued, "I wouldn't worry about it. If you want him back you could always have a sex op. Pucker up your hole and turn it into a fanny. I hear he likes that kind of thing." He swung his coat over his shoulder and walked out, trailing his pet behind him.

I was stunned. I could feel the heat of Eddie's embarrassment radiating across the table. Everyone could. Such a horrible thing to say to someone.

"Never mind him, love," June said softly. "He's only sour because he isn't getting any. Rumour has it he's impotent."

Charlotte chuckled.

George stood up and put his hand on my shoulder. "We're going to get something to eat. Would you like to come?"

Eddie shook his head. "I'm tired. I need to go home."

"Would you like us to drop you?"

"I'm fine. Thanks."

CHAPTER TWENTY-FOUR

We bought Chinese take away and went back to George's. With the cushions on the floor, we sat there, wrestling *chow mein* with chopsticks.

"That night, when you found me in the alley, you sounded like you were going somewhere with Sebastian. Why do you put up with him?"

"Seb's alright. He just doesn't listen to himself speak sometimes."

"But others have to. I caught him laughing about me with his friends in The Cambria before, telling them all about how sick I was and how he thought I'd attack you."

George paused. "What were you doing in The Cambria?"

"Having a drink with Eddie."

"Well, Seb's a lonely soul. He's his own worst enemy. I feel sorry for him sometimes."

"What do you mean?"

George chewed thoughtfully for a moment. "I don't think he ever fully came to terms with himself. His family were brutal to him. He never knew his dad, and his mum remarried a complete thug. He bullied Seb from the very beginning and used to taunt him for being a poof. If I were a couch psychologist, I'd say that Seb resented himself for letting it show. I think he was a camp kid; his step dad picked up on that. It's not like he could help it, but because of it he associates the way he is with being weak. It's twisted, but I get where it comes from."

"So he bullies other people in return?"

"You know how the cycle goes."

"Doesn't mean I have to let it slide."

"No. But Eddie's a big boy. He can look out for himself."

"Maybe."

"Picking on my girlfriend is a whole other matter though," he said, with a lascivious grin. "I'll have to have a word with him about that."

"You don't think I'm big enough to take care of myself?" I challenged playfully.

He put his plate down by his side and crawled over to me, taking my plate away, too. "I don't know. Are you?"

I knocked his hat off, and it rolled across the carpet. He watched it, then looked back at me.

"Best you can do?"

I took his collar in my hands.

"Is this designer?" I asked.

He tilted his head, quizzically.

I didn't wait for a reply. Yanking my hands apart, I held my breath as the buttons flew off in every direction, tearing the shirt open to his waist.

There was a moment of complete disbelief. I looked up, terrified I had overstepped the mark.

"You," he said, suddenly getting to his feet. Holding out his hand, he pulled me up with him. "You're coming with me." With that, he spun me in the direction of the door and slapped my bum.

Before I knew it, we were upstairs in the bedroom. He pushed the door closed behind him, and we were alone in the dark.

He tore off his jacket as he approached, throwing it to the floor. I threw my arms around his neck then slid them back down, undoing the last remaining button. Like the jacket, his shirt dropped to the floor by his feet.

We stood there, eyes like candles, aflame with possibility.

He reached down and, in one swift motion, pulled my top over my head, exposing my lacy white bra. He ran his fingers from my shoulder blades, lightly down across my breast.

Involuntarily, I rose up, pushing against him. Reaching around, he undid the clasp. The garment slid over my arms and joined his jacket on the floor.

Gently, he cupped my left breast and took it in his mouth. Just like my dream. A shot of heat ignited inside me, and I gasped. It caused him to stop, as though I had said something that caught his attention.

Slowly, his face came back to mine, and our lips brushed against one another. A sigh of wind through leaves; so softly it may never have happened. As though bending to his will, I found myself stepping back until I was pressed against the wall. He fell to his knees in front of me, unzipping my jeans and pulling them down with him.

His breath felt hot through the thin lace of my knickers. He teased me, not even touching at first; then lightly dabbing with his tongue. The sensation was exquisite. My heart thumped against my chest as he slid his finger beneath the seam and pulled the strip of material aside, blowing lightly against my skin until I felt goosebumps.

"Oh, God," I heard myself breathe, as his tongue touched the most sensitive part of me; lapping as though trying to drink me in. I could feel myself soaring too quickly. I didn't want the sensation to end, so I pushed him away.

"Slow down?"

"Yeah," I whispered.

He stood, and I tasted myself on his lips as our naked flesh pressed against one another.

With one hand around his neck, I let the other slide down to undo the button on his trousers. Running my finger around the inside of his waistband, I came back to ease down his zip. My fingers ran lightly over his boxers, then slid inside, and down between his legs. With my other hand, I pulled the elastic over his thighs.

I fumbled for a moment, then drew back, staring down at the place I had just touched. I found that I couldn't move.

It looked like mine.

"Hey, are you alright?" she asked.

"Yes, I'm- I'm-" Not fine, would be the correct answer.

She reached down and pulled her briefs back up. "It's okay. Ignore that for now. It's not important."

But already I was wriggling to get free, reaching for my clothes on the floor.

She stepped back, hands half raised in resignation.

"So you're leaving?" she asked.

"I have to. I'm working tomorrow."

"Working, right."

I pulled my top back on and did up my jeans. My bag was somewhere downstairs. I'd have to find it on the way out.

I glanced up. She was sitting on the edge of the bed, watching me. In the dim light her eyes looked coal-black, and a faint silver seam glowed across her chest as though someone had written on her using one of those birthday card ball-points. I stared for a moment, transfixed.

She raised her eyebrows as if expecting me to say something. It brought me back to myself, and I finished adjusting my jeans.

"I'll call you," I said as I walked out.

Downstairs, I grabbed my bag from the hallway and let myself out. I had no idea where the nearest bus stop was, or even if busses were still running, but I had my mobile. I used it to call a cab in a quiet cul-de-sac three streets down.

CHAPTER TWENTY-FIVE

I don't know what I'd expected. I couldn't pretend that I hadn't known. She had told me herself. I'd felt between her legs long before I took off her trousers. Of course George was a girl. I had known that all along.

So what was the problem?

I didn't know. No, I did know. I both knew and didn't know, all at the same time. I knew, but I wasn't going to admit it.

It freaked me out.

The chest, I could cope with. Surgery that backed up my image of her as a man. That, I could manage. After all, I was attracted to her masculinity. The thick voice, the haircut, that confident, cocky swagger and the clothes. She was a better dressed man than just about any real one. Even Mark had the occasional dress-down day.

She had it all. The entire package. The real deal. Everything that I had ever wanted. Polite, funny, challenging, clever, confident George. And the most important ingredient of them all: the spark. Chemistry like an amphetamine factory.

Everything.

But not a cock.

And the horror was that this was all my own self-delusion. I had known that moment was coming. I knew that we'd eventually get to that stage. I wanted it to happen. But I wanted one important difference. And that difference could not, and would never, be. It wasn't enough that George looked like a man. I wanted him to *be* a man.

I found myself shaking in the taxi. I couldn't believe what I'd done.

Anatomical. It was all purely anatomical. I knew that. I wanted George to be a man, but not nearly as much as George wanted to be a man. There was nothing she could do about that, absolutely nothing.

When I got home, I ran myself a hot bath and flicked on the radio to drown out my own thoughts. I took a couple of Nytol and read until I couldn't keep my eyes open.

Thursday was Miriam's half-day and she wasn't in. I went straight to Eddie's office. I needed to see him. I needed to tell him everything and see whether he could talk some sense into me over a drink at The Cambria. But he wasn't there.

I asked a colleague where he was, but she simply shrugged and gave me the flu story. That was blatant bollox. He hadn't been that ill last night.

Sitting back at my desk, I started to root through my e-mails. After deleting six spam messages, three circulars, and replying to two enquiries, I found myself feeling a little disappointed that there wasn't anything from George.

Both disappointed and relieved.

I said I would call him, so I stared at the phone for a full five minutes until it rang. Ignoring superstition, I answered it on the first ring, but it was just some guy enquiring about Sign Language courses. I gave him the number for the local Deaf Association and slumped back in my chair.

Then my mobile rang.

"Phoebe!"

"Who is this?"

"It's me," – always a silly response – "Ferris."

"Of course it is," I muttered.

"What?"

"It's good to hear from you," I corrected.

"You too. I didn't realise you got a new phone. Orla gave me your number."

Was there a hint of suspicion in his voice? "Sorry. I thought I e-mailed it to you?"

"It doesn't matter. I just wanted to make sure you're all set for Friday? All the attention's gonna be on you, Birthday Girl."

"Wouldn't miss it for the world."

"I guarantee you're going to like what I've got you."

Is that a money-back guarantee, I wondered? "Can't wait."

"So, I'll see you then? Henry's at seven?"

"You bet."

"Excellent."

I stared at the office phone for a further ten minutes.

"Miriam?" My boss appeared in the doorway. Her shoulder-length red hair was practically an 80's bouffant. "Oh," she said, stopping in her tracks.

"Miriam doesn't work Thursday mornings."

"Oh," she said again. "Then you'll have to do it." She walked briskly over and handed me a piece of paper. "I need a meeting with the manager of VAC next week. It's urgent. Here's the name and number."

As if George's name and number weren't already branded across my brain.

"Okay," I said heavily. "I'll get on to it."

"Good." And with that, she was gone.

The faint haze of cheap perfume lingered for a full half hour. Which is about as long as it took me to build up the courage to phone. When I said 'I'll call you,' this wasn't exactly what I had in mind. My vision was more one of not calling, ever.

"VAC, how may I help?" It was the prim administrator again.

"Hello, I'm calling from Disability First on behalf of Sheila Hewing. I was wondering whether it would be possible to arrange a meeting with George McCally next week?"

"It should be. Let me just find the diary." There was a moment of shuffling. "May I ask what the meeting is about?"

"Actually, I'm not entirely sure. I wasn't given that information."

There was a pause. A moment of understanding between one administrator and another. The moment that says *oh, you work for one of those, do you?*

"Well, Tuesday morning's free until about ten-thirty."

"Oh. That's great. Um, what about Wednesday morning?"

"Sorry, that's the only free space that week. I can maybe fit you in the following Wednesday?"

"No, that's okay. Tuesday morning it is."

So much for arranging my strategic absence.

CHAPTER TWENTY-SIX

I wanted to forget all about my birthday, but there was no chance of that with my phone buzzing every five minutes. First Orla, then Ferris, three friends from school and my cousin in Liverpool. Then there was Miriam's foot-high card on my desk. It stood as a headstone to the passing of another year, engraved by everybody I worked with.

"Go early," she said. "I'll cover for you."

So I did. Only half an hour or so, but I needed it. I soaked myself in a long, hot bath with extra bubbles. Dad had left a mini bottle of champagne on the kitchen counter, tied with a red ribbon. I opened it and sipped a glass in steam-enveloped comfort.

'Dress posh,' Orla had said. What's posh? Port-out, starboard-home? Sailor stripes, perhaps? I ran my fingers over my beaded blue dress, but I'd already worn it recently. Instead, I dug right to the back of my wardrobe and found a knee-length lavender pencil dress. I had a matching amethyst pendant and earrings. The addition of kitten heels made it just about passable. Once upon a time I had practically lived in this dress, but it's funny how even the most loved possessions get relegated to the back of the cupboard eventually. It was time for it to have its moment in the spotlight again.

I'd just finished applying my makeup when a car beeped its horn outside. I went to the window and peered out.

To my absolute astonishment it was Ferris, waving at me from a green Ford Puma. He switched off the ignition and stepped out. I checked my hair once more in the mirror and met him at the door.

"Look at you!" he said with an appreciative whistle.

"What are you doing here?"

He paused, arms outstretched, about to hug me.

"It's your birthday. I thought I'd give you a lift."

"But you'll be drinking?"

"It's your special night. I can forego this once. It won't kill me."

My questions were bordering on interrogation. I took a breath and relaxed my shoulders.

"That's so sweet of you." I smiled and let him gather me up in an embrace.

The smell of his aftershave brought back memories of that night under the bridge.

"Someone walk over your grave?" he asked, feeling me shiver.

"Just cold. Let me get my coat."

I left him standing on the porch and ran upstairs to find my jacket.

Orla, Andy, Sue and her boyfriend Tommy were all waiting for us when we arrived at Henry's.

"Surprise!" they shouted, letting off party poppers and throwing streamers. It wasn't much of a surprise though, considering I knew they would be there.

Within an hour, six other people had arrived, and I was rapidly drinking my way through a bottle of Chardonnay.

"Doesn't he look handsome?" Orla said, taking me by the arm.

I glanced over at Ferris, who was busy talking to Tommy. Probably discussing something like football, or fishing. Or whatever.

"Sure, he's handsome enough. In a Canadian sort of way."

She gave me a funny look. "Yes, he's handsome too, but I was talking about Andy."

"Oh," I said, embarrassed. Indeed, Andy was a catch. He was ordering drinks at the bar. "So you're still hooked then?"

She let out a melting sigh. "I've never been so hooked in my life."

"Ding, dong, the bells are chiming."

She slapped my arm playfully. "Who knows. We're going away together in the summer. He's booking a cottage in the Lake District. I can't wait."

I took another sip of wine.

"And?" she asked.

"And?"

"What about you? Any thoughts in that direction?"

I forced a smile. "Yeah, sure."

She sensed something wasn't quite right. Her sunny expression started to cloud, but before she could ask anything, Andrew arrived by her side, cocktail in hand.

And so the party continued. Some more people arrived, some of Orla's colleagues, a couple of Andy's friends from his course. I moved from wine to a Slow Screw and then wrapped my lips around a White Russian.

The room was starting to dance by the time Orla tapped a fork against her glass to get everyone's attention.

I was aware that people were gathering around me. I could feel that slow encirclement of heat from warm bodies and the scent of Lynx mingled with ladies' perfume.

I was staring along the bar. From my seat, I could see between the crowd, right to the other end. There was a person wearing a dark suit and a trilby.

"...very special woman..." I heard Ferris saying.

The person looked up. Was he looking at me? *Shit*, someone stood in my line of sight.

"...wonderful few months knowing Phoebe..."

I strained to see past Andy's shoulder. Was that him? How had he known that I would be here?

Half rising, I peered to one side.

"...become very close..."

There! He was walking down the bar towards me!

"...hope she feels the same...."

I stood and took a step towards him.

"George!" I called out.

The person turned towards me. He had a moustache and acne. Perhaps eighteen, hardly even old enough to be in here.

I became aware of the silence and realised that everybody was looking at me. The youth kept walking, wondering who this drunken woman was. I turned back to Ferris. He was looking at me like I'd called for a taxi on our wedding night.

"Sorry," I said. "Thought I saw someone from work. Must have had one too many."

Everybody laughed, buying into the joke. All except Ferris, who was still looking at me a little funny. I pieced together the threads of his speech and realised that I'd probably made a terrible *faux pas*.

"I can't really say more than Ferris already has. The past few months since meeting him have been a blast."

His face finally softened, and he came and put his arm around me.

"That's why I wanted to give you an extra special gift," he said, handing me a golden envelope.

Smiling around at all of my friends, I was grateful that our pulses weren't visible to the naked eye. Mine was racing with dread. What the hell had he bought me? A house? Were we moving in together? God, I hoped it wasn't a set of spare keys to his place. Maybe it was a voucher for the Early Learning Centre or Mothercare.

I peeled open the flap with trepidation. There, inside, were two plane tickets to Alicante.

"You and me, we're flying away together," he whispered, squeezing my shoulder.

From Henry's we went on to the Rhubarb Club, a night spot playing a mixture of salsa and samba. I sank a Martini, and we danced around our handbags for a while. The couples left first, except for Orla, who seemed to have temporarily returned to her factory setting and was flirting with every guy who walked past.

Some Italian stallion with slicked-back black hair and a waxed chest whisked me up and spun me around until I thought I was going to throw up. I had to go to the ladies' to powder my nose after that. As I came out, Ferris accosted me.

"Hey, are you alright?"

I nodded. "Why?"

"You look a little partied out."

"Yeah. I think I had a few too many at Henry's."

"Well, let's go home."

"I can't do that."

"Why not? It's your birthday. You can do whatever you feel like."

It was tempting.

Twenty minutes later I bowed out, saying my farewells to those I could easily find and promising Orla that I'd phone her in the morning.

Ferris took my hand and led me to his car. It was small in comparison to George's, but still good looking. I slid into the passenger seat.

"Back to mine?" he asked.

"Home, James, and don't spare the horses!"

I rested my head against the cool window and shut my eyes. I wasn't spinning. I wasn't sick drunk. I was just tired. Bed sounded like a really good idea. And a warm, occupied bed sounded even better than a cold, solitary one. Even if it was Ferris'. There probably wouldn't be a spliff involved, and no silly reminiscing about childhood TV. I'd probably have a really sore neck in the morning. But, what the heck. Ferris was every mother's dream son-in-law.

I caught myself thinking that. What did I mean? That George wasn't?

Like I even had to ask.

Too tired.

I felt the car slow to a halt. He poked me softly on the shoulder.

"Hey, we're here."

"Hmmm." I nodded and slowly pulled myself upright.

I'd never been to Ferris', and it was surprisingly alright. A spacious apartment like Mark's, only more wood, less stainless steel. The walls were sandy-coloured rather than white, mostly obscured by bohemian wall hangings. The musty smell of stale incense welcomed me like a furtive host. *Come in*, it said, *but expect the unexpected*.

"You're a hippie."

He laughed and went to the kitchen. "Drink?"

"Ugh, no. Sleep."

He came back towards me and pulled away a giant Indian throw to reveal a previously hidden cubby. On the floor was a snug fitting double futon. There were fairy lights hanging around the ceiling; their multi colours gave the impression of Santa's grotto in a fun, Christmassy, sort of way.

"Do you want a T-shirt?" he asked.

"No." I shook my head and started to undress, reaching to pull the zip of my dress down. His hand came up to help me.

Did I want to go home? Did I want a drink? Did I want a T-shirt? Considerate to a fault. One of life's truly good guys.

I turned to face him and found myself unbuttoning his shirt. His lips met mine. We were kissing again. How had that happened? We never know these things. But it wasn't like last time. It was actually nice. Soft. Not sloppy with first fumblings. Or maybe it was because I was drunk and therefore equally sloppy.

We descended to the covers, the throw falling back into place behind us. His mouth moved to my neck, and I used a finger under his chin to draw him back up.

"No?" he asked.

"No."

He smiled and concentrated on my cheeks, lips and eyelids. It was soothing. And then he took his love south.

Afterwards, we cuddled in a spoon, and I fell into a deep sleep.

CHAPTER TWENTY-SEVEN

By Monday, I was still suffering. I'd spent almost the entire weekend in bed. First with a hangover, then a twenty-four hour cold, which made my eyes water and my throat tickle. I propped myself up with Lemsip and Strepsils. Dad made me chicken soup on his day off, and we sat with the duvet on the sofa, watching repeats on the comedy channel.

Ferris had dropped me home the morning after, before the cold had started, and phoned on Sunday to see how I was. I told him 'fine' and that I didn't want to give him my germs – though I probably already had.

Sunday was another restless night. Dad woke me up coming home from work. It was ridiculously early, but I couldn't get back to sleep, so I took a shower, made breakfast and glared at BBC News for a while.

I had just put my bowl in the sink when there was a knock at the door.

"I wasn't sure if you were working Mondays now or not, so I thought I'd try and catch you in," Mark said, his fringe still ruffled but the stubble gone.

"What are you doing here?"

"I remembered it was your birthday, so I wanted to bring you something."

He handed me a little box with a paper bow.

"You shouldn't have."

"It's a 'thank you'. For the information you gave me. I called their helpline. They were really good."

"You've stopped snorting?"

"Near enough. I'm almost there. Look, do you want to get breakfast? My treat?"

"Actually, I was going to visit Mum."

"I could come too?" he asked, hopefully.

"You hate the cemetery."

"Well, yeah. But we're all going to end up there some day. I shouldn't hold that against the dead."

I stared at him. In the years that we'd been together he'd only been to Mum's grave perhaps three or four times, and then only at the beginning when he would have done just about anything to impress me.

"I don't know."

"Go on, I need some fresh air. And I'll buy you breakfast after."

"You're broke."

"I sold the flat."

That came as a surprise. Good riddance to bad memories. At the same time, it had been a place that I knew so well. I had stayed there on so many occasions. I sort of missed it. It would have been nice to give it one last farewell, if it hadn't been for the blazing, vase-throwing argument we'd had.

"Oh. Where are you living?"

"With Steve and Alice." His friends from work. Well, friends he had worked with, until recently.

"They've taken you in?"

"Just until I sort myself out. To be honest, I'm thinking of taking your advice. The sale has cleared my debts, so I may as well use what's left to go home and get back on the straight and narrow. Work out what I want to do next."

"You're going to tell your family?"

"Yeah. Maybe. It might be for the best. Dad always liked the booze. Maybe I get it from him. Maybe he'll understand."

I nodded slowly. Mark's dad had always been the first to crack open the wine whenever we visited. Then the gin, and finally the cognac. He usually fell asleep in his armchair before we left.

"Okay," I said, taking my coat from the hook in the hall and leaving his present, unopened, on the table next to the post.

We took the bus to the cemetery, stopping to buy flowers at the petrol station. I took the nail scissors from my pocket and trimmed back the grass whilst he went to find a watering can. After we doused it, I sat on my jacket, pushing stems into an oasis.

"So, you still miss her?"

"What do you think?"

"Sorry, silly question." He ran his hand through his fringe. "I ask a lot of those."

The self deprecation in his voice made me look up.

"Oh!" I said in surprise. "You're bleeding." I pointed to my nose and watched as he dabbed the back of his hand against his own.

"Shit, sorry," he apologised again, reaching into his jacket pocket and pulling out a large wad of toilet paper. "That happens sometimes."

It's not that I hadn't believe him before, when he told me that he had a drug addiction, but seeing the physical evidence gave me a jolt. It seemed ruby-red real.

"Are you okay? Should I take you to the hospital or something?"

"No, it's just a nosebleed. It'll stop in a minute."

I watched as a drop splashed to the grass around my mother's grave. Life and death in such close proximity.

"Was it worth it?" I asked. "I mean, the high. Was it worth all this?"

He shrugged. "I'd like to say 'no'. I wish it wasn't an either-or situation, but it was fun at the time."

"Fun acting like a tosser?"

He flinched. "Well, you don't know you are. That's the thing. You're all caught up in the moment." Mopping his chin, he sniffed hesitantly. The blood seemed to have stopped. "And as much as you hate to admit it, that moment feels good."

I pushed some more stems into the oasis and thought about what he had said. My contemplations were interrupted by another question.

"So, are you seeing anyone?"

"Yeah. He's Canadian. He's a nice guy."

"Ah, right."

"What?"

"*Nice?*"

"Yes, *nice*. As in not drug addicted, not violent, and not sleeping with other women behind my back. *Nice*."

He held up his hands in defence. "Okay, nice. I'm happy for you."

I took a deep breath and squinted up at the sky. It was still blue, but winter hadn't completely packed her bags.

"Are you happy?"

I gave him a withering look. "Are you?"

"Actually, yes. Maybe for the first time in my life."

I frowned.

"It's liberating," he continued. "Losing everything. It's like I've shed a huge weight off my shoulders. I was coked up because I needed to escape from who I was. I hated my job to be honest. I hated that flat. It wasn't me. So I became the sort of person who would live there. Coke really helped with that. I became the sort of asshole I imagined would have my life."

"And now?"

"And now, that life is gone. Now I get to find out who I really am. What I really like, instead of what I have to pretend to like. I still take the occasional line. Very occasional. But it does nothing for me anymore. It's served its purpose. I know what it is now, and I know what I am. I'm done. I don't need it anymore. I'm finally excited by life."

Excited by life. I thought back to the last time that life had excited me. "Isn't it scary, though? Isn't excitement just fear at what's about to happen?"

"Semantics. It's whatever you feel, that is real. Whatever breaks through your mundane day and takes hold of your senses."

I shifted uncomfortably. "But you can't just drop everything. It doesn't work that way."

"Why not?"

"You still have to face people. Like your dad."

"If I want a shot at being free, I have to accept that. Either he'll support me or he won't, but what's the other option? Rot away in a life I never wanted? With or without him, I've got a second chance."

"How did you know that you were unhappy?"

He shrugged. "I didn't. I guess my unhappiness found me. I always sort of suspected, but it's taken this many years to finally sink in. There's this saying that order always tries to return to chaos. Maybe that works the other way, too. Maybe chaos tries to return to order. It was chaos, wasn't it? All that booze, the wage packets, the bars - all that crazy shit?"

"Yeah," I smiled. "It was fairly hectic."

"Well, I guess it finally came to a head. In the midst of chaos I found order. I'm finally stabilising."

I shook my head in wonder. "It's amazing. You're perfectly sober, yet you sound stoned."

He laughed. "The power of the human mind."

"I'm kind of glad I met you before you found yourself. You would have blown my mind."

He grinned. "I'm really glad you let me come with you. I know I've been a total nob. I'm glad you gave me the chance to say I'm sorry."

"Yeah. Me too."

"But I'd feel a whole lot better about myself if he were more than *nice*."

I rolled my eyes.

"Don't settle, Phoebe. You're awesome. You deserve the whole schaboom."

CHAPTER TWENTY-EIGHT

I arrived in the office Tuesday morning, feeling a lot better about myself. I had opened Mark's present when I got in. It was a beautiful painted wooden pendant with an inscription on the back that read: *For the good times*. It seemed to mean a lot more since our talk. In four years I'd never suspected that there was such a deep, uncertain soul beneath that cocky façade.

"God, am I late?" Miriam asked, stumbling through the door with her handbag falling off her shoulder and her hair ruffled. "I overslept. Is he here yet?"

"Who?"

"Sheila's got a meeting with that guy from VAC this morning. I'm supposed to be taking notes."

I felt as though someone had just wired me up to the mains. With all the revelries of the weekend, I'd completely forgotten. "Oh, no. Nobody's here yet."

"Thank fuck for that." She dumped her bag on the table, fished out a hairbrush and groomed herself in her powder mirror.

I took her lead and went to the toilets to patch up my own looks. I was always shockingly pale in the mornings.

As I drew on my lip-liner, I caught my eyes in the mirror.

What are you doing?

I had no answer to that, so I finished up, straightened my blouse and went along the corridor to Eddie's office. I needed a drink with him. Perhaps he could tell me what I was doing. I realised that he was probably the only person in my life right now that I could actually confide in.

"Hey, Amy, seen Eddie?" I asked the woman he shared his office with.

"No, he hasn't been in this week."

I frowned. "Still ill?"

"Must be. I haven't heard anything."

Thanking her, I turned up the hall towards my own office and stopped in my tracks. Coming along the corridor towards me were Sheila and George. He was wearing the sharpest pin-striped suit that I had ever seen. Wide collar, minus the hat.

My heart rate shot up like a rabbit's on the central reservation. There was nowhere else to go but forward.

As I approached, Sheila stuck her head around the door to my office and said something to Miriam. She appeared behind them with her notebook as they continued towards me. I tried to focus straight ahead, as though nothing out of the ordinary were happening.

"Ah, Phoebe," Sheila said when we were a foot apart. "Bring coffee to the meeting room."

I nodded and floated on past.

Once in the safety of my own room, I sank into my swivel chair and rocked from side to side. Taking a few deep breaths, I picked up my phone and sent Eddie a text.

Hope you're okay? Where have you been? Need a drink? x

Then I almost succeeded in convincing myself that I was a grown woman, got to my feet and went to the coffee machine.

Each drip of the filter felt like a lifetime. I wanted in and out and over, as fast as possible. When I'd finally filled the pot, I put it on a tray with two cups, a bowl of sugar cubes and a jug of milk.

Showtime.

Plastering an air hostess smile on my face, I knocked politely and entered the room.

George was sitting in the chair facing me. He had the ankle of one leg crossed over the knee of the other. A typical male pose. Sheila sat facing him, legs neatly tucked beneath her seat and crossed at the ankles. At-a-glance tableau of gender conformity. I wondered fleetingly whether Sheila knew. I was fairly sure she must, given how long she'd been in the charity sector. She probably kept a rolodex of backgrounds on her desk. All the better to manipulate people with.

Placing the tray on the table between them, I turned and walked out, aware of George's eyes on me.

I headed to the end of the corridor, and then kept going. There was a newsagent's half a street up. I bought myself a pack of cigarettes and sat on a bench to smoke one. The phone could answer itself for ten minutes.

My stomach was doing summersaults. Utter confusion was the name of the game. The little men in the back room of my mind were working overtime. I could hear them screaming for more flip chart paper and a PowerPoint projector.

I flicked ash at the pavement and thought back to the time that I had run into George on the high street, sheltering from the rain. Examining my memory of us drinking in the pub, I tried my hardest to think of him as her. It was too hard. Something had hardwired in my brain. The images were frozen, and I couldn't seem to superimpose this new knowledge over them.

I gave up trying. Instead, I forwarded to the time outside The Millers, just after I discovered the truth. I felt the warmth on my fingers as I pressed them between his legs. The tingling sensation as I realised there was no cock there.

Taking a deep drag on my cigarette, I kept going until I arrived at the night we spent smoking dope and laughing about the state of my neck. I felt the warmth of the feather eiderdown, the smell of his aftershave, the giddy high as the drug worked its magic.

And then I came to *that* night. The night we were finally going to do it, and I walked out. My face burned with shame. I couldn't believe how I'd reacted. I was mortified at myself. All I had to do was cool it down, tell him that I wasn't ready. But I couldn't. I couldn't admit that *I* wasn't okay with it. So I made George feel like it was his fault. I placed the blame firmly on his physique. It wasn't good enough. It wasn't what I'd expected. It should have been different somehow.

"Oh God," I groaned, squeezing my forehead with my hand. Looking up, I realised that my cigarette had burned down to the butt and gone out. I reached over and dropped it in the bin. There wasn't time for another, however much I wanted one.

Back in the office, I checked the answer machine – nothing. I couldn't face my in-box yet, so I looked at my mobile, which I'd left on the desk.

Eddie hadn't replied.

On a whim, I walked over to Miriam's side and searched in her top draw for the keys to her filing cabinet. I opened it and flicked through the personnel files until I came to Beal. Pulling Eddie's file out, I wrote down his home number and address on a Post-it.

Sure, it wasn't ethical, but he'd forgive me.

I used the work phone to call his home number, but there was no response.

Just as I was about to try his mobile, Miriam entered the room. I quickly tucked the Post-it into my bag. A moment later, Sheila entered, followed by George.

"And this is the administrative side of things. We have two part-time staff who deal with the day-to-day running of the office. Miriam you already know, and this is Phoebe." She indicated me with a flick of her hand.

"Pleased to meet you," George said, his eyes holding mine for no more than a second. As though we had never met before.

"Well," Sheila continued, shepherding George out, "it's been a very productive meeting." Their voices faded to a murmur in the corridor.

"Christ," Miriam said, leaning across her desk conspiratorially. "He's a bit of alright, isn't he?"

"Yes. He is."

George was certainly packing today. Sharp suit, sharp haircut, sharp posture. He smelled of executive confidence. I tried to think of any excuse to go out there and have a last word in the corridor, maybe go down in the lift together. My mind raced but came up empty. There was no professional way that I could do it. Not with Sheila on the loose. And besides, what on earth would I say if I did catch up with him? I had no idea.

I made it to one o'clock and collected my things. "See you tomorrow," I told Miriam as I walked out.

When I got to the street, I was about to turn for the bus stop, but instead I pulled out the sticky note from my bag and looked at Eddie's address.

It was about fifteen minutes away, in the opposite direction. I tried his home number for the second time, then his mobile, but there was no reply from either.

Chewing my lip, I made the snap decision to visit him. Something just didn't add up. He'd looked rough at Weavers, but not terminal. Why was he still off work?

CHAPTER TWENTY-NINE

I had to ask the driver to tell me where to get off, and then it took me another five minutes to find his actual street. Delmar Avenue. Twenty one…twenty three…twenty five.

Staring up at the semi-detached, I noticed that all of the lights were off and the downstairs curtains were drawn. A high hedge meant that I couldn't see anything in more detail, so I opened the little wooden gate and walked along the side of the house to the door.

I knocked.

No answer.

Next to me was a tall, solid gate leading to the back garden. I tried the latch and discovered that it was unlocked. Behind the house was a small garden with a tool shed and a washing line. Nothing out of the ordinary.

I went to the kitchen window and peered in. There were several empty beer cans and a half-empty decanter on the side. Two or three plates were stacked in the sink but the kitchen door was closed, so I couldn't tell if anyone was in.

I rapped on the window and waited.

Making my way to the side door again, I pushed open the letter box and peeked inside. A pile of letters were scattered across the rug.

"Eddie? Eddie, it's me, Phoebe," I called.

I heard a door open behind me and turned. Separated by a low chicken-wire fence, Eddie's neighbour stood on her porch, looking me over. She was an elderly woman around seventy, with white hair, fake tortoiseshell glasses and a thick sky-blue jumper. She was wearing her slippers.

"Hello," I said. "I work with Eddie. He hasn't been in for a while. I wanted to see if he's okay."

I watched her eyes make the slow transition from suspicion to acceptance.

"I think he's on holiday, love," she said.

"Where did he go?"

"I don't know. He usually tells me when he goes away."

"When did he go?"

"Oh, last week sometime, I think."

"Before Wednesday?"

She thought for a moment. "Somewhere around then."

"Only, I saw him last Wednesday, and he didn't say anything about going on holiday."

We came to a conversational stalemate.

"I'm worried about him," I confessed.

"Well," she said, unconvinced. "I do have a spare key. He leaves one with me in case he locks himself out or loses his."

The sentence hung in the air, the idea forming in the space between us. But it was clear that she wasn't going to offer.

"I don't suppose there's any chance you could let me in?" I ventured.

"Oh, I don't think so. He didn't mention any visitors."

"I know, but really, I'm very worried about him."

She tapped her foot gently. The suspense was enough to make me scream.

"Wait there," she said. "I'll just tell my husband where we're going."

Christ, I thought. Next door, that's where you're going. But I understood her need to make me aware that she was not alone. That someone would miss her if anything happened.

Two minutes later she came tottering down her path and up Eddie's, key in hand.

"What did you say your name was?"

"Phoebe. Phoebe Gelber. I work with Eddie at Disability First."

"Hmm," she muttered, sliding the key into the lock.

The door opened, and I followed her in. To the right were a set of stairs leading to the floor above. The rest of the corridor led around to a doorway which I assumed to be the living room.

Immediately, we knew that something was wrong. We stopped and looked at each other.

"Do you smell that?" I asked.

The woman nodded and allowed me to go first, pushing open the downstairs door.

I couldn't even scream. I covered my mouth and felt my legs give way beneath me as I collapsed to my knees.

"Oh!" I heard the woman gasp behind me.

We simply stared in silence for a long time.

Eddie's lifeless body was suspended from the light fitting by a length of electrical wire. It had cut deep into his neck, his face purple and bloated. His swollen tongue bulged like a ghastly balloon between his lips. His eyes were open and bloodshot. The smell was unbelievable, but I was too stunned to react. I was frozen to the spot.

"Oh, Eddie," I whispered. "Oh, Eddie."

"Come on, dear, let's call the police."

"You go. I'll stay with him."

I heard her shuffle away. From somewhere by the chair in the corner I heard the sound of his mobile phone beeping, indicating a missed call. My missed call. I wondered how many other calls he had missed since deciding to take his own life.

Shaking, I carefully got to my feet. I knew that I shouldn't touch anything before the police arrived, but I had an overwhelming urge to cut him down and to change his soiled clothes. I wanted to make him look respectable, beautiful, even. His humiliation was over. Whatever he thought he could not face was beyond reach now. There was no need for others to see it.

I knew that I had to stop myself from doing that, so I pulled out my own phone.

"Mark."

"Hey, Phoebs, what's up?"

"I need you to come and get me."
"Where are you?"

By the time he arrived outside the house, a police car and an ambulance were parked up and several of the neighbours had gathered around.

They'd already taken Eddie's body away, but I was sitting in the back of the second ambulance with a blanket around my shoulders and a cup of sweet tea in my hands. Shock was at bay, but I could feel it prowling at the edges of consciousness.

"Phoebe!" he said, pushing his way through. "Are you okay? What happened?"

"Where's your car?" I asked.

"I sold it. But we can get a taxi."

I nodded.

"What happened?" he repeated.

"Um. My friend…he killed himself." I began to shake violently.

"Okay, come on," the paramedic said, helping me onto the bed. "Lie back, I'm going to elevate your legs." He reached back to close the door. "Coming in?" he asked Mark, who stepped inside. "She's in shock," he explained, propping a medical box and a pillow beneath my calves.

I felt my breathing steady slightly.

"Christ, Phoebe!" Mark said, standing next to me and holding my hand. I was grateful that he didn't ask any more questions. I wasn't ready to process what had happened.

After half an hour and another cup of tea, I felt good enough to get into a taxi. Mark took me home and tucked me up on the couch with a blanket and a Cup-a-Soup. He stayed with me all afternoon, watching wildlife documentaries.

"I really should tell work," was all that I needed to say for him to take my mobile phone into the garden with a cigarette. I heard his voice, but couldn't make out what he was saying. I was grateful I didn't have to make that call.

"Do you want me to call anyone else?" he asked when he came back in. "How about your Canadian?"

I shook my head.

I was completely drained. The after effects of shock meant that my entire body was in freefall. Mark carried me up the stairs and helped me into bed, then held me whilst I fell asleep.

CHAPTER THIRTY

I woke around six in the morning, my mind convinced that I was late for work.

"Need to go," I said, reaching over Mark to the alarm clock that wasn't even beeping.

"It's okay," he said. "They're not expecting you today."

I accepted what he told me and fell asleep again.

The next time I woke, I was alone in my bed.

Pulling my dressing gown on over the work clothes that I was still wearing, I made my way downstairs. Mark was cooking a fried breakfast. I sat at the counter and watched him.

"Morning," he said, as he flipped the sausages.

"Morning," I croaked.

He slid me a cup of coffee. "You need to eat something."

I allowed him to fill a plate and place it in front of me.

"What did you tell work?"

"The truth. You're off for the week."

I stabbed a rasher of bacon with my fork and moved it around in circles. "Did you see my dad?"

"Yeah. He came in as I was heading for the toilet. Good to see him again."

I buried my head in my hands.

"I didn't tell him. I didn't know if you wanted me to."

"No. Thanks."

"But I don't think he believes you let me crash because I lost my keys."

I shrugged. "It's okay. So long as he doesn't know about Eddie."

"Why?"

"I'll get through this better if I can just deal with my own emotions. I can't cope with other people's."

Mark took a sip of his coffee and nodded. "I get it," he said.

I left the food on my plate. "I'm going back to bed."

"You sure there's no one else you want me to tell?"

I paused by the stairs. There was one person that I desperately needed to tell, but somehow I didn't think a call from Mark would be the best way of breaking the news.

"No, I'm good."

"Look, just promise me you'll give me a call if you need me, okay? For anything. However silly. I'm around, and it's not as if I have a job to go to."

"Thanks."

I slept for about an hour before my phone went.

"Phoebe? It's Miriam. Your friend called yesterday. Is it true? I wanted to see if you're alright?"

"Yeah, it's true."

"And are you okay?"

"Not really."

"Sorry, that was a silly thing to say. Can I do anything? Do you need anything?"

"No, I'll be okay after some sleep."

"Oh, God! Did I wake you up?"

"It's okay."

"I'm so sorry! I just can't believe Eddie's gone," I heard her voice tremble.

"Hey, Miriam, it's okay."

"Why did he do it?" She was about to cry.

"I don't know."

"God, it's so awful."

"Yeah."

There was a long silence.

"I'd better go," she said eventually.

"Bye. Thanks for calling."

We hung up and I lay there on my back, staring at the ceiling.

It didn't take a genius to figure out why he'd done it. I was sure that it was because of his divorce. For all his faults, Eddie had really loved his partner, Tim. I remembered how happy he'd looked at their wedding. How he was always bringing Tim up in conversation. How that had stopped one day, without any of us really noticing.

He was broken hearted, and none of us had seen it. All his witty comments and dry humour. It plastered over the cracks. Hid his defeat.

My stomach knotted in the knowledge that I had been so close to him every day, yet never truly grasped the magnitude of his despair. I had chatted away like a Duracell bunny, about what? Things that never really mattered. All that time, talking over his unsaid words.

Was there ever a point at which I might have said something that would have changed all of this? If I had shut up for five minutes, would I ever have gotten close enough to make a difference?

I buried my face in my pillow and prayed for sleep.

CHAPTER THIRTY-ONE

I woke around one in the afternoon. My mouth was dry and a mild headache pounded for attention.

Dragging myself to the kitchen for Panadol and a glass of water, I put my phone on the counter and stared at it.

Finally, I had a legitimate reason to call George. And for all the world, I wished that I hadn't.

An image of Eddie's face flashed before my eyes, and I pressed my forehead into the heel of my hand until it went away. Panic was starting to build. All of those conversations we would never have. I went there to talk to him, and now we would never talk again.

I held the side of the counter for balance and focused on trying to breathe: *in...out...in...out...*

The dizziness subsided.

I put the kettle on for a cup of coffee and returned to my handset. The clock glowed 13:38, and I remembered that it was a Wednesday. What would George be doing? Would he be in his office, or out on visits? Maybe in a meeting, or talking at some Third Sector conference?

The kettle clicked, but I didn't move.

After a few more minutes of winding myself up, I pulled up my address book and selected his mobile number.

It rang twice and then an automated voice explained: "The number you have dialled is currently unavailable. Please leave a message, or try again later."

Had he rejected the call? A mobile doesn't usually go to answer phone after just two rings. Not unless the phone is turned off, then it goes to answer phone immediately.

I hung up without leaving a message, then kicked myself. He would see a missed call from me with no message. Maybe he would think that I was calling about yesterday, at the office. Maybe he would ignore it. But if he had rejected my call and I called again, would he think that I was harassing him?

Christ, I was becoming Orla – inventing alibis for the simple truth. Taking a deep breath, I called again. This time it went straight to answer phone.

"Hi, it's just me, Phoebe."

I paused to steady my breathing.

"I just wanted to call to let you know that Eddie passed away. They found him at his home yesterday. I thought you would want to know."

Short and to the point. I was proud of myself. Very mature. I even said 'they' had found him. Not 'I' – this was nothing to do with me.

My bottom lip wobbled. I sank onto a stool, burying my face in my hands.

It was *everything* to do with me. Poor Eddie. Had he had anyone to talk to? Is that why he took me for a drink? One last-ditch attempt at finding a friend who would understand. Who wouldn't judging him.

Fuck, he placed the wrong bet there. Phoebe Gelber, hardly an open book. Even George had enough sense to see that and steer well clear.

I turned the telly on and flicked to the comedy channel. There was a panel show on, but I was only half listening. Nothing seemed that funny anymore.

A knock at the door woke me up. The VCR clock announced five-thirty. Thinking it was probably Mark, I answered it.

"Hey, sweetie-" Orla stopped mid-sentence, looking me up and down in all my ruffle-haired, dark-eyed glory.

I stood back to let her in.

"Are you ill?" she asked, as we made our way to the kitchen.

"No, I'm just tired."
"What happened?"
"Someone at work died." I refilled the kettle.
"Actually *at* work?"
"No, at home."
"Who?"
"Eddie Beal."
"What, gay Eddie?"

I paused, finger resting on the power button. Gay Eddie. Nice touch, Orla. At least he'd be remembered for something in his life.

"Yes, gay Eddie." I flicked the switch.
"God. What happened?"
"He hanged himself."
"When?"
"Yesterday."
"And you just found out?"
"No. I found him."

I busied myself cleaning a teaspoon in the sink so that I didn't have to watch Orla's jaw drop. It wasn't necessary – you could practically hear it hit the floor.

"*Shit*. That's incredible. What were you doing there?"

Good question, Orla, glad you asked. I was actually going to talk to him about these feelings I've been having for a transgender girl who used to think I was hot. It was all going rather well until I decided I couldn't cope with her lack of an appendage and my own emotional crisis.

"I needed to drop off some files."
"And he was just there, hanging?"

"Neighbour let me in." I eventually turned and brought our mugs to the counter, sliding one over to her.

"Have you been on your own this whole time?"

"Yes," I said, knowing better than to bring Mark's name into it. She'd be mortally offended if she knew that I hadn't called her first. Then she'd be offended that I hadn't told her that Mark was back in the picture. Then she'd probably make the leap of assumption to us being back together and him having proposed. Orla had a mind that just sort of worked like that.

"You should have called me!"

"I needed to sleep."

"God, I can't believe it."

We sipped our coffee in silence for a while.

"Why do you think he did it?" she eventually asked.

I shrugged. "He was getting divorced. I think it hit him harder than he wanted to say."

"He was *married*? Is that even possible?"

"It's called a civil partnership."

"Oh, yeah, I've heard of those."

"You work in a law firm. I would hope so." My tone was sharper than it needed to be, but I was tired, and sometimes I felt like Orla deliberately chose to say stupid things just to get a reaction. She wasn't short on IQ, but now and then she preferred to hide it.

"Sorry," she said, instantly causing me to feel bad. "I just didn't realise you two were so close."

We sipped quietly for a moment.

"So, are you excited about Alicante?"

I stared at her. It was one of those defining moments in life when you realise the allowances you make for friendship. When you look at your closest friend with fresh eyes and see the flaws. How could anybody make the leap of conversation from 'I'm sorry your friend is dead' to 'by the way, have you bought a bikini for your holiday?'

"To be honest," I said slowly, "I haven't had time to think about it."

"No, of course not."

For the first time that I could ever remember, Orla and I sat in uncomfortable silence.

CHAPTER THIRTY-TWO

I was still watching the telly at half-past eight when Dad came down to start breakfast.

"Alright, love?" he asked.

"Yeah, not bad."

He looked around the room, then back at me.

"Have you been home today? Thought I heard someone in the house earlier."

"Oh, that was me. Did I wake you?"

"No, you're alright. I was just dozing. Are you ill?"

"No, we had some bad news at work. One of my colleagues died." I could hardly lie to him. Best to get it out of the way.

"Oh, dear. What happened?"

"Suicide."

"I'm sorry to hear that. Are you alright?"

"I will be."

"Is that why Mark was here?"

"Yeah. We were just catching up."

"Things back on with you two then?"

"Oh, no, nothing like that. We're just friends."

He seemed to take that in, then nodded. "Can I get you anything? Would you like a cup of tea?"

"I've just had one."

"Breakfast?"

I smiled and shook my head. "Really, I'm fine."

Good old Dad, he always knew how to look after me. He'd have taken the night off work if I'd asked him to. But I didn't. I was enjoying my own company. Just me, tea, and BBC Three.

I slept well that night, simply because I was exhausted. Too tired even for flashbacks or regret.

The next morning I forced myself to get out of bed and shower. I felt better for a change of clothes and some makeup. Better, until I saw the cold light of my phone glowing back at me. No texts, no messages. Had I really done so much wrong that George didn't even want to call me, even now that Eddie was dead?

There was another knock at the door.

Mark, Orla – who could it be this time?

Opening it, I didn't recognise their faces at first. A tall, middle-aged man with greying hair and a narrow nose standing next to a shorter, dumpier woman, wearing a green cardigan.

"Ms. Gelber?" the man asked, holding a protective arm around the woman's shoulder.

"Yes."

"I'm Martin Beal, and this is my wife, Samantha." She held out her hand, and I shook it in slow motion. "May we come in?"

Nodding, I stood back and allowed them to pass, indicating the sofa with my arm.

"You're Eddie's parents?" I asked, as we seated ourselves. Just to be sure that I wasn't imagining things. The whole situation seemed surreal.

"Yes. We were given your name by the police. I hope you don't mind, but we looked you up. We wanted to come and see you. To tell you how very grateful we are that you found him." His voice was thick. His wife pressed against his chest, her chin dimpled.

"Would you like a cup of tea?" I asked, suddenly feeling ashamed at judging Orla so harshly. Faced with the gravity of such a tragedy, it was easier to grasp at light conversation than risk breaking the very thin ice upon which you now stood.

"That would be nice. Thank you."

I went into the kitchen and flicked the kettle, savouring the vital few moments I had to get my head together. Eddie's parents were sitting in my front room! Why? Well, I'd have to go back in there to find out.

I put cups, sugar and milk on a tray.

With a pinch of horror, I realised that Dad was snoring upstairs. They would be sitting through there in silence, listening to him. I felt the need to explain. So, as I carried the tray in to them, I apologised.

"It's just my dad. He works nights."

"You live with your family?" Mr. Beal asked.

"Well, just until I can move out. It's not easy at the moment. I only work for Disability First part-time."

"And that's how you know Eddie – you work together?"

I let the present tense hang in the air between us.

"Yes, we've worked together for about five years."

It was comforting.

Martin reached for his cup of tea, but kept his other arm around Samantha, who was studying me through watery eyes. She sat almost ridged, like a flood barrier holding back the tide.

"He was a really good guy," I said, knowing that it sounded insubstantial.

"You found him?" She finally spoke. "What made you go to the house?"

"He'd been off work since the previous week. It wasn't like Eddie not to come in."

"He worked hard," his father nodded with that look of recollection in his eyes.

"Yes," I agreed. "I tried phoning but there was no answer, so I went over."

"Thank you," his mother said.

It was the most awful thing to be thanked for.

"They think he died some time on Friday night," his father added.

It left me feeling cold to think that he had been there, suspended by his neck, for four days.

"I'm so sorry," I said. "I didn't know."

"I know you didn't." His mother leant forward on the sofa. She seemed to have warmed to me. "You couldn't have. We're just so grateful that Eddie had a friend like you. Who cared enough to go and see him."

A hot rush of tears spilled down my face.

"See, Eddie's partner, Tim – he left him a few months ago. I don't think he ever recovered." There was such tenderness in his father's voice; clearly nothing had mattered to this man more than his son's happiness.

"I remember the wedding," I said. "They seemed like such a good couple."

"Yes," smiled his mother. "Yes, they were. Tim isn't a bad man. He just never seemed to know what he wanted. He wasn't settled like our Eddie. I think they married too quickly."

We fell silent for a moment, each following our own memories back into the past.

"We wanted to come and see you," she began.

"Yes," he continued, when her voice faltered. "We wanted to ask you something."

"Please," I said, opening my hands in my lap. They could pretty much ask me anything; I couldn't refuse.

"Would you read at the funeral?"

I nodded slowly. "Of course," I said.

"He'd like that so very much," his mother said. The look of enthusiasm on her face was heartbreaking, a woman drowning in the flood, desperately gazing up at the grey clouds for even the slightest silver lining. "We'll bury him next weekend, on Saturday, if that's okay?"

As if they had to ask for my approval. I smiled the brightest smile that I could muster. "I would be honoured." And I meant it.

After they left, I broke open the remainder of Dad's dark rum and poured myself a generous measure before calling Mark.

"Hey Phoebs, you hanging in there?"

"Yeah. I just had a visit from Eddie's folks."

"Wow. Heavy."

"They asked me to read at the funeral."

"Did you say yes?"

"Of course. But I was wondering what you're doing next Saturday?"

There was a pause. I was sure I could hear him smile.

"I'm all yours."

"Thanks, appreciated."

CHAPTER THIRTY-THREE

The week dragged towards Saturday. I went back to work on Tuesday. The atmosphere in the office was sombre. Nobody asked me anything about Eddie. Miriam could barely look at me. There was a huge elephant in the room called Phoebe. Everybody wanted to know what had happened – what I had seen – but nobody was going to ask.

It's funny how we tiptoe around death. It's impolite to enquire, to even acknowledge it at times. One of two events that happen to all living creatures, and it's 'rude' to ask. Watch a group of new mothers discussing the intricacies of cutting the umbilical cord, and you'd think there were no aspects of birth that remain off limits. But see the mother whose child didn't make it, or the elderly woman who lost her husband, or anyone who has ever lost someone – you just don't go there.

What are we so afraid of, crying?

One of the e-mails at the top of my in-tray was from George McCally at VAC Services. I assumed it was a general circular until I opened it. It was a circular, but a selective one, announcing a change of mobile number. For whatever reason – it didn't say – George had lost his phone and done exactly the same thing that I had done when I lost mine.

But there seemed little point in calling. He would already know about Eddie. The gay community was tight-knit, and the grapevine would have done its job by now.

I spent the rest of my time panicking over what to read. His parents had advised against anything overtly Christian.

"He was a humanist," his mother had explained.

I opted for writing my own tribute to Eddie, finishing with a short stanza from a poem that I had always liked. There was plenty of time to think about it, as nobody dared come close enough to give me any work to do.

By Friday night I was less and less sure of myself. Would my words be right? Was the sentiment strong enough? Had I said enough? Should I say more? Or less? It was one of those speeches you only get a single shot at.

As the taxi pulled up the driveway to the cemetery, I remembered it as a young girl; how much longer it had seemed then.

A crowd had already gathered. I could see Eddie's mum in a flowing grey skirt and blouse. Almost everyone else, like me, had opted for black.

Mark walked around and opened the door, helping me out.

"You alright?" he asked.

"Think so."

"Breathe."

Taking a deep breath, we stepped into the throng.

Almost immediately, I spotted George. He was wearing a clean-cut black suit with his trademark wide-collared shirt. His back was to me, and he was talking to June and Charlotte. I wanted him to turn and see me, but he didn't. My brief trance was broken by Mr. Beal appearing at my side.

"Phoebe, we're so glad you came. We weren't expecting such a turnout."

He was right. There were a lot of people. Not just work colleagues, but half the local gay community and several managers from across the Voluntary Sector. Eddie had been well respected and liked. It gave the day a bittersweet edge.

We filed into the room, and I sat with Mark near the aisle. When it was my turn to speak, I made my way carefully to the lectern. For a moment, I found myself daunted by the faces staring back at me. But then I felt a warm rush across my shoulders, as though Eddie himself were standing behind me.

"Sorry, sweetheart," I almost heard him whisper. "Didn't realise you'd have to go through all this." I smiled and cleared my throat.

"Eddie Beal was my friend and my colleague. We had worked together for almost five years. For most of that time, we simply passed each other in the corridor and got drunk at Christmas parties." Quiet laughter rippled around the room. "But in the last few months of Eddie's life, we spent a lot more time together. We became friends. And I would like to think that, if Eddie were standing here today, he would still count me amongst the people he was glad to know. As I was glad to know him. His warmth and generosity of spirit were matched only by his humour and artistic talent. Amongst the photos of family and friends, he always kept some of his drawings on his desk at work. One of these has been chosen for the Mardi Gras poster this year, which Eddie was helping to design."

A round of applause went up from a large section of the mourners. For a moment, I faltered, as I realised that I had been mistaken. Not everybody was wearing black. I could see a red PVC bowtie, a peacock-feather hat, and a pink shirt among them. Eddie would have approved.

"But Eddie also had the ability to laugh through the tough times. Sometimes you came to feel that his wit became his defence, making it hard to see what was at the very heart of him. In the words of Shelley:

"A Sensitive Plant in a garden grew,

"And the young winds fed it with silver dew,

"And it opened its fan-like leaves to the light.

"And closed them beneath the kisses of Night."

I sat back in my seat, trembling. Mark's hand closed over mine, reminding me to exhale.

The final speech came from Eddie's father. He spoke about Eddie as a boy, about his career helping disability projects to succeed, about how he met Tim, and their wedding.

I looked around the room, but couldn't see Tim anywhere.

"My wife and I would like to end by saying thank you all for being here today. It has meant so much to us, seeing all of

Eddie's friends and knowing how much he meant to other people. How many lives he touched. And thank you also to George McCally, for organising a collection for Eddie. The money raised was – well, it was substantial, and has helped us to give Eddie the best possible send-off."

My eyebrows were halfway up my forehead. A collection? Why hadn't I heard of any collection?

"Are you okay?" Mark whispered.

"Yes, why?"

He looked down at our hands, and I realised that I had squeezed his almost white.

"I'm fine," I repeated, loosening my grip.

Six of Eddie's friends, including Mitch 'with the keys' and the guy with the red bowtie, carried him out to a classical piece of music. We all followed in procession. They placed the coffin on a wheeled trolley, and we walked it across to the other side of the cemetery where a fresh grave yawned like an open mouth.

As I stood, listening to Eddie's cousin reciting *Miss Me, But Let Me Go*, I chanced to look up and catch George's eye. The late morning sunlight reflected rich green in his stare. I returned with my own steady, blue gaze. It felt as though the world around us were melting away, broken only by the first handful of earth being cast. It pattered lightly against the wooden coffin. Farewell, *Edward John Beal*, see you on the other side.

CHAPTER THIRTY-FOUR

The reception was held in a side room of the main building. It saved Mr. and Mrs. Beal having to do the catering themselves, and guests from finding transport to their house.

It was a standard spread: sandwiches, crisps, finger food. From the readings to the buffet, it was hard to identify any aspect of the ceremony that had not been done a thousand times before. It hardly reflected the vibrant, engaging life that had gone before it.

Mark was busy choosing between egg and cress or ham salad. I didn't feel much like eating, so I decided to go outside and look at the floral tributes. They were laid out in a paved square alongside the reception room: white lilies, red roses, carnations, hyacinths, even orchids. A touching collage of colour, more befitting the real Eddie. Their scent formed a sickly perfume that took me back to my mother's grave.

The day after she was interred, Dad and I went back alone. Just the two of us. All of the flowers had been carried down and placed on top of her grave. The unsettled soil formed a high mound which acted as a podium for the withered cuttings. Each bloom sliced off in its prime, separated from the vital nutrients of life, like my mother. The smell made me dizzy.

"...notice he didn't turn up."

I became dimly aware of a voice, and turned. I could see cigarette smoke rising from behind the far corner of the building. People were having a crafty fag out of sight.

"Yeah, well, would you? I mean, everyone knows he's the reason he did it. Who'd want to turn up at a funeral to be universally hated?"

"You can't blame it all on Tim." I recognised the voice and found myself drawn towards it. "I mean, seriously, I don't want to speak ill of the dead or anything-"

"Oh, come on. Tim was putting it around to anyone who'd stand still long enough."

"Hah, I of all people know that, darling."

"Seb, you didn't? You never told me!"

"Water under the bridge. But it wasn't easy for him, you know. Eddie was such a stiff."

"Well, he certainly is now!"

I stepped around the corner as they burst out laughing. Ellis saw me first and fell deathly quiet, causing Seb to turn. He put on a sombre face but couldn't quite control his giggles. I felt like a teacher catching two errant school children having a smoke behind the bike shed. Only they weren't children; they were supposedly Eddie's friends. And I wasn't a teacher. I was hurt.

"Oh, hello – Phoebe, isn't it?" Sebastian raised an eyebrow and took another drag.

"What are you doing here?" My words fell with deliberate gravity.

"What does it look like, sweetheart? We're havin' a *fag*." He emphasised the double entendre.

"No. I mean, what are you doing here, at Eddie's funeral, when you obviously thought so little of him?"

Ellis looked as though he wanted to dissolve into the wall, but my attention rested with Seb.

"Darling," he said, over his shoulder. "This is that girl I was telling you about. The one who threw up on my shoe."

Ellis simply swallowed and gave me a nervous smile.

"Nobody thinks you're clever, Sebastian. Nobody thinks you're funny. You're just poisonous. You went out of your way to humiliate him at Weavers, knowing how much he was hurting. You did it on purpose."

His eyes lost their glitter for a moment, cigarette poised at half-mast.

"And what would you know, miss fag bangle? You drop into one gay bar for a drink, and you think that gives you the right to comment? Snap those pretty little lips of yours together and go back to your middle-class sexual repression."

"That's it? That's your come-back?"

"What do you want, a floor show?"

"A little honesty, perhaps. An ounce of remorse. A 'sorry for being an arsehole'."

Ellis stepped forward. "I think we'd better go."

"No!" Seb held up his hand, "let this bitch speak. I want to hear what she has to say. How she passes off her own guilt on me."

"My guilt?"

"Well," he said, taking a step closer and flicking his cigarette butt at the floor. "You were the one who found him. What was it – *four* days late? Some friend you turned out to be. Me – I never claimed to be one."

"You spiteful little shit."

"Seb, really, I think we should-"

But Ellis never got to finish his sentence, because I hit Seb in the face. The flat of my hand landed squarely across his right cheek. The sound was like an ill-fated Shrove Tuesday pancake hitting the kitchen tiles. Messy, yet satisfying.

Seb took a moment to run his tongue around the inside of his cheek before squaring on me. His eyes had a lizard quality about them, something cold and calculating.

"Maybe you are butch after all," he jeered.

"And maybe you weren't paying attention to your step daddy's lessons."

It was a cheap shot, but I'm not like Seb. I don't sit and scheme. When something needs saying, I say it. And, right then and there, he was the red rag to my internal sense of fair play.

It worked. He came right at me, pushing me backwards. I grabbed his coat tail and dragged him down with me. We landed on soft, muddy grass. He was on top of me, pulling my hair. I'd never seen a man fight so much like a girl. I aimed for his face with clenched knuckles and managed to get a rough left hook in.

I was just rolling him over to push his face in the dirt when I found myself weightless. My legs flailed, but met only air before landing heavily on the path.

Before I knew it, Seb was on his feet, wiping mud from his lip and coming for me.

From out of nowhere, Mark blindsided him, shouldering him off-course and putting out his arms to contain him. Seb tried to push through, but against Mark's comparative height he stood no chance.

"Jesus Christ, I only came out for a cigarette," I heard George say behind me. He released his grip on my arms and I turned around. His jacket was open and stained with streaks of mud. He made a futile attempt at brushing them off, then gave up.

"What the hell is going on here?" he asked.

"Good question," Sebastian spat. "Why don't you ask your girlfriend?"

I felt the bottom of my stomach fall out. Mark, arms still raised in case Seb made another dash for me, turned with a look of complete surprise. I couldn't bring myself to meet his eyes, so I looked back at George.

He didn't look impressed. Rubbing the back of his hand against his jaw, he simply held Seb's accusing glare.

"This is Ed's funeral," he said levelly. "What the hell are you two playing at?"

I felt a twist of shame. What were we playing at? Neither of us had an answer.

"We can't go back looking like this," he said. "We'll have to go around the side so that no one sees us. Ellis, take him home." He nodded towards Seb.

"So, that's how it is." Seb gave a derisive snort.

But George wasn't having any of it. He looked him right between the eyes until he visibly shrank, like a dog tucking its tail between its legs. Ellis started to walk away and, with momentary hesitation, Seb followed.

Then there were three.

"Come on, Phoebs," Mark said. "Guess we'd better get going."

"Yeah," I nodded. "Could you give us a moment?"

Looking between us, he said: "Sure, I'll be just over there having a smoke," and disappeared behind the corner.

Then there were two.

I looked at the ground. There were small blades of grass pushing up between the slabs of stone.

"Death at a funeral," I said, humourlessly.

He leaned back, hands in pockets, one foot against the wall.

"That was nice what you did, all that money for Eddie."

"His family aren't rich," he shrugged.

"You should have let me know. I would have contributed something."

"I didn't know you were the one who found him," he countered. "That must have been tough."

Standing in silence, both acknowledging our equal avoidance of the other, I wondered whether I had made a mistake. Perhaps I should catch up with Mark.

"So, how have things been?" he asked.

"Not so good."

"Was that your boyfriend?"

"Once. We're just friends."

"It was out of order, Seb saying what he did in front of strangers."

"That and everything else he says," I piped, a sudden flash of anger giving vibrancy to my words.

George raised an eyebrow and smiled. "Well, he sure got under your skin."

"It's not a joke. He's a nasty piece of work. You may not want to see that, because you're his friend, but he's got a talent for hurting people."

"So, what, you were going to teach him a lesson?"

I couldn't tell whether he was being sarcastic.

"Strong Phoebe, fists clenched," he smiled.

I didn't like his tone, so I went to walk away.

"Hey, hold on a minute."

And I did, turning back to face him.

"Okay, I'm sorry. But you sure choose your moments. At a *funeral*?"

I couldn't help smiling, too.

"Yeah, I guess." I stared back at the ground, kicking my toe at some of those tufts of grass. "I choose all of my moments. I thought you knew that by now."

"Ah." He was watching me carefully. I couldn't tell what he was thinking.

"Look," I said. "I'd better go and get myself cleaned up."

"Sure," he nodded.

"Sure." I stayed where I was, landscaping blades of grass.

"What am I supposed to say?"

I shrugged. "I don't know."

I turned to walk away. Just as I reached the corner, he called out: "Weavers, eight o'clock. We're having a bash for Eddie."

CHAPTER THIRTY-FIVE

"Five minutes," Mark said as I approached, referring to how long the taxi he'd just called would take. "I told them to meet us at the entrance."

We started walking. He offered me a cigarette but I declined.

"Christ, I could really use a line right now. What on earth was all that about?"

"Sebastian. He's a tosser. He said some mean things to Eddie before he died. It just got to me."

"You put up a better fight against me."

"Wish I had your left hook."

We both laughed. Funny how fate brings you to that point occasionally.

By the time we had traversed the entire length of the drive, the taxi was already waiting. We hopped in the back and gave my address.

"So," he said.

"La, ti, do."

"Ho ho."

"So," I repeated, waiting for him to phrase the question.

"This George fella. What's that about? Is he a..." He ran out of sentence.

"Transgender. Yes."

"Right. And are you two..."

I paused for too long, trying to fathom the answer myself.

"Wow!" he laughed. "No – seriously? I mean, for real?"

"We kissed. That's it."

"But there was serious chemistry going on there!"

"You think?" I was genuinely surprised.

"Magnesium strip. Do you remember doing that at school? White hot spark."

I laughed. "You don't think it's weird?"

"Whatever turns you on."

I frowned. "I suppose that wouldn't really bother you, would it. You did shag Jessica after all."

"That was a mistake, by the way. Should never have happened. But yes. And you know what else?"

"I probably don't want to, the amount of drugs you were on. Does it involve bestiality?"

He chuckled. "Not quite. But this stays strictly between you and me, right?"

"Okay," I said slowly.

"About a year before we met, I ended up chatting to this guy in a bar one night. We just got on really well. One drink led to another, and capow!"

"You shagged a bloke?" I was open-mouthed.

"I went down on him, yes. And he did it to me. Totally weird experience. I have no desire to repeat it, but it was fun at the time."

"Stop – here!" I shouted to the taxi driver, indicating a pub on the main road.

The taxi dutifully pulled over.

"Come on," I said. "I feel like I'm getting to know you all over again. We need a drink for this."

He laughed, and we piled out onto the pavement.

With a G&T safely in hand, we squirreled ourselves away in a quiet corner.

"I can't believe you did that," I said, "and never told me!"

"Oh, come on. Think about it. You can laugh now that we're two mates having a drink. But imaging how you would have reacted if I'd brought that up in bed."

He was right. It would have been a completely different story.

"So, come on then. Spill the beans."

"Well," I ran an absent finger around the rim of my glass. "It's kind of a long story. And kind of your fault."

He smiled. "Now I really need to know."

"That night with Jessica-"

"Oh," he groaned, "can we not mention that."

"Well, that's how it all started. I got blindingly drunk and ended up with this stranger helping me get home. That was George. Only I didn't know at the time, because I was so drunk. Then, by accident, I found out that he's manager of VAC, this really big organisation we work with a lot."

"So he is a he then?"

"Yes, well. Yes."

"I thought so, but I wasn't quite sure."

"He started as a she, but now she's a he."

He frowned, which was better than I'd expected. I was bracing myself for laughter and a quick quip.

"So, down there," he pointed.

"Look, it's difficult, okay? Up here," I pointed to my chest, "he's a he. Down there," I mimicked him, "he's a she."

"How come?"

"I don't know. I didn't ask. Something to do with testosterone."

"Well, okay. The important stuff – how does he make you feel?"

"Like the day has just begun."

"Then that's it. You don't have an option. You gotta go with it."

"What?"

"Come on, Phoebs, this isn't like you. You see something you want, usually you go get it. If it doesn't bother you, where's the problem?"

"Because it does bother me," I said quietly.

"Why?"

"Because I thought he was a he when I first met him. When I found out, I freaked out. Then I thought that I was okay with it – but I wasn't."

"What's so hard about it? You're obviously attracted to him."

"Yeah, but physically-" I pointed down there.

"What's the big deal? It's all just body parts."

I smiled. "Yeah, I dunno. It's not that I don't want to."

"You just wish he had a cock?"

I bit my lip.

"Why?" he pressed. "Is it about pleasure?"

"No," I shook my head. "No, it's not that."

"It's about what people will think."

He had me. I felt my cheeks flush. Phoebe Gelber, are you really that shallow?

"Am I judging you?" he asked.

"No."

"Too right. I'm happy for you. He's a damn sight better than 'nice'. I saw it in your eyes."

"But you're Mark. You're not exactly normal."

"Hah! Thanks. So, who else?"

"Orla. She hates gay bars."

"Well, no great loss."

I gaped. "She's been my best friend since school!"

"Yeah. No great loss."

"I can't believe you said that."

"Come on, she's not exactly little Miss Intellectual."

"She's really clever – she works in a law firm."

"That's not what I mean. Try 'social intelligence'."

"That's hardly fair."

"But it's true. I don't say it to offend you, but really, Orla's opinion is hardly something to base your own self worth around."

"Okay. My dad."

"Hmm. Tricky one. But then, so's mine. You just have to take that risk, and I know your dad well enough to know that he loves you unconditionally. You could probably join the BNP and burn down an abortion clinic, and he'd still think the sun shone out your ass."

I almost choked on my drink. "You're unbelievable."

"One aims to please," he grinned. "Life's short, Phoebs, get with the programme."

"I've got a question," I asked. "When we were together, how did I make you feel?"

"Truth?"

"Truth."

"Never quite good enough. But then, to be fair, I wasn't."

CHAPTER THIRTY-SIX

By the time the taxi dropped me outside my door, my head was spinning.

We'd had a few too many, but it was more than that. It was exhilaration. I had opened my mouth and told him this crazy secret, and he'd congratulated me on it! I wondered whether I'd ever actually known Mark.

I made a cafetiere of strong coffee and carried it upstairs to cool whilst I took a shower. I needed to sober up before heading out to Weavers.

As I stood with water cascading over my back, a flash of anger returned. I couldn't believe Seb was so cold-hearted. Was that the cycle of abuse in motion? Is that what an unhappy childhood does to people, turns them into complete cretins? I felt sorry for Ellis, witless enough to be dragged along in Seb's wake, destined for a social tsunami.

I felt a lot better after a hit of caffeine. It was good to be out of black, I felt like something from a gothic film. Showing due respect for the occasion, though, I decided to keep to darker colours and chose a wine-red skirt that reached my knees. Evening mourning wear.

A second cup of coffee later and I was back on my game. I smoked up my eyeshadow and ran a glob of frizz control through my curls. I'd just finished wiping my fingers clean when I saw the time.

Quarter to eight already! How had that happened? It felt like ten minutes since I was rolling around in the mud, but when I looked outside it was definitely dark.

A taxi would take too long, so I grabbed my coat and ran down the street to the bus stop. It took two changes to get to Weavers. The first got stuck in traffic, and the second was late arriving. By the time I finally stepped off at the other end, it was gone nine.

Cursing under my breath, I headed for the door. I could hear loud eighties music blaring through the walls. A small group of smokers huddled outside.

"Lovely speech, that," I heard a woman say as I approached.

I realised that it was June.

"Really lovely, that. I love Shelley, I do."

"Thanks," I smiled and was about to push past when she offered me a cigarette. All I wanted to do was to find George, but it seemed rude not to accept.

"Do you know who I am?" she asked, moving closer to light it for me.

"June, right? We met at the Mardi Gras thing."

"That's right, love." She took a drag as she looked me up and down. Even in the chill night air she refused to cover her midriff. I guessed she was probably in her mid-sixties.

"Such a shame about Eddie," she tutted.

"Did you know him well?"

"Me? I know everybody, love. Sort of the great matriarch around here." She elbowed me conspiratorially and laughed with the kind of dark cackle that reveals deep wisdom. I got the impression that there probably wasn't much in life this woman hadn't seen. "Everybody's mother, me."

"That's what George calls you."

She smiled and shook her head reflectively. "Known him a long time. Best of my sons, that one. Done well for himself."

"Handsome," I grinned.

She nodded in agreement. There was an aura about her. Something solid and secure, at odds with her quirky sense of style. It was hard not to warm to her. If not a mother, definitely an aunt.

"Still, it's not been easy on him, what with what happened and all. Times I thought we'd be having this little shindig for him."

I glanced at her and realised that she'd drifted off into her own little world, gazing out across the car park. Just as I was about to ask what she meant, the guy standing next to her stepped back without looking and accidentally knocked her into me. She gave him a playful slap on the back.

"Oy, watch yourself!" she laughed, and turned to their conversation without so much as a goodbye.

I stood for a moment wondering whether to try and muscle in on their group. Realising that nobody was paying the blindest bit of attention to me, I dropped my unfinished cigarette and continued into the club.

It was mayhem inside. Smoke machines and disco lights were on over-drive, and fifty heaving bodies formed a human wall of sweat between me and the bar. I couldn't see a thing, so I part walked, part crowd-surfed my way to the door on the opposite side. I plopped out into the corridor like an egg plops out of a chicken's bottom. In contrast, the drafty, brightly-lit annexe felt like part of another building entirely.

After taking a moment to regain my balance and my breath, I started up the stairs to the lounge.

Although the music still thumped through the floor, the lounge felt like a sanctuary of calm. Most of the sofas and tables were occupied by groups of people dressed in everything from formal suits to tight blue lycra. An array of mohawks, synthetic falls and quiffs chatted and laughed beneath subdued lighting. Mitch was standing behind the bar, serving drinks.

I walked towards him. He smiled as I approached. It felt good to see a friendly face.

"What can I get you?"

"Just a white wine, please."

He turned to fetch a bottle from the fridge.

"On the house," he said, sliding an over-filled glass towards me. "It was a good speech you gave." He poured himself a shot of Drambuie. "To Eddie."

"To Eddie," I echoed, as we clinked our glasses together.

He downed his shot and turned to serve the person next to me.

Taking a sip of my drink, I looked around the room. My eyes came to rest in the corner by the far window. George was there, sitting at one end of a long leather couch. He was still wearing his black suit and wide collar, ankle resting across one knee.

Perched on the arm of the sofa was a slim, attractive girl in a figure-hugging yellow dress. Her waist-length blonde hair snaked and twirled as she leaned down to talk to him. I watched as she twisted a strand of it around her finger, noting that George's arm was stretched across the backrest, encircling her. A tableau of intimacy.

They laughed at something, and I felt the back of my neck prickle as he reached up and pinched her chin. She stood up. Reaching down, she took him by the hand and pulled him from the sofa.

I turned back to the bar so as not to be seen, and watched in the mirror as she led him towards the stairs. He didn't seem to be putting up much resistance.

The wine suddenly tasted bitter in my mouth, and the club felt like an alien landscape. Somewhere I didn't belong.

Downing my drink, I headed back towards the stairs and descended to the corridor below. It crossed my mind to leave by the fire exit, avoiding the main club. But if it was fitted with an alarm then, far from leaving undetected, I'd draw everybody's attention.

Gritting my teeth, I pushed back into the disco just as a jet of white smoke plumed up from the floor. I felt like I were emerging as a singer on a television game show. Momentarily disoriented, I started elbowing my way in the general direction of the entrance, only to find myself lost on the dance floor.

The music changed. All of the bodies that had been bouncing about like Masai tribesmen gradually soothed to a steady calm. I didn't recognise the track, but several people took it as a cue to head for the bar, widening my limited field of vision.

A few feet away, I saw George dancing with the little blonde girl. My heart sank as I saw that he held one of her hands in his, his other resting on her bottom. It was a sickening flashback to Mark in the toilet cubical. The same thing all over again.

I stared on, mortified, wishing that I'd invited Orla. Anything would be better than being here all by myself.

CHAPTER THIRTY-SEVEN

I didn't know what to do.

Looking around, I could see men kissing in the corner, some women too. People were dancing up against one another, and others were huddled in tight conversation, shouting above the noise. It seemed as though everyone were consumed by tactile intimacy.

Was I over reacting? All they were doing was dancing. Everybody was having a good time; it didn't necessarily mean anything.

But deep down, I was squirming. Body language is the same – straight, gay, drunk or sober. That pinch of the chin, the twist of her hair – that was flirting. They were flirting.

Why was George doing this? Why would he invite me out to watch him eyeing up other women?

Only he didn't know that I was there. He had no idea that I was watching.

Every nerve in my body was telling me to get out. To run as fast as I could. To get home and scream into my pillow. This whole situation was ridiculous. What was I doing in a gay club anyway? I wasn't gay. I'd said goodbye to Eddie in my own way. How was this helping?

Get as far away from self-harm as you can. That would be the sensible thing to do, Phoebe.

If I did that, though – if I gave in to my inner voice – then here endeth all. Whatever spark there was between me and George would be gone. Extinguished. Smoke without fire.

I burned with a curious fascination to find out how George would react if he saw me. Would he look guilty, embarrassed – would it turn him on?

It hit me with absolute clarity that I was jealous.

I wanted to grab one of the girls next to me, drag her out onto the floor and snog her in front of him. Just to prove I could. I wanted to beat him at his own game.

What a stupid thing to think! The last person to mess with my head had been Mark, and I was damned if I was going there again.

Disgusted, I was about to turn away when something caught my attention. I noticed that the girl in the yellow dress was standing rather awkwardly. She seemed to be staggering, as though supporting George's weight. His head was resting on her shoulder, hidden by the rim of his hat.

All of a sudden, he grabbed her long hair and tried to lift himself up, pulling her head back at the same time. Someone walked in front of me, obscuring my view, and the next thing I saw was June stepping out of the crowd and assisting the blonde girl. They were clearly struggling, and he was stumbling as though he could hardly stand upright.

I watched as they propped him against the pillar by the side of the dance floor. The girl walked off in the direction of the bar. As I continued to watch, I saw June press her hand against George's chest and kiss his shoulder in a gesture of maternal concern. His head sagged. He tried to sit down, but she held him under the arm so that he couldn't.

Anger forgotten about, I weaved my way across the space between us.

"Hey," I said, making my presence known whilst hovering just beyond their personal space.

George didn't look up, and June simply raised her fingers against his chest in casual acknowledgement. She continued to lean into him as a human support.

The girl in the yellow dress reappeared, carrying a bottle of water. Without looking at me, she twisted off the top and tried to lift it to George's lips. June helped by using her free hand to hold his chin up. I was starting to feel frightened.

"What's wrong with him?" I asked, but the music was too loud, and the two women ignored me. It was as though I had stumbled across an accident in the street that all of the people with medical knowledge had got to first. I wanted to help, but I didn't know how.

George lifted his hand and brushed the bottle away, almost sending it flying. The girl took a step back, and June whispered something in his ear. He tried to sit down again, but she wouldn't let him. It started to dawn on me that I understood his behaviour. It's how I act when I'm very, very drunk.

"Hey," I said again, stepping closer so that they couldn't ignore me. "Let me take him home."

"You know where he lives?" June asked, twisting her head to look at me.

"Of course. I'm his girlfriend."

The two women stared at me for a moment, then the girl in the yellow dress passed me the bottle of water and melted back into the crowd.

"Let's get him outside," June relented. "Take that arm."

So, with me under one arm and her under the other, we made our way out into the car park.

"Can't let him sit down or he'll never get up again," she said, leaning him against the wall.

"I'll call a taxi," I said, reaching into my bag and dialling a reliable number.

As I spoke, I could see June standing in front of him. He was looking into her eyes, barely able to keep his own open. All the while she was whispering to him, rubbing his arm and tenderly stroking his cheek like a mother hen.

"Ten minutes, they reckon," I said. "Will he last that long?"

"He'll be alright. Seen him worse." With George temporarily stable, she reached into her bag and pulled out her cigarettes. She offered me one, and I took it.

"So," she said, passing the lighter to me. "You two been together long?"

"Not really, it's sort of new. We work together."

She looked me over with a sharper eye, as though weighing up this new lamb in her flock. For someone used to knowing everything about everyone, I could tell that she didn't know what to make of me.

We stood and smoked in silence for a while.

"You'll be alright getting him home then?" she eventually asked.

"She'll ge hine," George's slurred words drifted from his limp body.

June glanced over her shoulder at him. It was a greater endorsement than I could have given her, and she seemed to accept it.

Thankfully the taxi was true to its word. I was getting cold outside, and the sound of its tyres on the gritty tarmac came as a welcome relief.

June and I supported George to the door and sat him down in the back seat.

"Not you again!" the driver said, glaring out of his window. "You two take it in turns or som'n?"

I wasn't sure what he meant. As I turned to get in the other side, June flung her arms around me and gave me a kiss on the cheek.

"Take care of that one," she said. "He's a special boy."

Feeling a little uncomfortable, I squeezed her hands and assured her that I would.

CHAPTER THIRTY-EIGHT

We sat in silence on the journey home. George rested his head against the window, and I stared straight ahead, trying to remember if this was the route we'd taken before.

The relief I felt at seeing his car outside the house was short lived. As I paid the driver and opened the door, I realised that George was in no fit state to walk by himself. A quick search of his pockets provided me with the front door key, but no matter how hard I tried, I couldn't get him to stand up.

"Oh, for Pete's sake," the driver grumbled, opening his door. "If he's sick on me, I'll sue you both."

Together, we managed to edge him along the driveway. I turned the lock, and the driver helped me to lay him out on the sofa. Despite his indignant air, he was the nicest taxi driver I'd ever met in my life, and I showed it in my tip.

"You two should think about rehab," he muttered as he walked back to his cab.

I closed the door and locked it.

Back in the main room, George was sleeping, hat over his face, one foot on the floor to stop the spins. It was clear that I wouldn't get any answers tonight, so I went up to his bedroom and searched in the cupboards for a spare blanket. All I could find were T-shirts and jeans. I thought about using the one on his bed, but then I'd have nothing to sleep under.

Trying the door to the right, I stepped into a small office. There was a computer, a desk, some shelves and a filing cabinet. No blankets.

I went along the landing and tried the door to the left of the bathroom.

"My God," I whispered.

The entire room was filled with cardboard boxes. Floor to ceiling. Big ones, little ones, medium sized ones – plus a couple of duffle bags. It was like someone had been saving up for the car boot sale of the century.

Tentatively, I took a step inside and ran a finger over the nearest tower. Was this some crazy form of house insulation?

I knew that I shouldn't, but I couldn't help it, so I carefully lifted the lid on one of the boxes. Inside was a set of kitchen plates and a green vase. I tried the one next to it, which contained more clothes. There were also some dresses, a knitted woollen hat, and a teddy bear. Further along there were two whole stacks full of books, and another with a set of board games like Scrabble and Trivial Pursuit. It was as though someone had packed away an entire lifetime. As though there was a whole other house hidden away inside this one.

Getting the creeps, I backed out onto the landing and turned off the light. Definitely somewhere I wasn't supposed to be.

In the bathroom I found an airing cupboard with fresh towels, bed linen, and a thin summer duvet. Pulling it down, I dressed it in predictable beige and took it downstairs. After throwing it unceremoniously over George, I went to the kitchen and filled a pint glass with water in case he woke up dehydrated. As an afterthought, I also emptied the plastic bin in the office and put it next to him. Then I went upstairs and flopped into bed.

It had been an emotionally exhausting day. The funeral, seeing George again, carrying George home. How was any of this happening?

Too tired to think about it, I closed my eyes.

For a moment, I didn't know where I was. I woke in that startled panic that you sometimes get in a strange house. Those moments between thinking yourself in one place, and realising you're in another.

It was pitch black, and I had been woken by the motion of somebody crawling into bed next to me. I lay perfectly still as they shuffled their way into a comfortable position, hot breath against my neck. Close enough to touch, yet not quite touching.

"George?" I whispered.

There was no answer, so I rolled onto my side, facing him. "You okay?"

I stretched out my hand and realised that he was trembling. That nasty, violent shiver you get when you're far too cold. Had he kicked off the blanket I'd left him?

There was a muffled sound. Before I knew it, his arm reached across me, drawing me close, and his face buried itself against my stomach. He began to sob uncontrollably.

I was startled.

I couldn't think of anything to do, so I gathered his head in my hands and simply lay there, letting him cry. It was the most desperate sound I had ever heard.

Eventually he slept, but I couldn't. I think I drifted off just as it was getting light. When I awoke, I was alone in the bed.

As I stepped out onto the landing, I could hear the sound of the microwave ping downstairs. After helping myself to shower gel and dental floss, I picked out some fresh clothes from the cupboard and made my way to the kitchen.

George was in the far corner, lit by sunlight streaming through the French window. He looked up as I pulled out a seat, the sound of it scraping across the tiles an early indicator of the awkward silence that was to follow.

"Morning," I said.

He nodded and turned back to the sink where he was rinsing out his bowl. The sickly sweet scent of instant porridge hung in the air. I could see by the oven clock that it was almost ten.

"How's your head?"

He shrugged. "Yeah, good."

When there was nothing left to wash up, he turned, leaning back against the counter but somehow not really looking at me. "Big meeting on Monday, I've got to get some things from the office. You need dropping anywhere?"

I stared at him until he reluctantly met my gaze.

"Town," I said.

I didn't bother with breakfast. We simply got into the car and left. We didn't say a word throughout the entire journey. He pulled up near the high street, and I opened the door to get out.

"I didn't think this was your style," I said, shutting it behind me.

I waited at the food court in the shopping centre for Orla to arrive.

"Some trend I don't know about?" she asked, referring to my faded baggy jeans and white T-shirt.

"Eighties are back in fashion."

"All you need is the mullet," she grinned.

We ordered ice-cream and sat back down.

"How was the funeral?"

"It happened," I shrugged.

"You okay?"

"Yeah, I will be." I started to wish that I had just gone home, but it was too late now. Here I was with the first big issue of my love life that I had no hope of explaining to my best friend. We were surrounded by shoppers, yet I felt completely alone.

"How's Andy?" I asked.

"He's adorable, as ever. Ferris says we should go to the pictures this weekend. Has he mentioned anything?"

I shook my head. "I haven't seen him in a while."

"Christ, girl, what's wrong with you? I've heard of 'treat 'em mean, keep 'em keen', but if you ignore him altogether, he'll go away. You have to put some effort in."

Orla's crazy bravado was uplifting, even if she was babbling away about an imaginary foursome that didn't really exist. For a moment I could almost see this alternative reality in which we planned our double wedding and went bridal shopping together.

"I don't think I like him that much," I said bluntly.

She paused, mid scoop. "Really? Why?"

"I don't know. He's lovely, but I just don't think he's for me."

"You haven't been seeing him long enough to know that!"

"Oh, come on. I've seen you decide in under twenty-four hours."

She sucked the end of her spoon and frowned at me. "There were very definite reasons for those decisions. One of them took me back to his mother's."

"You still slept with him."

"We were very quiet. And besides, I didn't actually meet her."

"No, but she knows what you sound like."

Orla rolled her eyes. "This isn't about me. The boy is beautiful. He's exactly what you need."

"Look, I agree – in theory, there's nothing wrong with him. It's me. It's all about me. I'm just not feeling it right now."

"Well," she said calmly. "I can't say that I agree, but you should at least tell him how you feel."

Before finding the Andrew of her life, Orla had worked her way through a string of men from all walks of life. Tattooed rockers, long-haired hippies, moody artists, suave accountants. I should have known that my dumping Ferris wouldn't come as any big deal to her. It was a weight off my shoulders.

CHAPTER THIRTY-NINE

"Hey, how are you?" Miriam asked, as I strolled into the office on Tuesday.

Actually, I was pretty good. Two days of unadulterated sleep, a four mile run, and a hot bubble bath had taken the edge off my frayed psychological state.

"Not bad. You?"

"Oh, still a bit teary, y'know. I just can't believe he's not coming back." She caught herself and forced a smile. "But it was a nice farewell, wasn't it?"

"Yeah, really good."

"That poem you read was lovely."

"Hmm." I sat down at my desk and booted up my computer. "I notice you've changed your status back to 'in a relationship'."

"Well, you know, after all that's happened I sort of thought 'what's the point in making people miserable'? Might as well enjoy life whilst you can. Try and make this world a better place and all that."

In her own twisted way, Miriam had hit on something. Best stay away from bother and pursue the things that are really important in life.

It was an uneventful day. The phone didn't ring, nobody dropped in to ask for information, and Sheila was at a conference, so not busting our balls. By lunchtime I was so bored that I started clearing out my backlog of unanswered e-mails.

Six down was the one George had sent me about the job with VAC. The deadline said Friday. I was about to hit delete, when something made me pause. It was the dumbest idea in the land to go and work for him after all that had happened between us. The way we'd left things at the weekend meant that it was over. Clearly something was going on that I wasn't privy to, and it had broken things between us. That was it. The end.

So, when everything is predictable, why not do something completely unpredictable? Just to break the monotony. Besides, an interview didn't mean taking the job. I could always look on it as practice. I'd have to leave this place sooner or later, and now that Eddie had bailed, there wasn't much to hang around for.

I stayed on a little longer than usual to fill in the forms and write my CV. Miriam asked what I was up to, and I simply told her that I was checking some documents for a friend.

A rush of adrenaline accompanied the click of the send button. The kind of rush that you only get from doing something you know to be dangerously insane.

Seconds later, my phone rang. I was just picking up my bag to leave the office so reached for it without reading the caller display.

"Yeah?"

"Phoebe?"

"Uh-huh."

"It's me. Ferris."

"Oh, hi!"

"What are you doing tonight?"

Shit – no time to spin the rolodex of excuses. "Um."

"Can we meet for a drink? We need to talk."

Where had I heard that line before?

"Okay," I said cautiously.

"The Millers, seven?"

"Uh-huh."

"See you there."

Well, that was one of the least participatory conversations I'd ever been party to.

"What's up?" Miriam asked, seeing my face drop.

"It's my boyfriend. Apparently we need to talk."

"Uh-oh."

"I think my best friend might have told my beau that it's over."

"Really?"

"Yup. Orla-ed again."

"What?"

"Nothing."

CHAPTER FORTY

"I just don't understand what I did wrong? I thought everything was going great."

I felt awful staring into the shattered hopes of this gentle, handsome man. When faced with such a delicate situation, it's always best to stick to tried and tested methods.

"It's not you, it's me," I explained.

"Oh, don't give me that. What happened? We were doing terrific. Did I say something, or do something?"

"No, really. You're a wonderful guy."

"Is there someone else?"

I winced.

"I knew it! There's someone else, right?"

"Not that it's any of your business, but no."

"What a load of crock," he snorted. "You could at least be honest with me."

"Okay, fine, if it makes you feel any better there's dozens of them. An entire football team, actually."

His face flushed scarlet, and he clenched his fists on the table. Not an encouraging sign.

"Look, Ferris. Really, you are an outstanding guy. Seriously, there's a wonderful girl out there for you – she just isn't me. It's biological or something, to do with genetics and smell – and stuff."

"What?"

"I don't know. Planetary."

He stared at me until I shut up and reached for my drink.

"So that's it then? Done. *Finito*?"

I nodded. Talking wasn't appeasing the situation, so perhaps being quiet would get us both out of there a little faster.

It sort of worked. He did a big feather-plumping ritual of storming out, leaving me with the bill. I guess that's the price you have to pay for agreeing to blind dates. Eight pounds twenty-six.

Strange, though. Finally giving Ferris the push was sort of empowering. I was my own woman once again. My body was my own – no more uninvited touchy feelyness. The indefinable cloud that had been hanging over me since that night under the bridge, suddenly seemed to lift. In its wake, a ray of self-appreciation shone through.

I ordered myself another drink, then went down to the river to smoke a cigarette and watch the ducks float past.

As I sat there, I thought a lot about George. It dawned on me that in many ways he was a lot like Mark, in that I didn't really know him. Mark had been a shock because I'd had three years of getting to know him, intimately, in which to build up a firm belief of who I thought he was. Having that image so brutally shattered had been hard to come to terms with.

I was glad he had weaselled his way back into my life so that I could get to know him again, properly this time. No hidden truths. I was discovering that I rather liked this new, vulnerable Mark. If we'd just left things the way they were, I probably would have hated him for the rest of my life. What a lot of energy to expend.

But George had been a bolt of lightning. Something exciting and unexpected. From our first meeting I had held all kinds of assumptions about him – her – him. I'd been drawn to his sharp-dressed confidence, turned on by the unknown possibilities of what may lie behind his cool exterior. I knew from the very beginning that I didn't know him at all. So why was I so surprised when he turned out to be different to what I had imagined? Wasn't that, in itself, to be expected?

Perhaps it wasn't the suave exterior that bothered me so much. Seeing him slumped down drunk, stripped of his trademark sophistication, wasn't so bad. It simply made him human. And that's a good trait, right?

But something darker lay beneath. Another dimension to my delusion was that, somehow, I always expected him to have my back. Picking me up off street corners, pulling me out of scraps, offering to go down on me without expecting the same in return, waiting until I was ready. Someone who genuinely cared about me. About Phoebe.

But Sunday morning had been brutal. A smack in the face from Mark had almost seemed the natural conclusion to our spiralling relationship. It was never going to end well by that point.

But a slap to the psyche from George was different. I was starting to open up. Deep down inside, fearful emotions were stirring. The hot flush of lust and sexual desire were gradually beginning to ease, revealing something more akin to... well, something a little more tender, perhaps.

Shut up, Phoebe, you dumbass. What are you trying to say? That you *love* George? Come on, really? He's a fantasy. A thrill. Nothing more.

And besides, Sunday morning had spelled out all too clearly that you belong in different worlds. Could you imagine George out for the night with Orla, Andrew – all of the usual crew? If you close your eyes, can you honestly imagine that it could ever work? Even if George agreed, he'd be shunned as a social pariah. If he were a gay man, sure. That could happen. The girls would consider him a novelty. They'd see him as cool and funny. Someone to confide in and taunt their boyfriends' masculinity with. The exact reason why Eddie was never a drinking buddy – he knew what he'd have to put up with.

But a female-to-male transgender guy? Come on, get real. Nobody would know how to act. The lines haven't been rehearsed. There's no protocol. If we ever kissed in front of them, they'd probably leave.

And think of it the other way around. Taking everyone on a night out to Weavers. It would be a hell of a lot easier at first. Most people nowadays don't have a problem with going to a gay club. The music's always good, and there's a great atmosphere. People are more willing to dance and chat to strangers. But it would still be superficial. Once a month, maybe. It wouldn't become a usual haunt, and the regulars wouldn't want that at any rate. Too many heteros spoiling the vibe. Even I feel uncomfortable there when I'm not with George.

Either way you look at it, you have to give something up. Best to stay on your own side of the fence, girl. Stick to what you know. Stick with the friends that you've always had – the ones who really do have your back. The ones who involve you in their lives instead of shutting you out, leaving you standing there like a lemon.

Still, it didn't seem like a very satisfactory resolution. If me and Mark could patch things up, surely it wasn't beyond the realms of possibility that George and I could find some common ground again? I'd hate to leave it this way with nothing left to say to each other, like strangers.

Was it all about sex? If I hadn't walked out on him that night, where might we be now?

CHAPTER FORTY-ONE

The weekend came and went. By Wednesday there was still no word about my job application. No 'sorry, you've been unsuccessful', but no 'we'd like to invite you for an interview' either. I speculated that it might take them the rest of the week to shortlist.

George had to be aware that I'd made the application though, right? After all, he'd be shortlisting for his own assistant. What had seemed like a good idea at the time, started to feel like a very bad one. What would he read into that? Maybe he just wanted rid of me, wanted me to fade into the distance like I'd wanted Ferris to do. Divine karmic retribution.

I finished up early, shifting an hour to Monday so that I could go into town and cheer myself up with shopping. I dropped into Boots to stock up on lip gloss, then perused the sale rails and discount shoe stores. There wasn't much that I wanted, but it was therapy all the same.

Picking a back street café, I tucked myself away with a cappuccino and a blueberry muffin to read the gossip columns of a glossy magazine.

"Phoebe? It is Phoebe, right?"

I glanced up to see a girl in casual office wear: grey knitted dress and black tights. Her fake dreads were scraped up into a tight ponytail and she sported a lip ring and a nose stud, eyes heavily coated in liner.

"Yes," I said, puzzled, as she sat herself down on the chair opposite.

"God, I'm so sorry. I really wanted to say that."

What, sorry that I was Phoebe? I may not be rich and famous, but it's not the worst job in the world.

"It's me, Jess."

The penny dropped.

"I didn't recognise you," I said. "You're all professional."

She gave a self-deprecating pout and nodded. "Yeah, I guess I do look a little different. I really hoped I'd see you around though."

"Right."

"Orla told me all about it, about Mark and everything. I am so, so sorry. Honestly, I had no idea. I just assumed he was single. He didn't say anything."

"Hmm."

"I feel like such a slut. I'd never do that to someone knowingly. Are you two still together?"

I gave a genuine laugh. "No. That ended. That night, actually."

"Oh shit, I'm really, really-"

"No, it's fine. Honest. We'd come to the end anyway. But we're still friends."

"You are?" Her eyes widened.

"Yeah. We make better friends than partners."

"That's amazing. I think I would have castrated him if he'd done that to me."

"It came pretty close."

We both smiled at one another. I remembered what I'd liked about her the first time we met. In her own way she was fairly grounded. Vivacious and easy to chat to.

"So where do you work?" she asked.

"Disability First. It's a charity up the other end of town."

"Yeah, I know the place. I think we do some legal stuff for them. What are they like?"

"It's okay, but I think I need a change soon. The boss is a bit of a ball buster."

"Anywhere lined up?"

I shrugged. "Not really. I just applied to VAC, but I'm not sure I'll get in."

"Really? I know George McCally pretty well, perhaps I could have a word. My girlfriend used to work with him at Stonewall."

I blew on my coffee to cool it down. "What was he like to work for?"

"Oh, George is lovely. I'd work for him any day. It's really sad what happened."

"Why, what happened?"

"God, it was ages ago. Four or five years, maybe. His partner got shot."

"Shot?" I almost shouted.

She nodded and rested her head on her hand. "Yeah, it was a really big deal. She was an aid worker, went out to Palestine I think it was. Got caught in the cross-fire. I wish I could remember. I think she was with Médecins Sans Frontières."

I was stunned into silence.

"Anyway," she said, picking up the paper bag of sandwiches on her lap. "I'd best get back to work. It was really nice meeting you again. I'm just sorry about the circumstances."

"Don't feel bad about it. You did us both a favour," I smiled.

I sat at my empty table after she'd left, watching my coffee grow cold.

Everything seemed to have taken on new significance. The house that didn't feel as though George actually lived in it. The room full of boxes – a storage space full of memories. Acting crazy after a funeral, getting blind drunk and dissolving in tears.

It wasn't Mark, and it wasn't George. It was me. How could I miss the blindingly obvious a second time around? Coke addiction, grief – I couldn't see a bull elephant if it were charging straight at me.

I went home and marched straight through to the kitchen, dumping my bags on the floor. Reaching for the phone, I dialled VAC's number and waited for the prim receptionist to answer.

"Hello, Voluntary Action, how may I help?"

"Hi, my name's Phoebe Gelber. I applied for the Executive Assistant's position. The closing date was last Friday but I haven't heard anything."

"Hold on a moment, Ms. Gelber, let me just check for you." There was a minute of key tapping and silence before she began speaking again. "Okay, yes – we're not actually notifying until tomorrow, but you will be receiving an offer of interview."

"Oh."

The little men in the back room of my mind had gone out for donuts. I hadn't expected that. My game plan was simply to withdraw my application. It seemed a little cruel in light of what I now knew. My worst-case scenario was that George had simply put it in the bin. But now it was my turn to be flummoxed. Not only had he seen my application, he'd approved it, with not a word said between us since that fateful Sunday morning.

"Hello, Ms. Gelber? Is that okay?"

Shit, I wasn't sure. Was it?

"Um, yes, that's fine. Great news, thanks."

"Okay. Is there anything else?"

"Nope, that's lovely. Bye."

I hung up. My panic response. I could always call back and withdraw once I'd had time to fully assess the situation. No point trying to blather my way through it live on air. Why would George offer me the interview? I realised that it was probably the most cordial way of letting me down gently. Simply refusing me an interview would have been rather brutal. Invite me, then giving it to a better qualified candidate. That would be the legitimate and polite thing to do.

I knew that the only real way to find out would be to ask George.

CHAPTER FORTY-TWO

I thought about the different ways in which I could do it. The interview offer landed in my personal in-tray on Thursday morning. I stared at it for a long time and then left the office without sending a reply.

Tomorrow would be Friday. I could dress up and go down Weavers. George would probably be there. He wouldn't expect me to turn up. But it wasn't very private – anyone could overhear, and they all knew him. Maybe it wasn't fair to do it on his territory.

What about going to his house? He might not be in. Or he might not let me in. And besides, there were a lot of memories in the upstairs room. Maybe not the best place to have a heart-to-heart either.

After thinking myself round in circles for an hour, I decided to send a text.

The Millers, 8pm.

I didn't put a question mark. I was going to take a leap of faith and leave it open. I'd be there, even if he wasn't. That way I'd know one way or the other. Either he'd come, and we'd talk. Or he wouldn't, and I'd drink myself into a stupor and take a taxi home. Perfectly neutral ground where nobody that we knew could eavesdrop.

By seven o'clock I was sweating. I'd pulled on my casual black wrap-round and my little ankle boots. My hair was up and my makeup on. Dad had gone to work, and the house was terrifyingly quiet. I descended the stairs with something akin to dread.

It took forty minutes by painfully slow bus to eke my way across town. The bar was fairly empty. Most people were at home bracing themselves for Friday night escapades, or having a quiet post-work drink closer to their offices.

I ordered a G&T and sat by the window, gazing at my own reflection against the darkness outside. My phone sat on the table in front of me, ticking like a time bomb.

Five-past came and went. Ten-past. He wasn't coming. Quarter past. The door swung open, and an old lady with a Shih Tzu trundled through to the restaurant.

By twenty-past I felt like the groom at a wedding where the bride had decided to flog all of the presents and take the guests on holiday to Ibiza instead.

I was almost at the bottom of my second drink, about to call a cab, when George walked in.

My entire body turned to butter. The same confident swagger and stylish get-up that had become so deliciously familiar. Everything between my legs started buzzing. Then I remembered why we were there. Cold sobriety returned like a bucket of icy water.

He glanced around and saw me, then turned to the bar and ordered a glass of red wine, which he brought with him.

He sat down, thumbed his nose and reached across for my phone.

"Twenty-five past. Not bad."

"Traffic?"

"Almost had to walk. Thought you might have left."

"You could have called."

"Spoils the fun."

I couldn't help smiling. So this was fun, was it?

There was a moment's pause.

"I'll get another drink," I said, tinkling the forlorn ice-cubes at the bottom of my glass.

"I'll be outside," he jerked his chin towards the back door and reached for the cigarettes in his pocket.

Now that I had him, I didn't know what I was going to say. So, with fresh drink in hand, I made my way outside and took a cigarette from his packet, allowing him to light it. We were the only two braving the night air, huddled beneath an inadequate heating lamp.

"I'm withdrawing from the interview," I said.

"Why?"

"I don't want the job." *I want you.* But my sentence drifted away with the smoke that I exhaled.

"So, why did you apply?"

"Why did you offer me an interview?"

He frowned. "You think I'm that cold-hearted?"

"What?"

"You applied for a job that you're qualified for. You have as much right to an interview as anyone else."

I felt a little discouraged. I guess I had hoped there would be something a little more personal behind it. Obviously not. "I think it would be a bit awkward, after everything that's gone on."

He shrugged, the perfect expression of noncommittal.

We lapsed back into silence.

"Are you okay, after the funeral?" I asked.

"Fine." A flash of annoyance, evidence of a raw nerve.

"I know what happened. With your partner."

His jaw knotted and he looked at me. "June tell you?"

"No. It seems everybody knew, except me."

His eyes suddenly softened, and he studied me for a moment before taking another drag and exhaling towards the ground. "It was a long time ago. I don't think about it much anymore."

"Which is why funerals make you sad?"

"Which is why funerals make me sad," he repeated.

"Is that why you stopped taking the treatment – the testosterone?"

He nodded. "Didn't seem much point anymore."

"What would it have done if you'd kept going?"

"Not a lot. I'd have a nice set of abs, and designer stubble."

I grinned. "No cock?"

He laughed. "I sense this is an issue with you?"

"No, I'm just curious. What does it do to you?"

"I'd need an operation for that."

"So why don't you have it?"

"Because, sadly, medical science is a long way behind human biology. Lot of pain, little gain."

"Would it work – like a proper one?"

"Some of them do, sort of. Or you can get a pump. Like having sex with a cyborg."

I couldn't help giggling. "Nice."

"Let's just say it's not something you want to go through without a lot of support. And I kind of felt like I was close enough to where I needed to be."

"But if your partner-"

"Leona."

"If she had still been with you, you might have done it?"

"I was heading in that direction." He shrugged. "That's a world of might-have-beens."

"Sorry, I didn't mean to make you think of it."

"That's okay. I'd rather you asked."

"I'd rather you told me."

Our eyes met, and a subtle spark leapt between us. I felt charged, like my veins carried high-voltage currents.

"So, whilst we're on truth or dare, why did you leave that night?"

I was dreading that question.

"Was it because I didn't have a cock?" he teased.

"Yeah, I was a little freaked out by that. I like you as a man. I guess I'd gotten used to the idea that everything about you was, well-"

"Anatomically correct?"

I smiled. "It came as a shock. It's dumb, I know. It's not like you hadn't warned me or anything. But it's worse than that. I was afraid of what people would think."

He wanted honest. That was honest. "Back to that again?"

I nodded. "I can't help it. I've never been on the gay scene. I've never been around people who would accept this."

"You're wrong."

I looked surprised. "No, really, my friends aren't the kind of people-"

"No, you're wrong. You can *always* help it. Your friends, they can help what they think, and you can help what you think. Don't shrug it off as some mystical fate dictated by God. If you want to change the way you look at things, you can. But that sometimes means getting away from the people who reinforce negative stereotypes. If those people are your friends, then it's a tough call. You have to decide what matters most to you. Living your life free, or living up to the expectations of others."

I was silent for a moment, absorbing what he had said.

"I just can't believe," he continued, more gently, "that before you'd even slept with me, you were already thinking about what people would think. It's not like anybody would even have known if you didn't want them to. But you walked out on something real, something good, because of what you imagined." He offered me another cigarette. "You have no idea how horny you left me."

I grinned like an idiot. "Did I?"

"You didn't feel that?"

"Oh, I felt it."

We bumped shoulders childishly in a gesture of secret pride.

"So, my turn," I said, letting him light the cigarette.

"Shoot."

"Maybe you don't remember this – you were categorically wasted at the time – but who was that girl you were dancing with at Weavers, the one in the yellow dress?"

His brow furrowed, trying to recollect. Then the *aha* moment hit. "Stephanie? Long hair, down to here?" He drew his hand across his waist.

"That's the one. You were flirting outrageously." I smiled, but he didn't. "Were you going to fuck her?"

"Don't ask such stupid questions." He brushed it off with a flippant Mark gesture, which meant that it wasn't a stupid question at all.

"George?"

He looked down at his feet.

"You have fucked her?"

"No. I haven't."

"But you would have?"

"I'm not going to have this conversation."

"Why not?" My voice was rising in angst. I felt very vulnerable. "I thought we were able to talk about anything now?"

He straightened up and stared at me hard. Then, after a moment, his shoulders relaxed and he spoke, calm and level.

"I was flirting with her because I didn't think that you were coming. I thought you'd stood me up. And yes, it did cross my mind that I could fuck her, in a pathetic, self-pitying sort of way. But I would have done it because all that I have thought about, night and day, for past two months, has been you."

For a moment, I forgot how to breathe.

CHAPTER FORTY-THREE

"I've never met a girl so much like a guy," I said in the back of the taxi as it made its way towards George's house.

"That's because I am a guy, in a woman's body."

"When did you know?"

"All my life, I guess. I always liked football more than dolls. But I think we're all genderless until puberty kicks in. That's when you notice – and when other people make you aware of it."

"I can't imagine you as a 'her'. Do you have any photos?"

He laughed. "One or two."

"How does it make you feel, when you look at them?"

"Probably like it makes you feel when you see yourself in Bermuda shorts and a florescent shell suit. You were a victim of the times, and of other people's sense of fashion."

I smiled. I could relate to that analogy perfectly. Somewhere in my treasure trove were pictures of me with a chemical perm and bright orange leg warmers.

I watched the houses go by, nervous thrill mounting in my stomach. George sensed it and squeezed my hand reassuringly.

I laughed.

"What?"

"You. I mean, if ever I doubted that you were a man, I'd just have to examine the logic."

"Huh?"

"Meaningless sex to forget about the person you really want to be with. How much more male can you get?"

He grinned sheepishly. I reached across and pulled his hat down over his face.

"Just here," I said to the taxi.

It pulled up in front of George's driveway and he paid the cabbie.

Once inside, he flicked on the mood lighting. I went up to the kitchen and poured two glasses of wine from a box by the sink. I passed one to him as we settled down on the couch, mellow music drifting from the speakers.

"So," he said, massaging my feet. "You planning on actually staying the night?"

"I reserve the right to run away screaming."

He smiled and took a sip of his wine. "Seriously though, I'm not asking you to do anything you don't want to."

Carefully, I placed my glass on the table and stood up, offering my hand.

In the bedroom we stood, face to face. He wasn't going to take control this time, patiently waiting, letting me decide. But my nerves were getting the better of me. I couldn't remember the last time that the mere presence of somebody had scared me. Scared and excited me.

I reached up and took his hat, placing it on my head, then threw it like a frisbee into the corner. He laughed and placed his hands on my waist, gently caressing the fuller, female form of my hips like a cat pawing a cushion. It felt nice. I ran my fingers along his smooth jaw, then his ear and the back of his cropped hair, pulling him closer so that we could kiss. The warm scent of his aftershave curled around my senses, drawing me deeper into him.

"I don't play games," he said, drawing back. "I want you to know that. What happened with Stephanie was a mistake."

"Shhh, I know," I said, placing my finger over his lips, then drawing it down his chin to the top of his shirt. Undoing the buttons, one by one, I slid the thin material onto the floor.

There was very little light in the room, so I moved to the bedside table and turned on the lamp. We were bathed in soft, orange light. He frowned at me, questioningly, but I had never felt this body-confident before, and I wanted to see everything.

"Do you mind?"

He shook his head and stood there, semi-naked, whilst I built up the courage to approach. The line across his chest looked as though someone had embossed him with silver. I felt the slight raise of scar tissue as I ran my fingertips across it. It was impossible ever to imagine there having been breasts there, like mine. He fitted his body perfectly. From his broad shoulders to his narrow, flat waist with its dark lick of hair just visible beneath his belly button.

I leaned down and kissed his stomach. I felt him shiver, goosebumps rising to my touch. It was a delicious sensation to hold such power over him, knowing that he had been thinking about this moment for so long.

He took the ties of my dress and pulled them, unfolding me like a butterfly emerging from a chrysalis. I reached behind my head and, as my dress fell to the floor, I released by bouncing mass of curls. Standing before him, in only my underwear and my black ankle boots, I felt exposed. Perhaps the light wasn't such a good idea.

"You're beautiful," he said, and his eyes matched the warmth of his voice.

Relaxing slightly, I stepped out of my boots and kicked them aside. Taking the button of his trousers between my fingers, I remembered how this had ended last time. Exhaling steadily, I drew down his zip. I could see his pulse racing in the dimple of his chest and knew that he was just as apprehensive, perhaps more so, as I had been the one to reject him.

When he was down to just his boxers, I reached behind and undid my bra. We were amassing a small pile of laundry between us, and it felt good to finally be rid of my feminine restraints. He watched, mesmerised, as the black lace of my knickers created a matching set on the carpet.

Swallowing, he slowly slid his hand around the waistband of his CKs, and pulled them down.

We stood there, completely naked.

"There's something missing," I said, shaking my head and staring at the space between his legs.

He looked uneasy.

"Your hat," I grinned.

"One condition."

"What?"

"The boots stay." He gave a lascivious wink and turned to retrieve his trilby. I was sitting on the bed, pulling my boots on, when he leapt at me. We tumbled back onto the duvet. Laughing, he buried his face in my neck and pretended to bite me.

"No!" I screeched, trying to wrestle him off.

Reaching over to the bedside draw, he pumped something into his hand, then moved one leg over mine and slid his fingers between us.

Oh!

I closed my eyes as a completely new sensation took hold. She watched me carefully as she pressed herself against me and started to move rhythmically back and forth. It felt as though we were kissing in the most intimate sense. I could feel every nerve on end, absorbing her motion.

"You okay?" he asked.

"Don't stop!" I gasped, and he leant down to kiss me again.

CHAPTER FORTY-FOUR

I woke lazily the next morning with George between my legs. His tongue was the best alarm clock I'd ever encountered.

Between cherry lube and the strap-on – not to mention George's expert touch – I'd never had an orgasm like it in my life! It was wicked, in every sense.

He surfaced from beneath the covers, and I tasted my wet self on his lips.

"Morning," he grinned.

"Morning."

"What time is it?"

"Eight. I don't feel well."

He laughed. "Me neither, but I can't play doctors and nurses today. I've got a VIP to attend to first thing."

"Who?"

"Your boss."

A fit of giggles took hold. It seemed so absurd that George was about to go and talk business with my boss using the same mouth that, just a moment ago, had been pleasuring the admin staff. Kind of poetic.

Showering together, we sponged warm soapy suds over our secret places. We got a little carried away, and it caused us to run late. He dropped me off outside the office whilst he went to find a parking space. This meant that at least we didn't raise suspicion by arriving together.

It was all I could do to keep a straight face when I delivered coffee to the meeting room.

I finished work at lunch time and phoned Mark for a drink.

"I'm leaving next week," he announced at the bar.

"Where are you going?"

"Well, can't stay with Steve and Alice forever. I think they're trying to start a family – I'm kind of in the way."

"Maybe you should ask to join in," I joked.

"Oookay. Who's got into you?"

"George. We finally, y'know."

"Nice one, Phoebs. How was it?"

"Mind blowing," I grinned.

"Was he better than me?"

"You both have your charms."

"That's a yes then," he pouted.

"Let's just say it was an experience I'm raring to repeat."

"Am I invited?"

"Certainly not."

We downed a couple of pints and discussed what he was going to do once he moved back to his parents'. He was totally off the coke now – no more nosebleeds. He had no idea about careers yet. It seemed sensible just to take one step at a time. Too much too fast could push him into a relapse.

Whilst we were talking it over, my phone went.

"Hey, babe." It felt unbelievably seductive to hear George's voice calling me his babe.

"Hey, sexy."

"You fancy Weaver's tonight? It's Friday."

"Sure. I'll go home and change. Meet you there."

"George?" Mark asked, after I hung up.

I nodded.

"Haven't seen you smile like that since I took you to Alton Towers for your birthday."

"I feel so god damn crazy – everything tingles. I think," I paused to take a breath. "I think this is it."

He laughed and bought me a rum and coke in celebration.

Back at home, I went through my wardrobe and pulled out the blue beaded dress. I could down-play it with a jacket and belt. And besides, this was Weavers – it would hardly even register amongst the decadent disco parade.

I felt excited. This was the first time we were stepping out as a couple. We could flirt and laugh and dance, and everybody would know that we were together.

My phone rang.

"Hello?"

"Hey, lady, where have you been?" It was Orla.

"Just working, mental as ever. How's you?"

"I'm great. Fancy a drink this evening? Andrew's out of town."

"I'd love to be your back-up plan, sweetie, but I'm out tonight."

"Where?" She sounded miffed.

"Weavers."

"Where's that?"

"Over near the river, next to The Millers."

"What, the gay bar?"

"Uh-huh."

"Why are you going there?"

I hesitated. "Some friends."

"Of Eddie's?"

"And mine."

"Okay. I'll meet you there. What time?"

Fucking Orla-ed again!

There was no getting out of it once she'd made up her mind. I told her that I'd be there at nine, which would give me an hour to chill out with George and forewarn him.

By the time I got there, half my head was bouncing like a bed spring, and the other half was filled with lead. My body was still ringing with the almighty orgasm of last night, whilst the thought of Orla turning up rather threw a wet blanket over the flame.

George was having a cigarette outside with June when I arrived. I walked straight up and kissed him on the lips. He smiled, surprised, then kissed me back harder, putting his arm around my waist.

"That's nice," June said, taking a drag. "Where's mine?"

I gave her a peck on the cheek.

"Slight glitch," I said. "My friend Orla kind of invited herself along."

"Great," he said, taking my hand and leading me inside before I had a chance to explain further.

By nine, I was drinking Tiger and laughing with George's group of friends. Charlotte was there, and June, and a couple of other guys and gals. It was so relaxed; I finally felt as though I belonged. Mitch kept taking the umbrellas out of the cocktail glasses and tucking them into my hair. I had about five of them and was starting to resemble a Thai ladyboy.

"You're vibrating," George said, leaning to one side so that I could reach between us for my phone.

"Where the fuck are you? I've been calling for ages!"

"Shit! Sorry," I said. "Be down in a minute."

By the time I got outside, Orla was clutching her denim jacket around herself like she was in the Antarctic. It was actually a fairly mild night, and I think she was doing it for effect.

"For fuck's sake," she huffed.

"Why didn't you just come in?" I asked.

"What, in there? I don't know anyone."

"Well, they're hardly going to eat you."

"Whatever."

"Come on, I'll buy you a drink."

I led her upstairs and ordered two beers. Mitch leant over and tucked another umbrella in my hair. Orla just rolled her eyes and grabbed her bottle.

We joined the group again. One of the girls moved over to share the large, square seat she was sitting on. Although uncomfortable, Orla did a passable rendition of civility. The girl she was sitting next to, Tanya, asked how she was and they exchanged a few words. The music was too loud for us to talk easily as I resumed my seat on the couch with George. He had his arm resting over the back, and I was leaning in to hear what Charlotte was saying.

I know it isn't how a best friend should act, but she had invited herself. What was I supposed to do?

Eventually, some of the crowd got up to dance in the cramped space in front of the live stage. A couple of saxophonists and a bass player were jazzing things up. I left Charlotte and George to chat, and hotched over to sit closer to Orla.

"What are we doing here?" she asked.

"Talking to people," I said, stating the obvious.

"Come on, we could still make Henry's."

"I don't want to go. I'm fine."

George caught my ankle with his foot, causing me to look round. He got to his feet and offered me his hand, using the other to button his jacket. Dapper to a fault.

Grinning, I accepted, and we made our way to the dance floor. I took his hat and drew it down at an angle as he spun me under his arm and pulled me close again. I could feel the heat between us, glowing like a hidden ember.

He took back his hat and leaned in, turning my legs to jelly with a teasing brush of his lips.

"Outside, now!" Orla barked, taking my wrist and dragging me away.

CHAPTER FORTY-FIVE

"What the fuck?" I shouted, as she pulled me round to face her in the deserted car park.

"No. No!" She wagged her finger at me like a school teacher. I realised that she was physically shaking. "*You* what the fuck!"

A taxi pulled up.

"Orla-"

"Who is this?" Her voice rose to a shriek. "This isn't the Phoebe I know! And who was *that*?" She jabbed an accusing finger towards the door. "Because you and I both know *that* isn't normal!"

"What do you mean?"

"Don't treat me like an idiot, Phoebe. I'm not blind. I know who that was in there."

"Yes. George."

"Jess told me all about her."

"Him."

"She's a fucking freak is what she is!"

My mouth opened and closed. It was as though she had slapped me.

"Is that what you dumped Ferris for? Christ, Phoebe! What the fuck were you thinking? It's *disgusting*!"

"Do you have an issue, other than your dress sense?" a familiar voice asked. I turned to see Sebastian standing next to me with a grey-haired gentleman.

Orla glared at him.

"Hurry along, sweetheart. You're lowering the tone."

Colour drained from her cheeks. I took an instinctive step back.

"Who the fuck are you?" she spat.

"I'm the one doing your boyfriend, darling. Apparently you were too big a cunt."

She practically staggered beneath the parry of wit.

"Phoebe, we're going."

"No, I'm not." I said softly.

Her eyes moved from Seb's to mine.

"You need to come with me," she hissed.

I kept my eyes to the ground.

"She's happy where she is," he said, breaking the silence. "Hop on your broomstick."

We watched as she teetered indignantly across the car park on her high heels.

I glanced at Seb, unsure whether to thank him.

"This doesn't make us friends," he said, brushing past me.

Turning, I saw George leaning in the doorway. As my lip started to tremble, he held out his arms and I buried my face against his jacket. I felt like a puffer fish that had just deflated. One minute *en guarde*, the next, cowering in a corner.

"It's alright, love," he said, kissing me on the forehead. "Happens sometimes."

I didn't feel much like dancing, so we took a taxi back to his house and ran a hot bath. We lay there, naked, sipping red wine and listening to the radio.

"I mean, I knew it wasn't going to be easy, but I didn't expect her to go crazy like that." My shock was starting to thaw beneath the warm water, replaced by utter bewilderment.

"How are you feeling?" he asked, blowing a white cloud of bubbles from his arm.

"Stunned."

"You think she'll call?"

"I don't think she'll ever speak to me again after that."

The reality of this sentence hit home. Orla had been my best mate since our first day at school. We'd done everything together, all the coming of age shit, but all the normal shit too –

ballet lessons, craft club, birthdays. We'd had spats, sure, but we'd never argued properly – not like that. If there was one person I always knew had my back, it was Orla. And all of a sudden she was now my greatest opponent. It made my head spin.

He slid his toe between my legs, causing me to smile.

"I just don't get it. We've been friends forever – I had no idea she was this…"

"Homophobic?"

I swallowed. "I wouldn't say that."

"Seemed kind of like what it is though."

We fell quiet for a moment, listening to a seventies classic.

"You know, they've done studies which have shown that the most vehemently homophobic men are also the ones who get most sexually aroused by gay porn."

I rolled my eyes. "Look, she's not a homophobe, okay."

"And if she is?"

I frowned. "What do you mean?"

"Well, how's that going to work out? Your best mate's got issues about your pre-op transgender boyfriend. Can't see that going down well over Sunday lunch."

"Are you asking me to choose?"

He gave his noncommittal shrug. "I'm just saying, it's not going to be easy."

"What were Leona's family like?"

George paused to take a sip of wine. "Great. She was adopted. Her folks were totally easy-going."

"That's a lot to live up to," I said, and immediately wished I hadn't.

"I didn't mean it like that. I'm just saying – not everyone is going to understand. Are you sure I'm worth it?"

"You think this is a mistake?"

"No," he sounded tired. "I'm offering you some thinking time. Some space to consider what you really want."

I knew then that he was offering me a way out, but it felt like rubbing salt in the wound. It made the situation black and white: stay, or leave. And it created doubt. If he thought that I could walk away from him so easily, could he forget about me, too? Taking a step back felt like running away, when what I wanted right now was a partner. Someone with whom I could analyse the problem and come up with a solution.

We lay in bed. Sex was the last thing on my mind. He sensed that, cupping my breast in his hand as we spooned together.

It felt like the longest night of my life.

CHAPTER FORTY-SIX

By the next morning, I still hadn't got any answers. I lay on my back staring at the ceiling as light started to seep around the beige curtains. George sprawled, back to me, across the other side of the bed.

I got up, showered, and dressed. Quietly opening his cupboard so as not to wake him, I borrowed another set of jeans and a top. Swigging orange juice from the fridge, I left a note simply saying *Call you later x*, and left. At least that way he wouldn't think that I'd skipped town again.

When I got home, I was surprised to find Dad cooking a fry-up in the kitchen.

"Can't sleep?" I asked.

"Ah, shifted my days around. Want a cuppa?"

I nodded and sat at the counter whilst he filled the kettle.

"Fancy doing something today?" he asked.

"Like what?"

"Well, I thought we could maybe go see your mum, then catch a movie or something."

I nodded, a little taken aback. Dad hardly ever went to Mum's grave. He once said that he didn't feel her there anymore. I think he thought it a bit pointless to lay flowers next to a stone when her spirit was all around him. Something like that. I liked the solitude it gave me, to sit there and talk to her. I guess we each have our own ways of grieving.

After breakfast I changed into my own clothes, and we headed out, stopping at the petrol station to buy flowers.

It was a bright, sunny day. The blue skies were starting to whisper the first hint of summer. We lay down our coats and sat there, faces tilted towards the sun.

"Orla came by last night," he said. "Just as I was getting in."

I felt my stomach tighten.

"She seemed terribly upset about something. You two had a row?"

"Sort of," I said, quietly.

"She seemed to think you'd taken up with some fella she didn't approve of." He lowered his head and gave me a slight smile. It was the look that he used to give me as a teenager when I'd done something indiscrete. It said he knew, but he wasn't going to say anything unless I wanted to talk about it.

"It's kind of complicated," I said.

"Life is, love. Life is."

I stared at Mum's grave for a moment, then took a deep breath.

"I met someone, through work. He's amazing." Dad simply sat, patiently waiting for the 'but'. "Only, he was born a girl. It's not his fault or anything. It's just biology."

I kept my eyes on the gravestone, cringing in the silence.

"Well," he said, philosophically. "I don't rightly see as you could help that. You know your aunt Mary was born with three nipples?"

I stared at him incredulously. "What?"

"Really, she had an operation when she was about your age."

Trust Dad to find the funny bone in any conversation. Too long hanging around hospital corridors, dealing with hatches and dispatches. I think you have to have a certain type of outlook to deal with that stuff.

"So, what did Orla say?" I asked.

"Ah, not worth repeating, love. I think she'd had a few."

"She must have. What time did you get back?"

"Seven. She was sat on the doorstep."

"God, I'm sorry."

"Don't be. She'll come around."

"Maybe," I said, though I wasn't convinced.

"So, what's the name of this new fella of yours then?"

"George."

He made a mental note and nodded. "Well, it'd be nice to meet him. Bring him round for breakfast some day."

I could have kissed him! Such easy, assured acceptance. Why had I expected any different? Then a thought struck me.

"Do you think Mum would have minded?"

He considered this for a moment. "You know, love, I don't think your mum would have minded anything so long as you were happy. You were the most important thing in her life."

I felt myself welling up, and that started him off.

"Come on, let's catch a film," he said, wiping the corner of his eye with his sleeve.

CHAPTER FORTY-SEVEN

It had seemed like a good idea at first, but now the reality was drawing near, I was losing my nerve.
Which mornings have you got free? I texted George on MSN.
Why?
Because you're meeting my dad.
In the morning?
He works nights. We'll do breakfast.
There was a long pause, but I wasn't relenting. This was something that I needed to do, both to show George that I was serious about us, and to get over the looming barrier of approval that still shadowed me. Despite Dad seeming to be fine with it, I still had this uneasy feeling that he might back out. It's one thing to accept something in theory but, when confronted with tangible reality, people have been known to change their minds. This was the last hurdle as far as me and Dad were concerned, and I was eager to clear it.
Hello?
Sorry, phone, brb.
I waited an interminably long time, listening to the tippety-tap of Miriam's nail extensions across her keyboard.
Thursday. If you're sure.
I picked up the phone and called him.
"I've never been more sure of anything."
"You're nuts," he said.
"I know. Love you," I said, and hung up.

Two tiny words, hurriedly burbled down a telephone line. Maybe he hadn't heard them at all. Maybe it would give him a little tingle in his tummy, like it had me.

"Who's that," Miriam grinned at me from across the room.

"No one."

"Didn't sound like no one. Spill the beans."

"I'm seeing someone."

"And who might that be?"

"Dishy George McCally."

"No way, from VAC?"

I grinned.

"You horny dog!" she laughed. "He's delicious."

"Do you think so?"

"I'm jealous."

Are you, I thought with an inner smile. Would you still be jealous if you knew? But it gave me a ridiculous amount of pleasure to hear her salivating over my new beau.

That night, I took a cab over to George's and turned up on his step with a bottle of wine. We hadn't seen each other for three days – my 'time to think' – and it was killing me.

"Hey," he said, opening the door.

I hadn't bothered to announce myself. I wanted it to be a surprise. It's the only way to tell what people are really thinking – to surprise them. No time to mask their inner feelings with a socially acceptable smile.

I needn't have worried. George's smile was genuine. It seeped into his eyes, giving them a warm, come-to-bed sheen.

"I wasn't expecting you," he said, as I stepped up to give him a kiss.

Before we did anything else, we made love on the couch. No toys, no distractions – just perfect body contact.

We lay there afterwards, my head resting against his chest, my hand cupping between his legs.

"I meant what I said on the phone," I whispered.

He ran his hand across my head, and for a moment the only sound was that of his heart beating beneath my ear.

Then the telephone rang, causing us to jump. He got to his feet and hastily pulled on his boxers before answering it.

"Hello? Hey…No, I can't, not the best time. Later maybe, or probably tomorrow…None of your business…Yeah, see you then."

I frowned as he replaced the receiver.

"Your other woman?"

He laughed at that. "Close. Seb."

I sat up and reached for my bra.

"It's quite something to watch him in action," I said.

"Have you spoken to Orla?"

"No. You know she went to my house and told my Dad about us?"

He looked at me whilst buttoning his trousers. "Is that why we got the breakfast invite?"

"Yeah, it sort of all came out."

"Look, Phoebs, I'm not sure about this. Isn't it going a little fast?"

Insecurity bit. "Isn't it better to find out now?" I asked, the hurt seeping into my voice. "At least if we discover it doesn't work, nothing's wasted."

"Hey, I'm sorry," he said, sitting down next to me and drawing me close. "I didn't mean it like that. I just don't want to throw you into something you're not ready for."

"I will be ready for it, if you're standing next to me. But you're making me feel like this is something I have to do all on my own. It's lonely."

"I didn't mean to make you feel that way. It's just that it's been a long time for me. I'm cautious."

"How long?"

He looked uneasy and reached for his shirt.

"You haven't been with someone since Leona?" I asked.

"Not in a relationship, no."

I frowned. "How long ago was that?"

"Five years in September."

"Is that how long the boxes have been up there?"

He occupied himself by doing up his shirt. "I just never really knew what to do with them," he said quietly.

I thought back to something that my dad had said when he stopped going to Mum's grave.

"She's not up there in those boxes," I said, placing my hand over his heart. "She's in here."

He put his own hand over mine and squeezed.

CHAPTER FORTY-EIGHT

When Thursday arrived, I had spent the night at George's house so that we could get up and dressed together. This time I'd actually bothered to pack my own clothes and a toothbrush.

George put on his smartest work clothes, as he was going on to the office afterwards. We drove over in his car.

"Nervous?" I asked.

"Just a little." He stared at the front door from behind the safety of the windscreen. "Does he know about the first time I came here?"

I laughed. "No, and he never will."

Holding his hand, I slid my key into the door to find that it was already open.

"Morning," Dad shouted from inside.

As we walked through, I realised with dismay that somebody else was in the kitchen, frying eggs. I couldn't believe that Dad had felt the need to bring back-up. The guy was tall and slim with a thick brown ponytail and moustache. He was dressed in the same blue overalls that Dad wore to work.

"This is Ben," he said, indicating the stranger behind him. "We work together up at the hospital."

"Ben?" George said, surprised.

The guy wiped his hand on a tea towel, then came over to shake George's in a familiar way. "Alright, mate?" he grinned.

"Unbelievable. How are you?"

"Good, mate, good."

"I thought you'd left town or something?"

"Nah, just getting on with my life."

I watched the exchange, puzzled.

"You must be George," Dad said, extending his hand.

"Yes. And you must be Phoebe's dad?"

"Call me Jim."

"Nice to meet you, Jim."

"Help yourself to a cuppa. Tea's in the cupboard over there, and milk's in the fridge."

I marvelled at the way Dad had used the disorganisation of his kitchen to organise our social well-being. Sure, things were so chaotic that he couldn't fetch you a cup of tea – but in bringing you into the mayhem, he made you part of the family.

Sitting myself at the counter, I watched as the three of them went about the kitchen frying eggs, microwaving baked beans, and brewing tea. It felt so incredibly right.

Ben went to the sink to rinse a saucepan and, as he passed, he flicked his tea towel at George's arse. Instantly, George's foot came up and caught Ben's in retaliation.

We ate around the counter rather than taking everything over to the living room table. It maintained the casual, friendly atmosphere.

"So," Dad said, "Phoebe tells me you work at VAC? That's that big charity place, isn't it?"

Dad had never been too good at keeping track of all the acronyms.

"Yeah, been there a couple of years now."

"What's it like?"

"Challenging some days, repetitive on others."

"Know the feeling," Dad grinned and pressed the top down on the cafetiere.

"I do some volunteering sometimes," Ben cut in. "Two days a month down at the Red Cross shop."

"The one on Barton Street?" George asked.

"That's it."

"I'll have to drop by some time."

"Yeah, it'd be good to catch up."

The rest of breakfast went by in a flash. There was hardly any pattern left on the plates, we were all so hungry. Then Dad headed off to bed whilst we gave Ben a lift into town, dropping him by the bus station.

"What was that about?" I asked, as we headed towards George's office.

"What, Ben?"

"Yes."

"Post-op. We were in hospital together after I had my boobs removed."

"Ben was a *woman*?"

"Yeah. Teresa."

"How come he's never at Weavers?"

"I guess because he just wants to get on with his life."

I contemplated this. "Would you still go to Weavers if you'd had the operation?"

He frowned, thinking about it whilst indicating to turn right.

"I don't know," he said. "I have a lot of friends there."

"But you don't feel gay?"

"Not exactly. I'm not a lesbian, I'm just… *sans l'appareil*."

I'd never really considered that before. If I'd seen Ben at Weavers, I would have assumed him to be a gay man. Yet part of me still knew that George was a woman – anatomically speaking. And because of that, it did make sense to see him there. Perhaps it was also his elaborate dress sense, which seemed at home in the vibrant club atmosphere. It made me a little sad to think that, after an operation, he might become like Ben – that he might not feel as though he belonged at Weavers. I didn't want him to change. I liked him just the way he was. So what did that make me?

He dropped me outside my office and I kissed him goodbye.

CHAPTER FORTY-NINE

I couldn't have wished breakfast with Dad to have gone any better. It had been perfect. Relaxed, humorous, not the least interrogatory. And I was still in awe of the fact that he had somehow known to bring Ben. It had really broken the ice.

But there was still one person that I had to tackle.

Ice-cream, one o'clock? I texted Orla.

A moment later, a simple *OK* came back.

I really didn't like the way things had ended between us, and I reasoned that the sooner we could talk it over, the sooner we could put it right. I wasn't angry with her – how could I be? I'd freaked out myself at one point. I just needed to make it alright again. To discuss it openly now that we had both had a chance to cool down.

When she arrived at the table, I could tell that it wasn't going to be easy. She hung her coat and bag over the back of her chair, then went to the counter without even waiting for me. I let her do her thing, taking my turn once she'd seated herself.

"How have you been?" I asked, returning with a bowl of mint chock chip.

She nodded and concentrated on her own dessert, spooning around the edges where the ice-cream had melted.

"How's Andy?" I asked.

"Good."

"Okay." I watched her for a moment, baffled by this strange Orla who I hardly felt I knew. "Are we going to talk?"

She held my gaze for a moment, then put down her spoon. "It's immoral," she said.

"What?"

"It's not natural."

This from a girl who had worked her way through the *Karma Sutra*, drunk, stoned and God only knows what else.

"I had no idea you felt this way."

"There's lots of things you don't know about me," she said, then struggled to think of any.

"We've been friends our whole lives."

"You're the one keeping secrets," she said. "You weren't going to tell me any of this, were you? Sneaking off to your secret club, mixing with those freaks."

"Don't use that word."

"Why? They are. That's what everyone's going to think. What about your dad? What's he going to say?"

"You did us a favour, actually." She blushed slightly, knowing the favour I meant. "Dad really likes George. They get on great."

She simmered in silence for a moment.

"Not everyone has the same prejudices," I added.

"It's not a prejudice, it's simple decency, Phoebe. You're not like this. I know you're not."

"Not like what?" I was finding it increasingly hard to keep a cool head.

"You could have any bloke you wanted, Phoebs – look at you. You don't need to reduce yourself to this sort of behaviour."

"Okay, that's enough. Where is this coming from? George is my partner. I love him, and we're happy together. Why can't you be happy for us? You're my best friend, Orla. I want you to be a part of this."

"You're sick," she spat, getting to her feet. "Call me when you come to your senses."

I felt numb from head to toe. If you had asked me before to imagine the worst row Orla and I could ever have, it would have ended in some sort of bitch slapping contest – or an ice-cream fight. Nothing truly horrific. But the sheer malice in her voice left me ringing.

Drug addictions, grief, and homophobia. The list of catastrophes I hadn't seen coming just kept on growing.

But unlike the other two, this one seemed pretty final. I couldn't see any way in which to patch things up. And that was because I didn't want to. Mark had clearly seen something in Orla that friendship had blinded me to. I knew that if George and I ever did split, I wouldn't be picking up the phone to her. If we ever did break up, it wouldn't be because I had 'come to my senses' – I was already perfectly in my right mind.

It finally hit home what Eddie had said to me once, outside The Cambria. If I'd always been gay, then I wouldn't have had a friend like Orla. Or perhaps she'd have accepted me in the same, warped, way that she accepted Jessica – at a distance, as a novelty. And if I'd always been straight, then I'd never have been at Weavers, and we'd never have had that row.

What seemed to have caused the problem was that I had confounded her idea of who she thought I was. In her eyes, I was some sort of bi – even though I didn't feel it. I loved George for the male in him. I fell for George, the guy, long before I knew he was Georgiana, the girl, and I accepted him with the calm understanding that, as Mark had put it – it's all just body parts.

None of us can help not being what we want to be. We all have images of the perfect body, the size eight dress, the full C-cup breasts, the rippling biceps, and the large cock that society worships like a false idol. Hands up who has never wished for something to be slightly different about themselves? I see no Mexican wave.

So, once the flesh has been examined and found to be wanting – what's left? Only the inside. What we think and what we feel. It may not seem like it, but this we do have a lot more control over.

I loved George. I wanted to wake up with him every day, to wash his back in the shower, to lick honey off his neck – and other places.

I was *proud* to be with him. That said, what else matters?

CHAPTER FIFTY

It was in this new spirit of emboldened enlightenment that I dragged George along to Mark's leaving party at Henry's.

Mark and I still shared a lot of friends from our days as a couple. Most of them were fairly surprised to see us sharing a drink and a laugh at the bar. It's nice to confound people like that sometimes – rising above the expected side-picking and boundary drawing to a transcendental plain of lasting friendship.

George and Mark shook hands, and George bought a round of drinks. We picked a table in the corner and started talking to Alice, Mark's former colleague and housemate, whilst he did the rounds.

"It's going to be weird without him," Alice said.

"Yeah, I'll miss him."

She looked at me a little strangely, her natural timidity giving her a church mouse approach to asking questions. "I didn't think you two were close anymore?"

"Well, he has hidden depths."

She smiled. "Will you stay in contact, do you think?"

"Maybe."

George swigged his beer and watched the room, not particularly interested in making small talk.

We were joined at the table by two of my friends from school, Trevor and Carla. I introduced George as my boyfriend, and they all nodded and smiled. No one suspected. He really was the picture of boyish good looks. I wondered how he did it. If you'd dressed me up as a boy, in a suit and tie with my hair cut short, I'd feel out of place. Sure, I wore jeans and sometimes looked a bit of a tomboy, but I still liked my makeup, perfume and high heels. I couldn't imagine cross-dressing to the point of believability. Sitting in a room full of strangers and feeling comfortable with myself. But that's what made George, George.

I put my hand on his knee and left it there whilst I continued to chat to Alice. Meanwhile, he bonded with Trevor over the rugby scores.

The room was buzzing by ten o'clock, and it was a squeeze to get to the bar. I'd done the full tour of school friends and former colleagues, and my feet were starting to ache.

George was somewhere in the crowd, completely at ease amongst the macho males. He had left his hat on the table and looked like a suited and booted business executive fresh from the city. It was breathtaking to watch. Like the most perfect piece of theatre. No one had a clue. There wasn't the slightest trace of suspicion.

I wondered how long that would last before someone like Orla made a loud speaker announcement and suddenly people started to find it hard to make eye contact. If she'd gone and told my dad, she'd probably tell the entire world at some point. But for now, everything was as it should be.

Spotting George at the far end of the bar, talking to a guy whose girlfriend seemed to find him sufficiently attractive enough to play with her hair, I made my way over.

"Hey," he said, sliding his arm around my waist.

"Hey," I smiled back, and kissed him. A smouldering, possessive kiss that screamed 'get a room'.

I drew back and saw the sparkle in his eyes. It was the first time we'd ever kissed in straight public. Something couples do all the time without thinking. And now, here we were – being a couple.

That night, when we got home, I asked him to show me the pictures of him as a girl. He rolled his eyes and, with a slightly inebriated sigh, went up to the room full of boxes and returned with a photo album.

At first, the girl staring back at me didn't look anything like the person sitting next to me. She had angelic blonde hair to her shoulders, and a big puffy fringe. She wore a pretty pink dress and was smiling with genuine, toothy happiness at the camera. The mottled blue background suggested it was an official school photograph. I guess I'd expected to see a moody, sullen face staring vacantly at the world. A disturbed child with too many adult problems on her mind. But she wasn't. She looked just like I did at that age.

It's only when I really stared hard that I started to notice the little dimples in her cheeks. Like a three-dimensional picture, something shifted and I was able to pick out the same nose and lips that now belonged to the man who was so familiar to me. It wasn't as easy as I'd imagined. Something monumental had shifted in George's appearance. It was a struggle to connect the distant past with the physical present.

"You look better as a boy," I said.

"Yeah, I think so."

"A pretty girl, but a handsome man."

He kissed my shoulder and rested his cheek there, watching as I flicked through the pictorial record of his youth.

"There aren't many of your parents in here."

"There's a couple. Look, there's Mum," he said, pointing to a blurred woman standing almost out of shot.

"Where are they now?"

"Retired to Devon a few years ago. I visit sometimes. You'll have to come."

It occurred to me that I really knew nothing much about his family. "Do you get on?"

"In moderation. We don't talk as much as we used to."

"What happened?"

He shrugged. "Not much. You just grow up, make your own way in the world."

George was only five years older than me, but I felt as though he'd travelled a lot further. I couldn't imagine not talking to my dad for more than a couple of days; he was part of the bedrock of my being.

We fell into bed and slept in each other's arms, tired and content.

In the early hours of the morning, I woke needing the bathroom. Disoriented and thinking myself in my own home, I opened the wrong door and found myself surrounded by boxes. It took me a moment to realise what had happened. Shivering in the dark, I reached for the light and stood there, staring at the cardboard mountain.

In the duffle bag closest to me, I spied the edge of a newspaper clipping. Unzipping it, I found half a dozen newspapers and a photograph. It was the first time that I'd had a face to put to the name 'Leona'. There was a very young looking George. His hair was slightly shorter, in a crew cut, without his swept fringe. He was grinning at the camera through sunglasses, sat on a low wall by a beach somewhere. Next to him, holding hands, was a mixed-race girl with a large bouffant of tightly curled black hair down to her chin. She had a beautiful smile. They looked touristy and windswept.

I didn't really feel anything for the girl. I was tired, and it looked like another lifetime ago. A bright, sunlit snippet from another planet. Out of place in the middle of my suburban night.

Replacing it, I picked up the news clipping.

British Nurse Killed in Sudan.

Apparently the tent they were using as a makeshift medical unit had been shelled by rebel forces. She'd been killed along with two French doctors and an Australian civilian. It said nothing about George, or her family and friends. Only that she had been twenty-five and that she had been in West Sudan for three weeks, working for Médecins Sans Frontières. The article beneath that one was a centre spread on whether aid workers should even have been in that area of Africa to begin with.

I wondered how many houses all of this stuff had live in. Had it been here, in this room, for the past five years? Or had George lived elsewhere? Had he gone to all the trouble of packing everything up and carrying it from house to house with him? All of these boxes came to twice as much as anything else in his house – anything he actually used.

Returning from the bathroom, I slid between the sheets and put my arm around his sleeping form. He stirred slightly and pressed against me.

CHAPTER FIFTY-ONE

The Cambria seemed dingy in the mid-day sunshine, like stepping into a cave. I'd been popping in on my lunch breaks and after work for the past week, but so far no luck.

Today was different.

I made my way towards the back, past the seat where Eddie and I had once sat. I recognised Ellis and the grey-haired gentleman from Weavers. As I approached, the table fell silent.

"Hi Seb," I said, trying to sound more confident than I felt. "Can I have a word?"

"I can think of several."

The table smirked collectively, but I ignored them.

"It's kind of important."

He twisted his glass in his hand, then gave a half-shrug. "I need a ciggy anyway."

Once outside, I pulled out my own packet. We weren't ever likely to be friendly enough to offer each other a smoke, but for the time being it provided a distraction under which we could feign common interest.

"What's so important?" he asked.

"It's George. You're his best friend, right?" This lick of flattery seemed to work.

"What about it?"

"Well, I wanted to run something by you."

After we'd finished talking, he went back inside the pub and I returned to work. Picking up the phone, I took a deep breath and dialled a number.

"Hello?"

"Ferris, it's Phoebe."

I thought he was about to hang up, but thankfully he stayed on the line.

My next port of call was the Red Cross shop on Barton Street. I'd been in earlier to find out which days Ben worked. He was steaming skirts in the basement when I arrived. The manager gave me special dispensation to go down and see him. I promised to make it worth her while.

"Hey, Phoebe," he said, as I picked my way across a room full of donated bric-a-brac.

"Hey, Ben."

"What can I do you for?"

"You knew George when he had his operation, didn't you?"

"Sure did."

"Did you ever meet his girlfriend, Leona?"

"That's where they met. She was studying as a nurse at the time. We were her pet project."

I smiled. "She must have been quite something."

He gave me a sideways glance as he swapped one steamed skirt for the next.

"Did you know he still has a room full of her stuff?" I asked.

"Well, that's probably natural."

"No, I mean an *entire* room. Like, fifty boxes."

He switched the steamer off and turned to study me more carefully.

"What's this got to do with me?" he asked.

The rest was fairly easy. Dad booked a day off work, I called the van hire company and – suspecting I was marginally insane – everyone turned up on time.

That's how we came to be standing on George's doorstep on Saturday morning. Me, Dad, Ben and Sebastian. I knew George would be in because I'd got him well and truly blotted at jazz night and piled him into a taxi home. There was no way that he'd be anywhere but in bed when we arrived at ten o'clock.

He answered the door in his boxers and a white T-shirt, scratching the back of his dishevelled hair and yawning like a sea lion.

"Huh?" He blinked in the onslaught of daylight.

"Christ, what a sight," Sebastian tutted, reaching for his cigarettes.

"Give us a moment," I said, taking George inside and shutting the door on them. We went through to the living room, and I sat him down on the couch.

"Phoebe, what on earth is going on?"

"I'm going to tell you, and you're not allowed to get mad."

"Okay," he said slowly.

"I needed to do this before you had too much time to think about it."

"Do what?"

"Today, we're clearing out your spare room. If you do it, you get this." I pulled a golden envelope from my coat pocket and propped it against an empty glass on the table.

"What is it?"

"Well, you only get to find that out once we've cleared upstairs."

He frowned at me. "I don't think that's such a good idea, Phoebe."

"Look, you said yourself – you didn't know what to do with it. Well, Ben works at a charity shop, we've got a van, and now you don't have to do it alone. We're here to help. But it's time, babe. It needs to be done."

We sat for a long moment until, tactful as ever, Seb rapped on the window.

"Come on, Sleeping Beauty, open the fucking door."

I rolled my eyes and squeezed George's hands between mine. He squeezed back and nodded.

"Okay," he said quietly.

"Okay?"

"Okay."

I opened the front door, and they made their way inside.

"Can you guys make coffee whilst I take a shower?" George asked.

Twenty minutes later, we were upstairs.

"Crikey, mate," said Ben. "You should have called me. You sure you're ready for this?"

"Yeah, I'm ready," George nodded.

And so the great clear-out began. But it wasn't about erasing the memory of Leona, it was just about giving her a place in our present. I dusted off the photograph I had found and positioned it on the bookshelf in the office. We took some of the plates downstairs, and the teddy bear and photo albums also stayed. Everything else went into the van, and Ben siphoned off most of it for the Red Cross. The rest we took to the shop at the tip, or delicately disposed of: half finished bottles of perfume, birthday cards, and toiletries. It reminded me of when Mum died, and how Dad and I had gone through her belongings, agonising over each little thing. Items that had seemed so insignificant when she was alive suddenly took on startling significance. Even Seb remained touchingly sincere.

When the last box had been loaded, and everyone else had taken the van on its circular tour of duty, George and I stood in the empty room. There were marks on the floor. Light beige squares contrasting conspicuously against the rest of the dust-settled carpet.

"You okay?" I asked.

He simply nodded.

I took his hand in mine, and he turned to face me.

"It's quiet in here," he said.

"It's a room full of possibilities," I smiled. "We'll fill it again, with laughter and good times."

His lip tightened. I saw tears in his eyes. He rested his head against my shoulder and I kissed it, smoothing his hair with my hand.

"I never thought I'd find you," he whispered.

I felt my own emotions spike, and pulled away gently. "Come on, I've got something for you."

Downstairs in the living room, I handed him the envelope.

Ferris had been too much of a gent to ask for them back, and it didn't feel right keeping them, so I arranged to buy the plane tickets from him and put them in a fresh card.

"Alicante?"

"Well, what's a holiday unless you can spend it with the person you really want to be with?"

He smiled.

"I love you, Mr. McCally."

Drawing me close and kissing me, his sea green eyes looked deep into mine.

"I love you too," he whispered.

GUADALEST

We didn't stay in Alicante. Within a couple of days we'd relocated to a small B&B near Guadalest, a medieval castle precariously perched on top of a towering cliff that overlooked the bluest lake I'd ever seen.

Its winding cobble streets were flanked by an abundance of little shops selling woven hats, lace tablecloths and colourful wind chimes. Glorious sunshine made it the perfect weather for an ice-cold glass of freshly squeezed orange juice at the local café.

It was the sort of perfect day that seems effortless when it happens, but that no amount of future effort can force into being.

"*Mi asno tiene dolor de muelas*," George sighed, gazing out across the endless horizon.

"What does that mean?" I asked.

He passed me the phrase book and waited patiently whilst I flicked to the page he had dog-eared.

"My…toothache…" I frowned. "My donkey has toothache?"

He grinned and shouldered me playfully. "Romantic language, huh?"

"You're an idiot."

He laughed and stopped a passerby, asking her to take a photograph of us. We stood by the wall with the mountainous sky in the background, his arm around my shoulder.

"What are you thinking?" I asked, as he looked at the image of us on the camera screen.

"How good we look together."

"Meant to be," I smiled.
"And how much I'd like you to move in with me."

www.ingramcontent.com/pod-product-compliance
Ingram Content Group UK Ltd.
Pitfield, Milton Keynes, MK11 3LW, UK
UKHW042002230426
12048UKWH00009B/493

9 780956 276636